PRAISE FOR SUSANA MEDINA'S *RED TALES CUENTOS ROJOS*

"'The novel can win on points, but the short story must be a knockout.' So said Julio Cortázar, a champion of both disciplines. Susana Medina's new collection adapts this formula, combining low blows with persistent fouling over the course of its eight stories."

—BEN BOLLIG, *TIMES LITERARY SUPPLEMENT*

"This collection will come as a total shock to mummy porn fans—E. L. James meets J. G. Ballard! Makes both writing and BDSM dangerous once again. Eat your heart out literary establishment."

—STEWART HOME

"A collection of eight explosive short stories ... Susana Medina's stories have an alchemical quality, throwing together disparate elements to create tender and terrifying reminders of what it is to be human: the danger and thrill of our appetites and the limits of our reason ... "

—JOANNA POCOCK, *LITRO*

"The everyday worlds of these stories are glamorous & disturbing, compelling & reckless; they are neural maps of consumer surfaces & psychological uncertainties, their inner landscapes demand our attention."

—STEVE FINBOW

"Medina's oeuvre mistranslates that of Borges. It is Borges's notion of mistranslation at work throughout. In the mode of Angela Carter and all those fantastic girls dallying in their bloody chambers, the trim metaphysical gestures and summarised plots contained in Medina's work re-render the marvelousness of fairy stories. The luminescent Marina Warner would feel most at home here."

—RICHARD MARSHAL, *3:AM MAGAZINE*

Philosophical Toys

Susana Medina

Philosophical Toys

A Novel

DALKEY ARCHIVE PRESS
Champaign / London / Dublin

Library of Congress Cataloging-in-Publication Data

Medina, Susana, 1966-
Philosophical toys / Susana Medina. -- First edition.
pages ; cm
ISBN 978-1-62897-086-9 (softcover : acid-free paper)
1. Young women--Spain--Fiction. 2. Desire (Philosophy)--Fiction. I. Title.
PR6113.E23P48 2014
823'.92--dc23
2014033474

Partially funded by the Illinois Arts Council, a state agency
This publication is supported in part by an award from the National Endowment for the Arts

www.dalkeyarchive.com
Front cover by Derek Ogbourne and Susana Medina
Printed on permanent/durable acid-free paper

To my dad, Francisco Medina Ángel, who bears little resemblance to the father portrayed here . . .

And yet . . .

The sex-appeal of the inorganic

Nina, my name is Nina, the same as my mother's. It comes from the Italian, from 'Antonina,' but in Catalan 'nina' means 'doll'. But it's not only my name. I talk of small things because they have been a recurrent cipher at the centre of my life. Also, those years, the years I'm writing about, toys had become ubiquitous, my friends kept giving me small toys as presents, kitsch gadgets, playful objects, I gave them similar trinkets and then I felt, I started to sense, that these trashy toys were relevant players in the hypnotic ritual of post-industrial life. That's what I said to Chris one Sunday afternoon when we were caught up in a traffic jam observing passers-by sucking lollipops while building the free toy from a chocolate kinder egg, These small polymer things, these trashy trinkets, there is a kind of spell in them, I said. My father used to call them Hong Kong rubbish, Chris said. Then a fragile adolescent running on stilettos crossed the street majestically.

When we got back home with shopping bags full of libidinal dreams and unpacked them, I stared at the mess of packaging and multicoloured stripy g-strings and thought about my mother's pair of black boots. I thought that I would have never thought about toys if it wasn't for Mary Jane. That I would have never linked them to my mother's shoes, Nina Chiavelli's high-heel shoes, if it wasn't for a chance encounter that forged my subjective dictionary to collapse them under the same concept. Then the words of a shoe fetishist telling me that for him high-heels became alive, flashed through my mind. That made me realise that I still hadn't told Chris about my parents' weird little secret, about my adventures.

Surrounded by these thoughts, while Chris prepared a mandarin and dragon fruit smoothie with the new magic-mix, I looked at my father's pocket-size photo album stuffed with snapshots of my mother's shoes, Nina Chiavelli's shoes, and wondered whether some objects were capable of recapturing the initial intensity of things.

Then I looked at a faded colour picture from when I was a baby. It was a familiar picture. I had once immersed myself in it in order to crack the mystery of things and failed miserably. In this picture, I was surrounded by toys against a blue wall. Toys of all colours, pale colours, bright colours, manufactured toys, handmade toys. Toys of all sorts of textures, fluffy beings, chewy beings, benevolent textures. I was in the realm of the sensuous rendered innocent. A domesticated, sanitised, unthreatening sensuousness. The whole fluffy animal kingdom rendered in a fantastic, simplified likeness that omitted danger, that omitted trouble, then the fantastic bestiary, equally devoid of genitalia, all soft, all cuddly, all belonging to the realm where everything was possible, where terror didn't exist, where crocodiles were docile, sharks benign, where monsters could be explored through touch. Pastel colours, happy colours. Later on, I must have been introduced to blue toys, pink toys, dolls for the girls, cars for the boys. Perhaps it hadn't always been like that, it wasn't like that for everyone, I could only think about what I knew, about my past. My first toys were all fluffy, soft, without sex, without gender, with little class distinction inscribed upon them. They all belonged to the realm of absolute make-believe, welcoming me sweetly into a fabricated safe world, the world of disavowal, mythical innocence, a world fabricated by guilty adults.

The toys in the picture disappeared into the background as I focused on the baby I once was. I was assaulted by a sudden flurry of self-deprecating thoughts—who would have guessed that beautiful baby would develop indomitable poodle hair, slightly horsy teeth, bulging eyes, a myriad of neuroses and keep on growing to an absurd height? I turned the picture quickly upside down as Chris came back into the living room. He was dressed in a khaki outfit that I had rescued from a charity shop. It suited him: black hair, black eyes, brown skin, khaki attire over tall body. He always looked impeccably unkempt, it suited him, like it suited him to be into gadgets and come up with an ancient fable when you least expected it.

They can be quite uncomfortable, it depends on your mood, but they were so cheap, they must have been a remainder from a posh lingerie shop, I said, savouring the smoothie while pointing at the g-strings. You're such a charity shop junkie, why don't you put them on? said Chris, slinging one of the g-strings on his head. Typical of Chris and typical of most men I had known. I had always admired Chris for not being afraid of ridicule. I didn't follow him into the kitchen, it was such a war zone and Chris, a brave soldier, g-string on his head, offered to venture into the unspeakable and prepare a light carrot-onion-potato-and-cream soup so as to use the new magic-mix again. As usual, he dealt with the cooking, he is a good cook, Chris.

When he returned with a tray in his hands, I snatched the scanty piece of underwear from his head, further dishevelled his black hair and relished the orgasmic soup. He had added a tang of orange juice and served it with garlic bread, and we devoured it on the fraction of the table that wasn't covered by paperwork, as the news delivered new barbarities. It's difficult nowadays to separate work and leisure as living rooms tend to be living room offices. We had work to do. And after dinner and coffee, Chris swivelled his chair towards his Mac and started working with photoshop on a new project. He worked so hard. We both did. I said I was going to do some thinking, please do not disturb, I said. Another dubious article for *Vague Philosophy*? he said. Yes, no, I said, I'm going to write about toys, about the sex appeal of the inorganic, just thinking. OK, he said, don't think yourself out, and I went into my studio which also served as a storage room, put the new things away and found myself rescuing my pale blue silk kimono from the wardrobe. I put it on. I hadn't worn it for a long time, it looked better now, I was fuller, I was a bit corpse-like before, although it had never looked quite right. In any case, I felt the pale blue kimono would be conducive to philosophical thoughts on the supernatural power of some objects. I was a third-rate philosopher, but a philosopher nevertheless.

En route to my desk, I also found myself rescuing a large red threadbare notebook from the time I ghostwrote about The Museum of Relevant Moments for the anonymous Collector. Shabby post-it notes in different colours and sizes bulged out from all its three sides and on opening it, you entered a zingy city of thoughts and moods made out of irregular patches of hand-written words that spoke about the unruly spontaneity of language. Written in black, blue, or green ink, the writing was sometimes wild and chaotic, other times it was sharp and neat, other times it was slanted or unusually large, other times unusually small and ordered. I leafed through this tangle of ideas, perplexed at how many things I'd written I'd entirely forgotten about. With a grin on my face, I recognised a piece about a small, headless, plastic elephant that I'd found in the street and raised my eyebrows at a free-floating fragment that I'd underlined: desire is a headless elephant . . . sometimes . . . sometimes. Other notes in the large red notebook spoke about shoes, amulets, objects, there was this long list that divided the kingdom of things into all sorts of subspecies and also a typed-up cutting about my father that I instantly recognised:

> Scrambled up chemical messengers. A
> wayward neurotransmitter. Boob in
> neurotransmission. Neurotransmis-
> sion script error. Like being col-
> our blind, confusing colours. Or

```
like being smell blind, getting
odours mixed up. Olfactory misread-
ings. A weird neural convergence.
```

Placing the red notebook on my empty desk, I lit a cigarette and started thinking that it was the year that I met Mary Jane, fifteen years ago or so, that my mother returned through a film sequence, the first encounter that transformed some of my certainties into indelible question marks. My mother's spectre first appeared through a pair of boots in a black and white film, then through her stilettos and then through work. Perhaps Mary Jane prepared me for it, she became absorbed with certain objects until she entered a different reality, she believed some objects had magical properties, she ended up inhabiting a disturbed playland tailor-made to her needs.

I was so young, so naïve, fifteen years ago or so. And yet I was back there at the blink of an eye.

Mona Lisa's demonic laughter

Twenty-one, that's how old I was fifteen years ago, a baby that had landed in London in search of adventure and the flux of history. At that time, my deceased mother had somehow been erased from my life. I rarely thought about my father. They had always felt as if from a different geological era, so ancient, so remote, my parents, so much older than my friends' parents. I was blasé about everything, as if I knew everything, when in reality it was all façade and intractable delusion. I just didn't look back when I left home, I was looking for stories, I travelled the world looking for stories, unaware that the strangest of stories awaited me at my father's loft in Almería, southern Spain.

I ended up going back to Almería all the time, backwards and forwards, grey skies, blue skies. I was brought up there, in a small house surrounded by tall buildings, a few scattered palm trees, an arid landscape exactly the opposite of the evergreen here. I had these ideas about intensity, living life to the full, living as many lives as possible. That is what I considered my purpose in life. Having strange experiences, reading books, going to the cinema, observing interesting details in everyday life, enriching my subjectivity through delirious adventures, doing anything that would enhance my perception, that is what I regarded as my work. I had strange ideas, musings of immortality, I was always interested in that which was beside the point, fascinated by the marginal, the rare, the peripheral, the inexplicable, not out of exquisiteness or justice but out of something that with time I have recognised as having the uncanny flavour of fate.

I became an artist, I became a drifter.

It was then that I came to this country, to London, Europe's largest megamall, as Chris calls it. I was in time to witness the last vestiges of the punk civilization and saw for the first time Indian women dressed in vibrant saris and Sikhs with turbans as long as their beards. Above all, I felt sexually curious about the porcelain white British boys that came from all over the country to gather in one point in space. I was relieved to find that I wasn't as tall here as I was in my own country, although I was still too tall, my body a bit lanky, weak, fictitious. I had always been too tall, the tallest in my class, the tallest in the playground, too tall for most boys, most boys wanted girls shorter than them, perhaps felt intimidated by my height, I had to learn not to feel uneasy in my own body, persuade myself it wasn't that I was too tall, it was that other people were so short.

That's when my adult life started, in this multicultural town. Adult life? I was three hundred and sixty degrees open to the world. Or so I wanted to believe. I wanted to absorb everything. Dyed my hair strange colours, took most substances, met strange people, people I would have never met in my own country: gangsters, tramps, and guys who were masters at screwing everything up with the impeccable alibi of being punks. I was addicted to sensations, forever new sensations, I was drawn to strangers who became intimate strangers, I was drawn to disaster men, sweet men. Had not realised yet that life was not a spectacle, it was the time when I believed life was an experiment, your head an immense laboratory to play with, the time when everybody wore black as a sign of individuality. Black, a uniform, it was a colour that defied for quite a while the supposed volatility and ephemerality of fashions, what changed was the design, slightly longer lapels, whatever design on forever black, swarms of people dressed in black signalling unbearable dystopia.

At that time, time didn't quite exist, it was exhilarating, the abolition of time. It was running time, reflective thoughts prevented you from running, they weighed too much, something deadening about reflection, I wanted to run. I ran in

all directions, relishing the fact that whatever I did, no matter how inconsequential, I was learning a new language. I relished arguments with boyfriends, where I learned new ways
of expressing anger, dark insults, absurd expressions like
'don't get your knickers in a twist,' and sometimes even visited my bank manager with complicated transactions for free
tuition in financial English. I soon noticed that most people
in this town, including me, spoke weird English. Everybody
was from somewhere else. During my teenage years, I had
learnt some English by listening to pop lyrics which I translated contentiously and sang to the top of my voice aware
that singing wasn't my forte. Also, I had learnt a patois version at school for three years with a sunny, beautiful woman who had managed to turn the English language into such
a perfectly Spanish-sounding dialect that it made me suspect
that she was audaciously practising a novel form of satire. Her
English words had an angular quality to them, her intonation
was perfectly Andalusian and she had transferred quite a few
sounds from Spanish into English, making it sound like a sophisticated catastrophe, a stylish accident awaiting a linguistic
study of rare English mutations.

The English I spoke when I came here entitled me to the
most basic of exchanges. I took evening classes with young
and unwitting missionaries who were travelling around the
world spreading the language of an empire that had moved
to the other side of the Atlantic. I did the homework, wrote
new words in a small red notebook. I learnt English with an
authentic English punk, John K. He sported a green Mohi-
can. He was a full-time disaster, but he was a real punk, to me
the equivalent of English royalty, a rare species that temporarily fulfilled my need for the unclassifiable. He was a full-time
disaster, because he couldn't be otherwise. His upbringing
was a series of events spelling out the word DISASTER. He
was from Mile End. He taught me how to ask for cigarettes:
'got a fag, mate?,' to say: 'innit,' 'blimey,' 'wa'er' and not to

say 'my' but 'me': 'me brother,' 'me grub.' He unpygmalion-
ised me his own way. I quickly developed an accent and a vo-
cabulary which astounded my English teachers. I didn't even
know I had acquired a Cockney accent. When I left him, he
stalked me for a while. He stalked me and stalked and stalked
me. Left a message on my answer-phone, whispering: sorry you could never get a word in edgeways ... please talk to
me. Then another one saying: rot in hell. Then another one:
I loved the way you ... while humming. Then another one:
did you ever love me? Then I changed my number. I suppose
I got tired of gritty realism. It was then that I met Mary Jane.

My linguistic ignorance was so pliable that I developed a
la-di-da accent when I became friends with Mary Jane. Mary
Jane Prendergast. I met her at the Slade School of Art, at a
strawberry-cream party in the quad. She came up to me, put
a strawberry in my mouth, extended her hand and said: Mary
Jane Whatever, pleased to meet you.

Mary Jane was older than me, a mature student, beautiful straight, long, red hair, on her cheek a large velvety mole
which was an unsuspected entry into another dimension. She
had been a dentist's assistant, talked with great fondness about
shiny implements, about prosthetics, she wore colour when
everybody wore black. We rented a flat together, a bit expensive. We weren't interested in paintings. We were more into
creating sculptures out of found objects, bizarre encounters of
things, entities that were disruptive in some sort of way, unsettling objects. Mary Jane made a monstrous all-seeing female eye with extra thick curled eyelashes. I made Pinocchio's
glazed noses that twisted into capricious shapes.

It's so weeeeiiiiiiiird, Mary Jane would say, raising her eyebrows, opening her eyes to their widest excess, stretching the
word to its limit, deforming it until the word decomposed
leaving a spectral trace hovering around her. She liked that,
transforming the perfectly normal into the weird. Weird. We
were into anything that was weird. Of course, normality was

definitely weird, sometimes we were interested in that kind of weirdness, but most of the time we cultivated rarefied situations. Cultivated anything that would shock us into a different reality. We were both fascinated by traumas, pathologies, compulsions, the blurring of boundaries, negative pleasures. We explored these in our lives, in our work. Repetition, desire, destruction, that's what we were into, disagreeable objects, the beauty of the abject, transmuting shit into gold and gold into feathers.

The invigorating effect of neon. Brightly lit colour against black nights. We used to hang around Soho. Soho, a neon back-drop promising a cinematic paradise where superficiality is finally redeemed, celebrated. Neon always complicated the senses, a visual attack that changed the chemical landscape of the mind. But then also Soho in the afternoon. We used to spend many Sunday afternoons in this Soho café, having late breakfast, looking at a *Mona Lisa* that hung on its nicotine-infused wall. Mary Jane used to say Mona Lisa's face was my most frequent expression. Sometimes she would call me Moaner Lisa, as if my enigmatic glance concealed a complaint at the world.

It was a good reproduction, this Mona Lisa with her enigmatic smile. Mary Jane would fantasise it was the real Mona Lisa, the real Mona Lisa unframed. The first time she did so she was messing about with a sausage, a fork, and a sugar pot. Art, especially contemporary art, becomes Art with a capital *A* primarily due to the space where it's displayed, she said slowly and repeatedly piercing the sausage with the fork. If you remove an artwork from a museum, from a collection and place it anonymously in a bar, in an average household, many people would probably cease to see it as great art. A celebrated art piece draws its aura from the status of the building where it's housed, the more empty space around an artwork and the more powerful the building smells, the more intense the presence of the work becomes. It's the collectors who decide what's great art and what isn't. Art has become a question of power relations, make it bigger and bigger, money, monumentality, wow-factor, she said lifting the fork and half-sausage towards her mouth and leaving it suspended in front of her nose. If you saw the *real Mona Lisa* with her enigmatic smile, unframed, in a cheap café like this one, it'd still be a good painting, but its aura would vanish, it wouldn't be the aura it has at the Louvre. Some aura, a celebrity aura, would adhere to it due to the fact that it was so well known, such a celebrity, but nobody would mistake it for the real one, nobody would ever wonder whether it was the real one, it's the consecrated building that lends it its hypnotic reality, *place is the message*, she said. In any case, the *real Mona Lisa* would mean little to somebody who had never left the Amazonian jungle, to an Eskimo in a remote polar land in the Artic Circle or to a traveller from outer space. It'd be an image of a woman bearing an enigmatic smile and that would be about it. Don't you agree? she said taking the aluminium sugar pot that was resting next to the salt and pepper and sprinkling it maliciously with a bit of pepper.

The *Mona Lisa* didn't have any aura at The Louvre, aura isn't the right word, I said. You know what I mean, kudos, prestige, status, she said placing the half-sausage inside the sugar pot and burying it with a roguish smile which meant: yes, this is my idea of fun, a hidden sugar-coated piece of sausage lurking in a sugar pot, ready to freak out and repulse whoever finds it. She then searched into my eyes for complicity and found it. Then she said: What if? And then: Can you hear, can you hear Mona Lisa's demonic laughter sniggering about the ultimate undecidability of things?

Look at that flower, it's so weeeeeeiiiiiiird.

Mary Jane taught me to recognise strangely libidinous flowers, to look at involuntary sculptures, to look at the shape, colour, and texture of natural and fabricated things. I didn't realise it until I started ghostwriting about Buñuel, but in a way, we were working within a tradition, the surrealist tradition. We must have unconsciously felt that this tradition wasn't exhausted, especially the tradition of uncanny objects, of perversely sexualised objects. We would have never linked our work to surrealism, for we saw it as a prehistoric and remote movement that had become entirely absorbed by advertising. But like Mary Jane and me, the surrealists had been interested in placing the visible at the service of the invisible, they had explored the sex appeal of the inorganic, like us they saw insanity as a site for artistic exploration. Like the Surrealists, we wanted to create an atmosphere of psychic ambivalence. We wanted to provoke through ambiguity, beautiful terror, abject beauty. We plunged into the depths of abjection in order to produce interesting work. Undoubtedly, some of the surrealists had hang-ups about women. We had hang-ups about men, but more so about our identities as women. We realised that in many ways we were playing a game of reversal. We didn't quite understand at the time that sometimes the object of desire is feared, sometimes desire with its boundless force is to be feared. It became increasingly impossible to ignore that we were turning fear into sarcasm.

We spent that whole year, the year we met, working these things out. Mary Jane slept on things. I broke writing down to its bare minimum. I used to write stories before I met Mary Jane. Stories about sweet disaster men, my whole life was about looking for stories. Then I got tired of stories. Had read so many. Written so many. Decided what I loved about reading, about writing was the way a sentence embodied an unsuspected truth, a perfect constellation of words, the rhythm, the complex pleasure of language. Stories became suspect, their illusion of meaning behind all this chaos a lie. I wanted to follow the logic of sounds, wanted to unlock the secret affinities of words, didn't want to sacrifice the life of words for the sake of a story. I broke down the stories into fragments. And then the fragments into further fragments.

Wanted something different. Fragments were so resistant.

Words. I loved them as much for their meaning as for their music. Loved the way they flowed together into unpredictable melodies, their pulse, their sound as matter, their texture. I loved words in all languages, but above all I loved Spanish words. I didn't want to sacrifice my own native language in order to adopt a new one, like some foreigners do when they slowly strip themselves of their mother's tongue so as to fit into the new culture only to find they won't fit in. It was a way of clinging to my identity, at least my linguistic one. I read avidly in my own language to keep it perfect. I wrote in my own language while learning English, even if I couldn't quite share with anybody what I had written: in general, the English tend to be resolutely monolingual, an embarrassing eccentricity, a scandal that has at its root a government that doesn't believe in investing in foreign languages *educashun*. Or at least, that's what a stranger who spoke fourteen languages told me at a party.

I became a dictionary addict. There was something disconcerting about looking up the translation of Spanish words into English and vice-versa. There were always slippery gaps in the translations. Chasms. There was something missing and something extra. One word meant five different words in one language, but it didn't mean half those words in the other, it meant a set of other words instead. Words strayed into other words, forming ever-changing constellations. Then I couldn't quite smell English words, I couldn't quite taste their flavour, their emotional environment. To me, Spanish ones always sounded better. My relationship to English was different. It was learnt, it didn't belong to me, it lacked the texture of years of experience, the texture of a highly subjective dictionary, although I did love listening to Mary Jane.

Mary Jane.

The importance of clothes. Clothes are so important. Clothes are sites of intensity, like lipstick is a site of intensity.

Mary Jane started and left unfinished many projects, but the one I remember best from that time was an anthropological diary about clothes and desirability. Why do men wear such dull clothes? Are they scared of fancying each other? she would ask. She wrote down her observations when wearing discreet clothes, repelling clothes, kinderwhore clothes. How men behaved. How women behaved. How she behaved. She reflected on becoming a skirt. A jumper. A pair of trainers. She took notes on indifference, false indifference, jealousy and admiration from women, even fear from men. She became narcissistically absorbed in herself as an experiment, derived a tingling pleasure from tracking people's gaze, consumed their attention with different degrees of detachment, explored the power of a certain combination of colours she was wearing, certain textures like white velvet, the way a top was cut to create discontinuities of flesh and fabric to emphasise certain parts of her body, the way a green top and red lipstick created an after-image of her lips.

Clothes became part of her libidinal everyday. It was a disguise, it was play. It's so so so in-te-res-ting, she would say emphasising every syllable. Some people look so serious! She relished disrupting that seriousness, the disruptive effect of desire, disrupting all that rational pretence, it was like a card castle, you just had to blow a bit and down it came. We all like to be desired, that is the conclusion she came to. Desire is an update on your desirability. Only disgust makes the other's gaze a foul caress. She couldn't wait for summer to finish her diary, when more and more flesh is exposed, when eyes that never ever look jump out of their sockets even when looking out of their corners. Summer! The weather had been indescribable that year. At the end of that year, I mean towards the middle of July, I started noticing the indescribable weather in this country, the fact that the word summer did not mean the same to me as to Mary Jane. It was at the end of that summer that my mother returned through a film sequence that started slowing down my pace, transforming fast time into slow time, gradually, a lethargic initiation into the fact that I wasn't who I thought I was, perhaps nothing was what it seemed to be, and what was exactly the way it seemed, I couldn't quite digest.

My mother's resurrection

Luminous days forever, the desert dunes, crystal clear beaches, my old father, school friends, and a quietness that I couldn't cope with for too long: that's what going home meant to me. I would go to Spain during the summer and Christmas holidays to visit my father, my friends, my past. I would always get this feeling of still time. It felt strange being at the house I'd been brought up in, the same ominous wallpaper with its dizzying geometrical pattern, the same new-looking old sofa, the same transparent plates, encountering again the same two cracked tiles in the corridor, the chipped one in the bathroom, things used to feel so close, yet so far, like a superimposed vision of the same space. I would see my cousin Antonio, some of my school mates, feel strange that so little had changed, that year after year people worked in the same shops, lived in the same places, as if nothing had really moved while I was away. I know it was deceptive, but I would get this feeling of time standing still, as if I had only turned my back for a second and on turning it again I could see the same faces in the same places. Other times, going home to Almería would be like opening a door here in my flat, rather than going from one country to another, it was more like going from one room to another through a special door. I opened that special door, and there it was, my past, a whole country, a handful of familiar faces rendered slightly different through a distortion in perspective.

I would always go there towards the beginning of September, to avoid the deathly caress of July, August, when the sun becomes a perpetual crushing embrace. My father, Jordi Joan, was Catalan, from Barcelona, but my mother and he and then his brother had gone to the south of Spain at the time when the whole of the south of Spain was immigrating to Barcelona. Almería had become a huge film set, the new American Southwest where Westerns could be shot with ludicrous budgets. My mother had vainly been lured by the prospect of acting in the Spaghetti Westerns that were being shot there, only to find out that it was a brutal and macho genre where actresses were mostly incidental. It was obvious, but they were in love and blind to everything they didn't want to see and when they got there, they witnessed the Spaghetti Western industry, which was supposed to flourish with the success of Sergio Leone's films, dry up after a few flops. They stayed there, though. They were both in awe of the lunar landscape, the desert, its rugged beauty, even if my father only had seasonal work playing the sax in a band at weddings and fairs, mostly during the summer. That must have ensnared my mother, the drawn out soulful notes my father played. He had a sweet perfect control of the sax, as though the sax was an extension of his heart, aorta, arteries, his solar plexus. He played mainly jazzy, improvised songs, had this masterly way with a melody. He didn't play the sax for years. Then he started playing it again for a local charity to raise money for a shelter for abandoned dogs.

I went back at the end of that summer. I was welcomed by a violently orange sky. I like your teddy boy shoes! Where did you get them from? That was the first thing my father said to me. I hadn't worn these teddy boys blue suede shoes for years. I'd gone to a Japanese retro party the previous evening and was wearing them in order to discard them and get a new pair of shoes in Almería, so as to minimise on luggage on my way back. It astounded me that he should like them. He had always slagged me off for not being feminine enough, for being a tomboy of sorts. I used to have a pair like that, back in the fifties! he added after a pause. Your mum bought them for me. I smiled with complicity while seeing him for a few seconds as he must have been way before I was born, wearing teddy boy shoes, a young man whose gentle features echoed his serene approach to life.

But in the next few seconds the vision vanished, he suddenly looked older than ever, a robust old man with sad dog eyes that probably mirrored those of the abandoned dogs he was looking after, something moving about my father that was almost tangible, yet sometimes I mistook for emotional blackmail, as if he was trying to strike within me an inconvenient chord, like when he said: I miss you.

He said the house wasn't the same without me around, the whole house missed me, he said. He then slightly turned his head to one side half-placing his hand on his mouth and when he turned towards me again, he showed me a toothless smile. He did it again and then his smile suddenly bore perfect gleaming teeth, a magic trick he must have practiced as soon as he got his new three-tooth denture. He was his usual playful self, but he seemed increasingly forgetful this time. I worried, seeing him like that. And he worried about me being far away, living in another country. What did I bear a daughter for, to have her bugger off to another country? And what are you doing in England? Look at what they're doing to Northern Ireland! They're pirates, the English, they've always been. They've always been so English. They feel superior to us! To everybody! I shook my head, said it was because they had this vision of Spain as a vast holiday resort, they were deluded about their own country, not everybody, that strange feeling of superiority is dwindling away, Dad, it's a stereotype, I said.

For years and years and years, my father had been a night porter in a four-star hotel, had witnessed English hooligans practicing the healing power of smash by smashing bars up, he had been frightened, shocked. He had retired two years ago. He knew not all the English were like that, he spoke some English and had friends from Albion himself, he was an anglophile, but he just wanted me to go back home. It was ridiculous to compare London to Almería, but my father did that, he said Almería was better, the weather was incomparably better, 3,000 hours of sunshine a year, the best place in the world, the people were nicer, more civilised. Yes, dad! Almería was an utterly forsaken town at the time, but anyway. I had to say something, though. England is an outlandish island marooned in the Atlantic, I said. Islanders are like that, they keep themselves to themselves, like the Japanese, I like it there, you can go down the streets in your pyjamas and nobody bats an eyelid, it's a nation of introverts and eccentrics, yes, there are pirates and hooligans, but there are also people so gentle.

Yes, so gentle that they've re-elected Thatcher, come on let's eat, my father said. He was being unfair and he knew it. He had cooked a special seafood platter that day, but he had boiled the shelled king prawns instead of grilling them with sea salt, and the squid was burnt. The seafood platter was a sorry affair, most unusual for him to ruin a meal, let alone serve it nonchalantly. Like Chris, my father was a good cook. He liked cooking exotic dishes. He would cook special recipes for me, dishes he knew I hadn't eaten for a long time, grilled squid with garlic, parsley, and lemon sauce, Hungarian goulash, Singapore noodles. Then he would vanish in front of the TV and I would vanish into nocturnal life. Everybody escaped into nocturnal life. The unbearable heat did that, postpone life until the evening. Nocturnal life. This time I didn't go out that much during my stay. I drew my thoughts instead, read delirious philosophers translated from the French, watched late night TV accompanied by the breeze from a portable ultra-modern fan which made the curtains swell up fitfully, gazed mesmerised at the animated curtains as if they were pregnant with hypnotic power.

Except for meal times, my father and I gently ignored each other, a loving indifference that had taken years to cultivate. He watched chronic soaps, went to men's bars, and played the sax at a few charity concerts. I had endless show-

ers and read voraciously by the ultra-modern fan. Time went
by in a flash. It was the evening before I was leaving, while
my father snored away in his bedroom, that I watched a video
that resurrected my mother and sparked off the strangest of
memories. I found it on one of the living-room shelves, it had
a beautiful scratched quality, it was a bad recording. It was a
film by Buñuel, the surrealist film-maker, *Diary of a Chambermaid*, set in the 1920s, in black and white, long panning
shots. That film was the first incident in a series of coincidences. It brought about a wayward neural storm. I have seen
it many times since, I don't watch it anymore, although at the
time, I almost switched it off. I suppose I was in that inter-
mediary area between vigil and slumber. Curiosity won over
slumber: Buñuel, Jeanne Moreau, a chambermaid in black
and white, beautiful long shots.

The film was about a Parisian woman who found a job in
the countryside as a chambermaid. Countryside people were
hostile. They were hostile because she was from Paris, they
thought she was sophisticated because she was from Paris, the
world's fetishised capital at the time. The opening sequence
focused on her shoes. She wore dainty high-heel shoes. She
was wearing the wrong type of shoes to begin with. Countryside working women didn't wear dainty high-heel shoes. They
were impractical. Moreover, they were exclusive footwear belonging to the beautiful people, the idle Madams.

A pretty chambermaid, uniforms, subdom games, such
come-ons to male desire. The colourful tacky sex-shops that
now sell traditional black and white maid costumes and updated rubber ones, came to my mind. Spanking the maid, the
maid spanking the master, that's what also crossed my mind
when I saw the chambermaid, a personal neural connection,
a book by Robert Coover I'd read. This chambermaid, the
chambermaid in the film, was sexually knowing. She playfully kept the house master at bay, mindful that some jobs required a certain type of flexibility. She wore perfume, black

stockings, high-heels, goods unavailable to rural servants. Her presence in the house spoke about the city, not just any city, but Paris, Paris and its emerging mass-produced market of goods accessible to a wider range of customers, even to a mere chambermaid.

A little girl was murdered in the film and when a little girl is murdered, rape is invariably the name of the game. The chambermaid had felt tenderness towards this little girl, offered her an apple, offered her her own bed. The chambermaid stayed to solve the murder, she slept with the murderer in order to solve the murder, she was going to destroy him so as to avenge the brutal act. She was called Célestine, was played by Jeanne Moureau. There was this old man, a gentle eccentric old man, a bit of a lecher. He was gentle but capable of contempt. He was supposed to be a man of refinement. His daughter, a rigid woman obsessed with expensive bric-a-brac and exotic English vases who referred to everything in terms of its financial value, thought his age justified him in having certain little whims, that's what she said. The old man called all his chambermaids 'Marie,' regardless of their names, as if all the chambermaids were interchangeable, all the same. He called Célestine, Marie. He called for her, made her read a bit from *Against Nature* by Huysmans, a bit where the whole of society is condemned. She read. He enjoyed her voice. She read beautifully. He enjoyed that. The beauty of a voice, as if her voice was detached from her body.

The video tape had been recorded from TV, it was interlaced with advertising breaks in colour, it was strange seeing old ads, their lack of sophistication, old faces and products engraved in the mind through repetition that now triggered the soft spot of nostalgia, of a time when everything seemed right. Then the main bit in the film came. The main bit for me. The bit where the eccentric old man makes the chambermaid wear a black pair of old boots and slowly fondles them.

A remote memory hit my neural circuitry as I looked attentively at the black pair of ankle boots, astounded by their overwhelming presence. These old boots were exactly like a pair of ankle boots my mother used to wear, a replay of lost moments, there was an identical match in my memory, a mirror image. They were the same, as far as I could recall. They had moderate high-heels. Buttons on the side. The leather wrinkled a bit round the ankle, the way my mother's boots wrinkled. My past lurked in those boots, a black pair of ankle boots with intricate tight-lacing. The old man in the film made the chambermaid walk. And then, my mother, Nina Chiavelli, came back in full. I remembered that way of walking, it was identical to the way my mother walked, she walked slowly, majestically. And then those boots, they sparked off flashbacks of my mother from her knees downwards, flashbacks of the leather from her boots slowly creaking, as if to create a counterpoint to the heel's tapping. For my mother, walking must have been a way of speaking, if some people cultivated a beautiful voice, my mother must have cultivated the way she walked.

I paused the film.

My nostrils detected for a fraction of a second an unmistakable smell: the wet sand of the desert.

I carried on watching the film, but my head was flooded by my mother, images of my mother, real images jumbled up with old photographs. It was the photographs in the old album that became all pervasive in my mind, the black and white snapshots, the hand-coloured pictures, and at some point the irruption of Technicolor.

When the film finished, I got my parents' photo album out, browsed through its rancid rice paper pages, wondered at these pictures that had been taken way before I came into existence, became immersed in them. My mother dressed up as an Indian, my father as a cowboy, my mother dressed up as a sheriff, my father as a saloon girl, my mother dressed up as a bride, my father as a groom, my father with an impeccable barman uniform. Then my mother with beehive hairdos holding me in her arms. Then a picture of her as a dead prostitute in a western she had featured in. And then, my mother mounting a cardboard horse in a fairground: a black and white snapshot that featured my mother wearing the black ankle boots I'd just seen in the film.

The memory of my mother's boots became in turn a magnetic field for other memories. Memories crystallised around them like in a speeded-up nature film. I was dizzy with memories. Memories, such beautifully unreliable stuff. I rewound the tape. Watched the frontal sequence again, with the boots walking towards you. The boots carried on walking towards me, they came out of the screen, walked towards the sofa where I was crouched down staring at them wide-eyed, and then they became larger and larger and larger until they filled the whole living room.

It was as if my head was working as a 16 mm film-projector. I fetched the remote control as if it gave me the power to be in charge of my own visions and pressed the 'off' button: the gigantic boot suddenly trailed off.

I wasn't scared. Just dazzled at the power of my head to conjure up a dream-like event while I was awake. It was like a gust of weird weather, a neural storm configured into an image that had made itself visible for a few seconds to then vanish back into obscurity.

I laughed nervously, hoping for something weird to catapult me into a fully bodied revelation. I rewound the tape again to compare my mother's boots in the fairground photograph where she was mounting a cardboard horse with the boots in the film. It was difficult to tell, perhaps they weren't quite the same. It was difficult to tell whether they really were identical. The snapshot was the size of a cigarette packet, the boots tiny in comparison to the close-up I'd just seen on the screen. I realised that didn't matter, if there was an object that condensed the odd flavour of my childhood, it was those an-

kle boots, a black pair of boots somewhere between the snapshot of my mother on a cardboard horse and Jeanne Moreau's
boots walking in *Diary of a Chambermaid*.

My mother, who was she?

My mother died when I was six.

My mother, Nina Chiavelli, was now resurrecting before
my eyes. I barely knew anything about her except that when
she left us, my father said she was doing films in heaven, that
it was much better than to act in films on planet earth. He
said it in a whisper, as if it was a secret and something to be
secretly proud of. He said it with such warmth and conviction that I believed him for years. It was a strange thing for
my father to say: he was an atheist. It was a great thing to do,
to do films in heaven, he would say. My mother died the day
after my sixth birthday. She died of breast cancer. Perhaps her
striptease career had consumed her. All those looks had consumed her, intensified a genetic curse that ran through gen-
erations striking more or less at midlife. She was Italian, my
mother. Stylish. She was forty-one when I was born, my father thirty-seven. We made puzzles together. She taught me
sweet Italian words. She took me to the zoo, to the circus,
shopping and to strange bars where men wolf-whistled and
paid lewd compliments to her arse that utterly baffled me as
in my small world the word 'arse' solely designated the place
where shit comes from. She had been trained as an account-
ant, the family profession. But then, a decade before I was
born, she made a U-turn, she went into acting, it became her
passion, pretending to be different people, visiting different
subjectivities, erasing herself to become the host of others.

I went into perhaps-mode.

Perhaps her career was thwarted when I was born and she
became quietly disappointed? She was a foreigner in Almería,
an unknown actress from an unknown town in Italy married
to a stranger from Catalonia. Perhaps the locals saw her as a
failed actress and a failed mother, with a cruelty that made my

mother drink even more? That must have been tough for her, for who can say what is failure, when most lives are spoken by so many different voices, so many different insurmountable constraints, so many situations forever happening out of time, timing forever elusive, forever playing hide-and-seek in a game of chance, even biological chance, where willpower might be a mere pawn in a senseless game played by random forces. The fact is that she tried hard, she worked hard and perhaps that's what did it, all the struggle, the trying, the erosion. The only roles available for women in Spaghetti Westerns were as prostitutes or widows and she once got a role as a female corpse. We had a picture of her as a dead prostitute. For that role, she had to dye her hair red, wear a red velvet nineteenth century dress with a scandalous décolleté and huddle in the corner of a saloon set, her head lolling on her naked shoulder, eyes closed, immobile. I later found out from my cousin Antonio that most acting she did was unpaid or poorly paid and the only well-paid 'acting' she could get was when they needed somebody in the nude, as if that was all she could be good for. She wasn't required to perform in a narrative, she was required to take her clothes off slowly, to reveal her well-lit body in well-lit shots. That must have angered her. She was a talented woman, delicate body, talented head. She must have thought if that was what was required in order to forward her career, she had to comply with it. But it didn't. That was her career: revealing bits of flesh.

Well-lit shots, shots, as if the camera was a gun. (. . . and as I write this, I realise that in English you might not think this thought, in English cameras shoot, whereas in Spanish, only weapons 'shoot': cameras 'film,' cameras 'take,' but never 'shoot').

I don't think my mother had ever set out to be a striptease girl, to slowly deduct her clothes by numbers. But even that was difficult to get. The fact is that they rarely called her. At least, that's what Antonio told me. She wanted to act. She wanted to be able to choose her own roles. And she had a thing about red wine. And brandy. And cava. And she also liked martini, with an olive skewered on a toothpick just before lunch-time. L'apéritif. And then, after lunch, *le digestive.* Calvados. With time, I realised that she was too fond of elixirs of quietude, she even drank at breakfast time. It wasn't just variety, but quantity. She just wanted to forget something I would never know about. She had an addictive nature, something within her that was beyond her. And then I thought that perhaps she was a wonderful mother and a terrible mother. Perhaps she was obsessed with herself, as some actresses are. Perhaps she would feed me, play with me, she would do this with love, but sometimes, she would do it as if it was a duty, an excruciating chore, something that stole her time from more important matters. Perhaps she would feed me in a rush, impatiently, waiting until I was in bed to fix herself another drink, watch films on the sofa, escape. I don't remember any of this, I am always looking for reasons for my sense of inadequacy, I only remember mostly good times. But isn't that what you are supposed to remember?

Undoubtedly, the brain spins and tweaks memories according to your needs. And undoubtedly. some of the photographs in the album were slightly at odds with my happy memories and confirmed what Antonio told me about. There were some faded colour pictures where she was holding me in her arms as if in bliss, but then, there were other pictures where she had this look as if she was truly far away, so far nobody could reach her, something akin to an irate desperation in her remote look. But was that my mother in the photograph album? The mother I remembered? I couldn't see in those pictures the mother I remembered. The mother I remembered was a warm and sad sensation, sometimes aggressive, unphotographable, and then I mainly remember vividly the way she walked.

My neural circuitry replayed the sharp tap of her high

heels against the fake marble tiles in the corridor. Perhaps that was the soundtrack to my childhood: tap tap tap tap tap tap tap. I looked forward to that rhythmic sound, there was mastery in that rhythmic sound. But also something cold and imposing, authoritative. Sometimes the tap tap tap tap tap tap tap was discontinued midway through the corridor. She swayed, she lurched, fell over in the corridor and my father took her to bed. She must have struggled with alcohol. She was my mother. She was wonderful. Had her dark moments. She would sit on the sofa, take her shoes off, play with me, then disappear into bed until late in the afternoon the following day. Blues would come from the bedroom. She would sing the blues, she was so pale my mother, she must have sung with an Italian accent. I suddenly remembered the blues coming from their bedroom, her voice, I couldn't understand the lyrics, I remembered her singing *Mississippi goddam*. How old was I? Three, four, five. I would carry on playing with my dolls, my girlie toys.

And yet in another memory we were a happy trio: my father played the sax and my mother sang made-up songs while I jumped wildly on their bed.

Bits from my childhood came back with my mother's black pair of ankle boots: accidents, mischievous deeds, petty theft, wonder, and an opaque sensation that took me a while to unravel. One of the things I remembered was repeatedly doing things that I knew I shouldn't be doing. I would burst into their bedroom when they were not in and engage in activities that were related to knowledge, to exploring: I searched their wardrobe, the drawers, the bedside table. I tried my mother's high-heels on and awkwardly dragged myself to the mirror, my feet were housed by immense ships. I returned to the mirror and clumsily smeared lipstick on my thin lips, not knowing at first how a lipstick worked.

But how could a black pair of ankle boots with intricate tight-lacing, a pair of boots that looked like another pair in a film, condense the spirit of my childhood? Did I used to crawl around in my mother's little high-heel boots? I now wonder whether in her absence, I'd play with them. They were probably still warm, they had a special smell. Perhaps I touched the soft, shiny leather, cuddled them, licked them, kissed them good tonight. Perhaps, sometimes my mother would warn me to be careful with the heels and then snatch them and hide them away. All this is mere rhapsody. I don't remember any of this, it all belongs to the realm of the per-haps, what was clear was that the memory of these boots was a back entrance to my childhood, that I must have learned an important lesson from this pair of black boots.

The photographs in the album stacked at the end, and ironically the belongings that my mother left me, the belong-ings I inherited from her when I was seven, were my own be-longings. My first teeth, a lock from my hair, first baby con-gratulation cards, a baby suit, a silver spoon where the ladle was placed horizontally with my name engraved on it, my first drawings, school reports, a single cream woollen bootee. All this she had kept in a large shoe box. I suppose many mothers must feel that impulse, to treasure a baby's bodily things, to build maternal reliquaries.

Inside the shoe box though, there were also reminders of death. Apart from my first belongings, there were a couple of post-mortem photographs of her parents: they used to do that at that time, use photography's death spell to take pic-tures of the dead, a double death to ensure they would nev-er come back, as it's happening now with video in the States, people recording their dead as a memento, a deathbed sur-rounded by mourning relatives.

When my mother died, my father kept everything as my mother used to keep it, everything except himself. He be-came a black sun. He mourned my mother's death for years and years. I looked after him for years and years. He proba-bly never survived it. He probably lived for quite a few years inside his own collapse. He stopped playing the sax, didn't see his friends and became adhered to the TV screen. He became a single father. He became a ghost of his former self. He did strange things like hugging one of my mother's boots in his sleep. That was one of the strange memories the wayward neural storm summoned to the surface: my father hugging one of my mother's ankle boots in his sleep, the boot that was identical to the boots I had seen in the film, Jeanne Moreau's boots. Unable to sleep the weekend siesta, sometimes I would stand by his bedroom door and see him hugging it in his sleep as if it was a teddy bear. At the time, I didn't think anything of seeing him hugging the boot. And then, in one of the few dreams I remembered from my childhood that boot had become a book, a book my father was sleeping with, a book that was not really a book but a boot. This old dream was one of the things that I recalled vividly about my mother's black pair of ankle boots.

My father never talked about my mother. Or if he did, it couldn't have added up to all that much, it was as if he inhabited a realm where life and death had lost their mutual exclusiveness. He must have thought that a gentle wall of silence protected me from his bleakness. All I remembered was his woe. How he didn't comb his hair, how he looked moth-eaten, he had become a neat image of neglect, but then he looked after me, he drove me to school every morning, he came straight from work to be with me, he helped me every evening with my homework. He must have stopped hugging my mother's little boot in his sleep when I was eight or so. I tried to remember when I last saw the boots. I had this vague memory of last seeing them inside a shoe box in the wardrobe in the corridor years and years ago, a remote memory that blurred the boundaries between dream and fact, like so many remote memories. They were shinny and soft, they had slightly worn-out heels. I went to the wardrobe in the corridor, searched everything, but they weren't there.

The eccentric old man in the film had survived through the cluster of memories enlivened by various chambermaids wearing old boots and shoes, the last memory perhaps proving too much: he died hugging the ankle boots. I think my father must have died when my mother died, one of the many deaths he survived. Like my father, the eccentric old man hugged the boots because they brought back memories, undoubtedly memories of affection, beautiful memories, irretrievable memories, the kind of memories that only come back in dreams. Like the old man, like my father, perhaps I also hugged my mother's black ankle boots one day, but that was different, a little girl hugging her mother's boots, that was perfectly acceptable.

Against nature, against the natural order of things, against death: those words rang rhythmically in my mind. In a way, you didn't know much about this old man, the old man in the film, I didn't know much about my father, nor about my mother. There was nothing that gave you a clue as to why the old man in the film cherished shoes so much, except for the title of Huysman's book, *Against Nature*. It took me years to realise that the old man's eccentricity was steeped in class distinction, if the chambermaid submitted to something, it was to that. At the beginning of the twentieth century high-heels were a sign of privilege, wealth, prestige, status symbols worn only by the privileged classes. The working class, peasants, couldn't afford to wear such impractical shoes. And this is what the opening image of the film referred to. A subservient maid who had all the signs of poverty inscribed upon her body and mind, could have never been chosen by the old man to wear such sophisticated footwear.

But, what did all this have to do with my father's hugging my mother's black ankle boot at night? Was my father a boot fetishist? How could my father, an anarchist indifferent to the sensual properties of things, be a boot fetishist? This film changed the way I viewed him, maybe he had a secret life. Maybe he was more interesting than I thought he was. I wanted to find out more. And more I found. To begin with I didn't like what I found out. I blushed for a second. I discovered my inner prude for a second. I realised that perhaps my rebellious streak was just a pose. I had always pursued anything that was different from the norm. But my parents? Parents are supposed to be proper. That's what I found myself thinking. I was only twenty-one, though. Excuses. I shrugged my right shoulder and laughed, but there was a slight delay in the laughter. I had to swallow, digest, flush my own unexpected hypocrisy.

I got up late the following day. When I went into the kitchen to make some coffee, my father was already preparing lunch. His radiant white T-shirt, the pale yellow furnishings in the kitchen, it all gave off light, emphasising the day's luminosity. I stood by the door watching him in a haze. I watched how he deftly chopped a red pepper into the finest of slices. How he then crushed some almonds into small triangles. As I sat at the table, I looked at him, and he looked back at me with a funny grimace that meant: *good afternoon.* Cod stew with red peppers, garlic, and almonds? I said. He nodded and said: And potatoes and a bay leaf.

While drinking my second coffee, other childhood memories came back. Things I knew I shouldn't be doing, forbidden things. In these memories, I would silently go down the staircase that led to my parents bedroom, tiptoe towards the door, carefully turn the handle and peep in. I would go down barefoot so as not to make any noise. The tension. The fear. I would carefully open the door, both exhilarated at the prospect of being caught and not being caught. The door ajar, a fragment of the bed, the white bedspread, the strange whispers. While remembering this, my head started radiating questions in all directions, questions that made me look at my father as a puzzling creature hiding behind a dejected face whose familiarity was a cipher of the unknown. Was my father a pervert? A pervert? Where did I get that filthy word from? I was a perfect adolescent, an adult's nightmare. Was my tendency to inhabit a permanent limbo related to something I had forgotten? Was my father bewitched by the way my mother walked? Was I a little peeping-tom? A dirty little girl who liked spying on her mum and dad? I myself had doubts about my identity, but only afterwards, not before. What was a pervert? What was a fetishist? Was it a question of degree? Was his life dominated by boots, by shoes, underwear or whatever? I myself had struggled to be different, had done everything possible to be different, but this struggle for authenticity was probably only a pose. Or worse, not a personal decision but something imposed from without. I investigated a bit, found out that the perversions as we know them were named, classified, articulated in the late nineteenth century, that it was then that psychiatrists turned their gaze from madness to perversion. I found out that there were social reasons, reproductive anxieties that demanded a prescribed version of normal sexuality. Perversion was a nineteenth-century medical concept, a juridical concept! Had my father been born two centuries before he wouldn't have been considered a pervert! Perhaps it would cease to be a perversion in the future. My father had simply been born in the wrong century. What was a perversion? Etymologically, the word came from Latin, it meant a different version, nothing pathological about it. So, different from what? Different from the law, from unenjoyable straight genital sex with a view to reproduction. But was sex ever really like that? I found it difficult to believe, sex was sex was sex was sex. How could sex have ever been detached from pleasure?

Did I think these thoughts at the time or was it later? Probably later, maybe a year and half later, when I emptied my father's loft. I tried to talk to my father the morning that he drove me to the airport, tell him about the film, about remembering the definite way my mother walked, about the boots. I couldn't ask him whether he was a fetishist. I know you're supposed to idealise your dead parents, but there was something definitely abrasive about my mother which she sometimes combined with her flare for the spectacular: she once pulled out the tablecloth from the dining table causing all the crockery atop to smash against the floor into myriad shards in an unforgettable crash. As I was about to go through Departures, I asked my father whether he remembered that, the unforgettable crockery scene. He was startled, he said that my mother was a wonderful woman, she always kept me on my tiptoes, he said. On your tiptoes? I repeated. He didn't say anything. I felt a fly buzzing in my ear. I've forgotten my sunglasses, I said. That's the last thing I said. Then spent the whole trip back to London taking pictures of the clouds, trying to avoid the plane's silver wing.

A cellar in a loft

I had three colour films of clouds. I developed them, got intoxicated with the simple beauty of clouds. Mary Jane was about to go to Pennsylvania for a couple of months, she had a new boyfriend there, she had abandoned her anthropological study on clothes and desirability, she was confusing too many people, she was getting confused herself, she was busy packing her things when I arrived. While she was packing, I asked her whether she had come across any guys who were seriously into high-heel boots. Not as such, she said. As a redhead, I've come across a few guys who have an unhealthy obsession with redheads, she said. And as a mole-on-the-cheek owner, same. And there are guys who are into dental braces, believe me, and gloves, wigs, nylon, spandex, and nappies, she said. Nappies? I said. Yep, and asphyxiation, she said while putting multi-vitamins in a stripy toiletries bag I hadn't seen before. I once met a guy with a moustache who was really into dressing up as a flashy, tacky woman, he was really into it, I said. Then I told her about my father hugging one of my mother's ankle boots in his sleep, about the film, it was probably the wrong time. She made a grimace of disgust followed by laughter and apology, then said she loved it, you should do a piece about it, that's definitely bizaaaaarre, that's *so* weird, she said, not as weird as necrophilia though. And what about princesses kissing frogs, isn't that weird? she added. That's definitely weird, I said. If you saw my father, you'd think my mother was into bestiality, she said. What's wrong with weird? I said. Your dad hugging your mother's boots in his sleep, that's completely insane, that's *so* very weird, she said with a lingering ironic look on her face.

So very weird?

I blushed on my father's behalf.

Give us a kiss, she said. Then her molecules disintegrated and re-formed in Pennsylvania. She was gone. I had the whole flat to myself. I had never lived by myself before. It was strange being by yourself. I suppose I was lost. I thought being lost enriched me. Without Mary Jane around, I would wander around the flat naked, hearing the cacophony of my thoughts, lost before the window, sometimes observing my next-door neighbour washing his car. He washed it twice a week, he washed it slowly, caressing it with a yellow sponge soaked in luscious foam, sprinkling it with water slowly coming out of the hose, then he would polish it with wax until it became shiny, pristine. Now and again I mulled over my mother and the film and my father hugging one of my mother's high-heel boots in his sleep. It had the presence of a gigantic hallucination. It was hard to shake off. How could my head fabricate such a monumental absurdity? I sleepwalked to the Slade everyday, went to the pub with my classmates and to art parties where you were supposed to become inordinately drunk. I also became a dedicated art student while the leaden sky foreboded, day after day, the end of the world.

Time is elastic. It can also shrink into an unremarkable amorphous mass. That's what happened that year, time disappeared down a drain hole of endless rainy days. I catalogued my cloud pictures into high clouds, low clouds, and rain clouds, realizing that the amazing thing about them was that they were suspended in the immensity of sky, which could not be conveyed in a photograph. I was lost for a long time. I wandered around the streets of post-industrial life looking for the chance encounter with my identity in material objects. Wandered around looking at shop windows, looking at people, seeing people talking to themselves, sometimes wanting to talk to people, tell them soothing things. I took forever to decide what to buy in supermarkets, so much choice, bought things and then exchanged them, browsed through charity shops as if in that array of sad objects I would find something that would release me from my trance, looked in expensive shops, in cheap stores, sometimes inhabiting a flaccid time, other times intoxicated by what seemed to me a spectacularised world, receiving thousands of contradictory messages, a chaos of stimuli, a chaos of ambivalent visual dealings, chaos. In busy streets, I gazed at the frozen mannequins on the windows, looked at people, felt sad about the ghostly solitude of all those bodies lost in time and space, wonder why people looked miserable when they were by themselves.

I would look at some people wondering whether they were unkissed people, the unloved. I would also deliberately lose myself behind the main streets, looking for the feel of their innards, the rare alleyways. All these houses that looked identical until you realised all of them had slightly different architectural details that differentiated them, fluting on a shaft, an extra window. So quaint, so different from the environment where I grew up, such an anachronism, undoubtedly a convulsive fairy tale, a rancid imperial dream, that's what this architecture became with my wandering. Sometimes I enjoyed the brutal indifference of the rows of houses. Other times, I stopped at derelict sites, observed the debris encroached upon by weeds, wandered around until the air became thick with ghosts.

On a few occasions, I tried to leave the flat and found it impossible. It took me forever to wash, to brush my teeth, to get dressed, to find the keys, to find my wallet, to trace my favourite lipstick. The flat kidnapped me, hid things away to test my patience, the furniture encroached upon my body slowly until I knew I wouldn't be able to get out. Then I would be rescued by a telephone call. I liked the classmates I was going to the pub with. But I always found Mary Jane's voice the most grounding, even when she told me that she was going to stay in Pennsylvania a bit longer. There was something that tied me to the flat, and once in the streets, something that trapped me outside. I drifted along libidinal streets, sinister streets, listless streets, dirt, beauty and the ubiquitous smell of burnt petrol occasionally discontinued by slithers of chlorophyll. Perhaps, once in the streets, I was secretly collecting all those ossified moments, all that life, all that death, inhabiting a zone beyond life and death still to be named.

There was something I needed to process, but I didn't know how to do it.

I became unresponsive to men's mating calls.

Somehow, I felt sexually lazy.

I ticked off sex from my diary: I had done it, overdone it, it got a bit samey. Sex without love tends to leave a mere anecdotal trace. Availability, used to be my motto. It was a motto invented in order to counteract my clumsy looks, my insecurities. Erotic survival made me willing and always the one on top. Maybe I needed a rest, time to digest. I needed silence, to recoil into myself. I had no sex drive at all. That didn't bother me in the least. I was indifferent to most earthlings and predators. It was as if my own physicality didn't exist anymore, and at the same time my body felt heavy, unfit. I was doing jobs, little jobs. And then, I was getting on with college work while listening to depressing music which I found uplifting. I had to work harder on the essays, since it wasn't my native language, but then many art students thought in images, not in words. Over a year slipped by without anything memorable happening. I hardly noticed the seasons changing. And before I knew it, I was in my final year and it was Christmas again. When Mary Jane came back, she was full of strange stories about Ohio, Ontario, Virginia, and endless deserted motorways. The guy from Pennsylvania . . . she wasn't all that sure about him, familiarity breeds contempt, she said. She spoke whinging and whining, taking the piss out of the mighty swell Americans. She had been to New York a few times and loved it, but these other states, they are 'kinder neat,' they are fragments of the real America, there's a suicidal sadness in the air that I like, she said. Everything is

large, cheap and sad, she said. She tied up her long red hair
in a pony tail. And now head down, back to order, she said.
She then plunged into college work with a dedication I hadn't
seen in her before. We decided not to go home at Christmas,
to carry on working, even if we slowed down our pace. We
found a perverse satisfaction in completely ignoring Christmas Day and New Year's Eve.

Around the middle of January, just before art school started, I was summoned back to Spain. I got this call from my
cousin Antonio. Bad news. Your father is losing some of his
memory paths, he said. He forgets to switch the cooker off,
gets locked out, forgets to pay bills until the darkness in the
house enlightens him. He can't live by himself. He has become sick with forgetfulness. Not exactly an absolute danger
to himself, but he needs somebody to look after him. Did he
really have nursing needs? It was difficult for me to accept. I
couldn't live there with him. Sacrifice my life in order to look
after him. Father. Then my father rang me. Said some of his
mates were kicking the bucket, mortality sucked, it's time for
me to go to an old dinosaurs' home, a friend of my GP has
started up this community for old dinosaurs like me, my GP
has already arranged everything, some of my friends have already moved there, it's near the desert, the best of all possible
worlds, he said. An old dinosaurs' home? I asked. It's only for
old wrinklies, it's a commune, a cooperative, he said. He was
adamant. And I knew there and then that something wasn't
quite right.

I opened the special door that connected London to Almería and there he was, my father. But this time I saw a slight
difference in him straight away. His head seemed to be hi-
jacked by an intermittent, hazy atmosphere that came and
went in random gusts. He was in high spirits. He talked about
his childhood with a rare streak of nostalgia which flushed his
face, sang anarchist songs that he had learnt from his mother and treated me like an adult for the first time, with more

care than ever, a robust old man confused by a derelict mind. That's what he said when I first saw him. He said, I'm OK. I'm just losing my mind, it happens, don't worry about it, it's nothing. He was dressed impeccably. His sad dog eyes became sadder for a prolonged instant. Don't worry, he said, I'll be playing the sax, I'll have an audience, they'll cook for me, I'll have company, you get on with your life, he said. And then he added something that could be translated as: I'm not afraid of going, when you gotta go, you gotta go.

Homes were considered dumping sites, where you deposited your unwanted relatives. It's still a bit like that where I come from. That is the way homes are thought of. Unless the circumstances are extreme. It was my father's choice. But this wasn't a home, it was a commune, a cooperative. That's what my father's GP said. I could look after him myself, move back home. I thought about my life. What would I have sacrificed from my life? My desultory art degree? My disagreeable objects? My beautiful clouds? Were clouds more important than people? That wasn't the way to think about it. Except for a few lapses, my father seemed fine. Just odd that he would want to go to an old people's commune, but he insisted that it was the best possible cure for his loneliness. Neglect. I threw away everything from the fridge, sad at the evidence of degeneration. All the fruit and vegetables in different stages of decay. All the well-out-of-date jam and mustard pots, the yoghurts, other foods where the date had been erased. I helped him pack his things. At the time, I didn't quite take in what was happening. It affected me, but I found there was within me a denial, as if by not acknowledging the frailty of life, it simply ceased to exist.

On the day he was leaving, I thought I'd cook something, a special treat, but my father didn't trust my culinary skills and I ended up buying an expensive, ready-made meal. Roast duck with orange. Duck? He didn't like duck. He started laughing. He then quickly turned his head to one side half-covering his mouth with his hand and when he turned towards me again, raised his eyebrow and showed me a toothless smile. It quickly became his habitual magic trick. He then ate the duck while going: quack, quack, quack, quack . . . He had a great chuckle. We exploded in continuous, expanding laughter as he repeated: quack, quack, quack, quack . . . He was in good humour. The duck episode became a recurrent joke that underwent cow, sheep and dog variations with time: moo moo, baaah baaah baaah, woof, woof.

But the one that persisted as a trigger to infinite laughter was: duck a l'orange quack, quack, quack, quack . . .

There is the shock of the new and the shock of the old, my father's GP told me as he wrote down the address of this special new commune he had already talked to my father about. My father was both lucid and confused in equal measure. I went with him to the care home, which was called *El Refugio*, the haven. He became friendly with a woman called Eva, with the others, he seemed happy there. At the time I thought that his forgetfulness was just a sign of old age, I didn't know that it was Alzheimer's, but that's what it was. Middle stage of Alzheimer's. Alzheimer's is a word that dissolves all hope. It's a slow-motion word for death. When the GP briefly spoke about memory cells dying during old age, emphasising that it was as normal as deep wrinkles, white hair and gum disease, he put it in such a way that it seemed there was nothing to worry about. I didn't know he was speaking about senile dementia and was eventually told that my father had asked all the doctors he came across not to mention the 'A' word to me. He asked them not to talk in front of me about *severe* degeneration of brain cells or senile plaques accumulating in the brain substance or neurofibrillary tangles. He asked them to always tell me that he was well. *Shhh shhh shhh shhh.*

In order to help cover the costs of the commune, the house had to be rented, as his savings weren't enough. My father didn't belong to a throw-away culture. I had to sort out the detritus of years and years of life, my father's life. How could he have accumulated so much trash? But of course, what to me was trash, to him must have had some kind of value. Foreign coins, old passports, postcards from exotic places from friends. Gas, electricity, insurance and telephone bills going back more than twenty years. Perfectly ironed handkerchiefs, two huge safety boxes impossible to move, rusty tools, suits from when he was young running up to the present, impeccable ties that took you throughout the last fifty years of fashion, all these vintage clothing and then Russian magazines from the Iron Curtain time, my toys, most of my toys were still there.

And then, the loft. Did I have to empty the loft as well? Couldn't it be sealed off and forgotten forever? We all have collections of useless objects erected in memoriam to identity, sentimental museums reminiscent of those we had in childhood, our treasures made up of bizarre trinkets. Throw away everything, my father said. He said it was all rubbish in the loft, I could throw everything away, old radios, record players, vinyl LPs, singles, Glenn Miller, Elvis Presley, Tito Puente, The Beatles, Jeanette Birking, Louis Armstrong, American comics from the '50s and then boxes and boxes, lots of cardboard boxes. How could I throw away these things? My father's past? How could I dispose of my father's wedding ring even if he hadn't worn it for years? How could I dispose of my father's old trinkets, even if they were cheap things? I got a ladder while thinking about people who loathe cheap things, people who hid their sentimental museums behind the façade of financial value, measurable value. I felt sorry for them. Status-crazy people. They needed expensive, tangible objects to show their value to the world, without the status of things they became nothing, invisible, expensive things could conceal their insecurities or an inner ugliness, allowing them to love themselves better via the love of others towards their expensive things.

We all use things as extensions of ego-needs, embodiments of the immateriality of the soul, but for some people things were their deepest secret, they had a secret sentimental museum.

My father's secret sentimental museum, the loft.

It was there, in the loft, that I found these huge cardboard boxes full of shoe boxes full of exquisite shoes. Were all these exquisite shoes my mother's? Some of them had never been worn. They were completely new. Others had their bottom tips slightly worn. Sandals, stilettos, slippers, platforms, marabou mules, high-heeled, flat, orthopaedic, playful, sensible shoes, threatening spikes, laced boots. I opened the boxes, making sure each pair ended up in its box. I listened to the stories these shoes suggested. I took off my slightly smelly trainers, tried a pair of invisible plastic sandals on, tried some other shoes on, but they were all far too small. I looked at my feet as if I had never seen them before, observed their hairy toes, their unvarnished rough nails, bowed down in praise at the effort humanity had made to soften the impact of ugly feet through beautiful hocus-pocus. I held a red shoe up to the beam of light coming from the crack on the roof and marvelled at the architectural beauty of the design, the sensuous line of the arch, the sensual beauty of the natural red coloured leather, the excess of the pointed toe, the undulating lines. Then I held a perfectly poised stiletto, the heel the height of absurdity. I realised that I was seeing these shoes in terms of form and texture. I was seeing them as sculptures. These were ingratiating shoes. Flirtatious, heroic, romantic, delicate, witty, frivolous, aggressive, defiant, unwearable. They were irresistible. There was something redeeming about them, even about the ones that were tacky. Function? Comfort? These were sculptures of hypothetical utility. These shoes pointed to playfulness, to allure, to excess. Some of them were a utopia of androgyny translated into a shoe, others a dream of simplicity, yet others were revoltingly girlie, a walking parody, a dark nightmare of pinkness so sickly feminine that they could only possibly be worn with really hairy legs.

Were these shoes just shoes or were they more than shoes? Shoes have acquired the status of mythological objects. You put a pair of shoes in an empty space and a story soon begins to emanate. If clothes became limp when not worn, shoes were three dimensional forever, like hats. If a man could mistake his wife for a hat, didn't we see in shoes a particular presence where sex, age and personality were quickly arrived at? I counted the shoes. Ninety-five pairs, ninety-five stories. I looked at an ornate slipper. At a lime green sequin stiletto. I felt sorry all these shoes didn't fit me. Ah, the scoundrels. There it was, the immateriality of thought translated into matter, a collective fantasy of excess sculpted into skin-like leather.

All these shoes echoed my mother's feet. Did I remember my mother's feet? Were there any photographs of my mother's feet? How could Cinderella wear glass shoes? Did my mother occasionally wear outrageous stilettos for effect? Would my mother play act more than the usual play act? Was my father fatally dominated by these shoes because they were my mother's most cherished excess to the point that she and her shoes became indissoluble? Or were they ultrafeminine gifts from my father pointing to a secret obsession, my mother being an accomplice? Or was it both? Did the fact that my father slept with one of my mother's boots mean that he was a fetishist or was the boot an innocent evocation of my lost mother? An innocent evocation? Was my father a man who had a cellar in his loft?

I didn't want to drown in a pond of facile psychologism. I looked in the photo album again. My mother's bulging eyes. Perhaps her eyes looked too much like Bette Davis. Also, her extra long forehead, her bitter lips, her elongated triangular face. Maybe that was the problem. The reason her face would not be considered for acting. Today, she could have made a fortune as a Bette Davies look alike, been hired out for exclusive parties, for commercials advertising bitters, for audience grabbing programmes where she would have been voted the best Bette Davies. I am not sure she would have liked that. Her eyes popped out too much, and then perhaps her nose was a touch too big? Also, as an Italian, a '50s Italian, her breasts weren't big enough for acting. How could have she competed with Anita Ekberg, Sophia Loren, Gina Lollobrigida? A flat, short woman, with bulging eyes that echoed those of the formidable witch?

Perhaps my mother wore beautiful shoes to distract the gaze from her face, perhaps she didn't appreciate her odd beauty. This eclectic collection of shoes spoke of her eloquent addiction. But my father must have thrown some of her shoes away. I looked for Jeanne Moreau's boots amongst the boxes and there was no trace of them. I went back to the photo album. My mother with a roll-neck minidress, boots made for walking, false eyelashes, my parents in a white convertible with friends, my parents posing next to their first television set. Then there were a handful of pictures at the back of the photo album that hadn't been mounted on the rice paper pages. I realised that the mounted pictures ended when I was about five, probably a reminder of my mother's initial demise. There were all these photographs, but what had happened beyond their frame? I looked for hand-written letters, diaries, notebooks, testimonies. I didn't find anything. I took everything down from the loft. I sorted everything out with the idea of taking it to the Red Cross. I couldn't possibly keep all these things, all these records, all these shoes. The Red Cross? I imagined a starved woman somewhere in a remote dusty village in Ethiopia going to a well in the next village wearing my mother's absurd stilettos and gently rejected the mental image as politically incorrect. Was my primal scene dominated by a cruelly red stiletto?

Were all these colourful shoes, things of darkness? These

shoes resurrected the dead, spiced things up. Golden shoes and then black, green, magenta, red, silver, yellow, white: there was a pair of shoes for every shade of feeling.

Some shoes had been walked to pieces, danced to pieces, others were intact, others I just didn't understand. During the following days, I unpacked more shoes, admired them, tried on a few, thinking that maybe I should cut my toes off like Cinderella's stepsister in order to fit into an ideal of female beauty. Then one evening, I came across these extraordinary fake camel-fur knee boots that distracted me for a few days from my father's memory holes. So finely made, so elegant, so sensual. I measured them against my feet, tried them on, stood up, walked. They did fit, but my feet were in an absolute prison, I could barely stand up, they were so tight. They were extraordinary these fake camel-fur knee boots, so shinily hairy, with flat soles, a wonder from the '70s. I couldn't wait until the following day to take them to a shoe repairer to be stretched. So I went down, drowned them in a bucket of water to expand them, waited while immersed in the TV flow, then tried them on again soaking wet so the inner leather would continue to expand.

The fake camel-fur boots ritual started.

A ritual that was just a prelude for my inexhaustible capacity to do dumb things.

The fake camel fur didn't look wet, it was water resistant, the trapped water inside the boots made a sucking noise, they weren't painful if I stayed still, if I sat, but after a few minutes I experienced the first discomfort somewhere in the circuits of pain. I took them off, surprised to see that my feet were a bit bluish, drowned them again in the bucket pressing hard on the inside, thinking I should cut my toenails, even an infinitesimal millimetre off that tenacious matter would count. As I was cutting my toe nails, confronted by the ugliness of my feet and the yellowish thick layers of sedimentation from my ingrown toe nail that I had to file to diminish its outstanding depth, I realised these boots were definitely libidinous objects, sophisticated animals, that as such they were entitled to put forth their conditions. What was pain in comparison to the privilege of wearing such extraordinary artefacts? Wasn't the extraordinary worthy of sacrifice? I tried them on again, walked carefully along the corridor, feeling the sacrificial tightness in communication with all the other muscles of my body. I looked for different things, tomato soup tins, jars, plastic glasses, placed them inside to check the tension against the inner leather. I finally placed a pair of aromatic lemons inside the boots and pushed them against the instep, excited by the prospect of overnight boot expansion.

I tried them on as soon as I got up, tried to walk a bit with them, but they were still quite tight. I took them to a shoe repairer to be stretched, but didn't think my mother would have liked that man, there was something suspect about him, something beyond the calendar with an image of the Sacred Heart surrounded by orangey pictures of pin-up girls torn from magazines held to the wall by gaffer tape. Shoe repairers became suspect. It took me a while to find the right one, a shoe repairer who said he couldn't stretch them lengthwise, only the width, he would try his best, I could pick them up in three days. When I picked them up, he suggested I wear them everyday for an hour the first week to break them into my feet, then gradually wear them more and more. I put them on there and then, at the shoe-repair place. I went shopping for razor blades for my father, shopping for the unknown, but after twenty minutes or so of intense pressure travelling from my feet up to my head, I entered a phone box and changed into my trainers, welcoming the unbelievable respite. Maybe they would never ever fit, after all they were a size too small, the design was for slender feet, my feet were wide, maybe they were as impossible as a squared circle. I immersed myself in the fake camel-fur boots ritual as soon as I got home, a bucket of water, tins of tomato soup, until they fitted on perfectly, a five-day ritual that distracted me from the fact that my father had become a double stranger, from my sad hours at El Refugio where I was introduced to the gentle world of forgetfulness.

The paradise of forgetfulness

Alzheimer's is a bewildering illness. It slowly steals away your personality, your humanity. We are nothing without memories. Alzheimer's destroys the invisible wires that enable communication between different thinking regions, leaving the victim at the mercy of neural cul-de-sacs. If my father would end up confusing me with people on TV or treating me with the politeness you may treat a complete stranger as his illness progressed, I slowly learned to react as if I shared the same confused reality as him. But that daunting word wasn't part of the landscape, it had been hidden from me, my father wasn't ill, he was merely senile, he just forgot now and again about recent events, although his secret sentimental museum seemed to have been completely deleted from his memory, otherwise he wouldn't have told me to throw everything away. When I told him that I was emptying the loft, that there were all these shoes, my mother's shoes, he laughed, blushed, and then reacted as if he didn't know what I was talking about: shoes? What shoes? Ordinary shoes?

Extraordinary shoes, I said, mum's shoes.

Mum's shoes? What are you talking about? he said.

The loft, I said.

He then lost his patience and shouted angrily: I told you to forget about the loft, how many times do I have to tell you? It's all rubbish up there. I was surprised by this sudden bout of anger since it wasn't an emotion he was inclined to show. Had he really forgotten about my mother's shoes in the loft? Did his forgetfulness configure into some kind of pattern or was it a somewhat chaotic demolition of memory paths that could capriciously erase an entire memory zone? But it wasn't forgetfulness. He probably didn't want to talk about it. Forget about the loft, he said again. He then said that he had enough savings to pay for El Refugio, that I didn't have to rent the house, forget about it too, he said, and started talking about a mechanical toy car that he had as a child. I played with it everyday and then one day it just went missing. I looked for it everywhere, even in my mother's loft, he said. You never talk about your childhood, I said. Many people from his generation didn't talk about it or if they did, they skirted around the Civil War. It was too long ago anyway. But the lingering effect of trauma after the Civil War and the recurrent waves of censorship that ensued had first consolidated into a collective, mournful muteness that had given way to a prolonged silence which couldn't be broken until the euphoria that the process of democracy brought about had been superseded.

Personal memory added a different dimension to historical memory, sometimes pushing tragedy right to the background. What do you remember about the war? I suddenly said. You couldn't see a cat around, he said. But you were happy, you always say how happy you were, I said. Terrible happy times, they were intense times, he said vividly recalling his childhood at the end of the Spanish Civil War as his happiest time, his fiercely anarchist mother, the anarchists' ideals of justice and fraternity, his first encounters with my mother. Almost every trace of my mother had been erased from his memory, every trace except their first encounters in an anarchist theatre group in Rome. He spoke about the sheer excitement of the air raids, the hair-raising sirens, walking amongst the debris of so many shattered lives as if a prolonged naïveté had blinded him to the reality of war. He vividly remembered listening with his whole family to the news on the radio, listening to the nobility of human sacrifice, the heroes, they had truly believed the collapse of the Republic would lead to a future without hierarchies, without leaders, with the responsible freedom of self-government, but then such a senseless game, the war, all those sacrificial bodies, he said. He had changed his mind in retrospect, he had later come to admire Gandhi.

That evening, my father slipped into a fold in time whereby he inhabited simultaneously the late 1930s in 1991. He recounted stories that I had heard a few times before but this time he retold them with an enchanted air and he was obviously emotionally charged. He spoke about his mother's glorious escape when she was eighteen, how she ran away to Barcelona with a fugitive lorry driver to join the anarchists, how she joined a small theatre that made alternative plays about freer ways of living and different ways of relating to others, how that was when she became a singer of bawdy songs, a cuplés singer, a popular musical genre at the time. His mother had fought for abortion rights and women's equal pay. He had forgotten that I had written a short-story about it, 'Yaya,' that it had been published in an anthology and that he was proud about it. He didn't remember it. This was in the 1930s, he would emphasise, his face aglow with emotion. There was talk of 'free love' in the air, he laughed. All these ideas that are taken for granted now, abortion, divorce, were shortly put into practice at that time, some of the anarchist ideas were ahead of their time, they were put on hold for thirty years, they were taken up again in the '60s, but still so much to do, he said. It was a crucial moment in history, change was nipped in the bud, history could have been something else, he said. He then spoke about this guy who had become a human bomb by tying tonnes of dynamite to his body and throwing himself to the enemy's tanks, like Palestinians do now, he said.

Another evening, I heard him say something that has remained in my head. He said, mother, there is only one, but she cannot be an umbilical chord forever, not even during the first years of your life. My father, Jordi Joan, had a permanent audience now. He could play the sax anytime and a small group of oldies would gather and listen and clap. Now and again, he would play awkward notes and make jokes to erase the traces of his confusion. My father, he looked the same amiable self, the same fine features, same sad dog eyes, same sensual lips, same hair style. And yet, he was slowly becoming in part somebody else, a robust old man whose memory paths increasingly led to the same places: childhood, the war, anarchism, his mother, his happy childhood amidst the chaos. My mother had been such an important part of his life, and yet he never talked about her, her presence had almost been erased, relegated to the realm of acquaintances, an anecdote in his life that was fading to the point of virtual disappearance. Do you ever dream about mum? I said. Not anymore, he said, I used to when she died, but then she vanished from my dreams.

El Refugio was a special old people's commune. It was run by volunteers, a pilot project that seemed to be working. The patients were encouraged to set and clear the table, wash the linen, sometimes they cooked. The atmosphere was gentle and caring, perhaps a side-effect of the powerful drug cocktails in their systems. When I think about it, even the stray dogs that wandered in the courtyard seemed to be inhabited by a narcotised softness. The project had been set up by Dr. Alvarez, a financially savvy flower child with black locks whose presence was like a mild breeze. I was pleased such place existed. It was the perfect place for my father. He would have hated to go to one of those aseptic limbos where bureaucratic design numbs everything with its deadly caress. I'm in Eden, he said. This is Shangri-la, he said.

An adulterated citrus fragrance enfolded El Refugio. A deaf-blind person would have guessed its position between citrus fields and a busy main road, solely through the sense of smell. I kept taking trains backwards and forwards to see my father. El Refugio was an immense villa that had been recently restored. Dr. Alvarez had recruited volunteers and raised funding to deal with the restoration. It was a beautiful white building of simple lines. And at the back of it, there were field after field of greenhouses, an enormous alien sprawl swathed in plastic solely populated by a community of promising vegetables. It was cold. And sometimes the greenhouses were chilled. I liked those frosty mornings with the sun gently lighting the day, but powerless about changing its low temperature. Experiencing the luminescent frost made me wonder about the traumatic effects upon the psyche of living in England, a country whose sky was struck with sharp mood swings. Was I staying longer around my father partly because of that, the gentle, nourishing light, the persuasive sun?

With the discovery of my father's secret sentimental museum, my mother's shoes, I began to listen to him with a new heightened sense of awareness, waiting for a comment that will make me understand him better. It seemed that he had forgotten about his secret sentimental museum, he had forgotten my mother, but he would passionately quote Durruti's words, the Spanish anarchist's well-known words, which he must have heard so many times from his own mother: *We have always lived in slums and holes in the walls. We'll manage. It was the workers who built these palaces and cities here in Spain, and in America, and everywhere else. We can build others to take their place. Better ones. We're not in the least afraid of ruins. We're going to inherit the earth. That's a fact.* He would remark how much he loved those words, *we're not in the least afraid of ruins.* And as his memory was becoming precisely that, a pile of ruins, I loved him all the more for remembering those words, although with time I began to wonder whether it was also an oblique reference to his preference for libidinal fragments such as my mother's shoes. My father spoke about Durruti and the anarchist's unforgettable experiments, but other patients didn't remember any of that, the war, the ideals, the loss. Perhaps they preferred silence, the war was just too far away, perhaps what they remembered was precisely that, the silence, these people's secret for happiness was to be found in the fact that they didn't remember much, amnesia, that's what their happiness was made out of.

I spent three weeks going to visit him, growing fond of all these old people who would give me stale biscuits hoarded for special occasions, played mnemonic games with them, realised it was a torture for others to see them like that, not for them. I listened to some of their relatives, heard stories about previous hospitals where their demented parents and uncles forgot to tick the menu order sheets and were left starving for days.

Soft, soft, soft, ever softer, that's what I became with these people who carried their hearing aids and dentures in their pockets, who suffered from long strings of illnesses, who were walking pharmaceutical cabinets, who took slowly one step after the other. Extraordinary white-haired heads, then grey, then silver. I had never been with so many old people before. In the world I inhabited, old people were more or less invisible. And now I entered a whole new world that was strange and genuine at once, a gentle world where pretence had been discarded in favour of humility. The world these people sick with forgetfulness had built seemed to be shaped by a new vision, a vision based on empathy and genuine caring. This particular group of people, in these particular circumstances, a self-governed home, had definitely reached a concord about empathy. Somehow, through them, I learnt to look at old people in a new way. I had always thought of old age wisdom as a myth. Of course, some of them were stubborn, some others moaned, others talked incessantly to keep dangerous silence at bay, but my fondness for these gentle amnesiacs who carried their spare parts in their pockets, grew with every visit to my father. While I was there, I experienced a strange sensation that I could be there forever. And I knew it would be necessary to leave sooner rather than later. Had I found paradise? Were they preparing themselves for a lengthier stay in heaven? Would all this softness soon start to asphyxiate me?

I joined my father, the others, in their prescribed games.

We played Scrabble being open about spelling, any spelling was allowed as long as the word sounded right. This way of playing had its fans, but also its fierce critics. My father profoundly disliked this small violation of rules, perhaps because his spelling had always been good and although he couldn't remember his closest relatives' names, he still had his own spelling intact, perhaps spelling was for him an ideal of order without which the world would collapse into a myriad of splinters.

Then at times, I wondered whether I was idealising these people, whether I was denying the reality of their fragility. The joy some of the old men felt as they kissed me on the cheek was something new to me. When my friends kissed me, it wasn't a big deal, a kiss. My friends took kisses for granted. These old people had abandoned all the nonsense of being competitive, the senseless race, the senseless hurting each other through action, through lack of it. They had abandoned all this in favour of being empathic, sentient beings. I learnt. I respected their strengths, blurred their weaknesses, being aware that perhaps, if I had stayed there longer, I would have started to perceive them in a different way.

Soft, cute animals, that's what the female patients had in their rooms. Some of the women had been given cute teddies, fluffy bunnies, ducks, penguins, as if their senility had transformed them into cute little girls rather than old women on the road to the final regression. The men didn't get these flannel worlds as presents. The men got warm gowns, chequered sleepers, aftershave, useful things, as if men weren't capable of such regression, as if their world was one of pure functionality. I myself had got my father a couple of paisley silk pyjamas, a pair of navy blue espadrilles like the ones he usually wore. My father, a piece of history. He wasn't a child, he was an adult made vulnerable by increasingly devouring memory gaps. If we don't entirely choose what we remember, he certainly hadn't chosen to forget bits of who he was, who he had been.

He became good friends with Dr. Alvarez, an indefatigable presence always dressed in medical white. I soon realised that Dr. Alvarez needed his patients as much as they needed him. I admired the man for being so simple in his methods, focusing on the patients strengths to show there can be joy and purpose in senile decay. He gave them diets rich in anti-oxidants, omega 3 and claimed curry was good for memory. He made them walk backwards, he also made them count from 100 to 1 backwards, wear their watch on their right-hand or left-hand if they were left-handed and watch pictures upside down. It was all about breaking habits as a way of exercising the brain.

My father also became friends with this feisty seventy-five-year-old woman, Eva. She was still quite agile, a few of them were quite agile, their age didn't correspond to the youthfulness they showed. But then, why should it? At exercise time, as I heard some of their bones creak, I came to admire Eva, who had asked a nurse to remind her everyday of her running time. It was arranged for the trainer to go along with her. Eva didn't seem to mind. She jogged around the grapefruit fields for half an hour every morning, sometimes bringing a grapefruit back and peeling it with her hand, relishing the grapefruit's spray as the peel was removed with her rheumatoid fingers, the fragrance, the adhesive perfume it left on her finger tips. My father had always looked younger than he was, as if all those years of celibacy had softened the ageing process of his skin. At El Refugio, he became close to Eva. And I could see in the way he talked to her, in the glint on his iris, in his final joining her for her half an hour run, that he was falling for her. But then that was what I told myself. How could that happen with a shaky short-term memory? Did he recognise her everyday, was everyday forever the first time?

Then I thought that the fake camel-fur knee boots were perfectly beautiful objects that perhaps could trigger my father's secret memories. It was none of my business, but I had been thinking about it now and again. Questioning my motives. Questioning whether the idea of triggering his secret memories by wearing my mother's fake camel-fur knee boots wasn't an alibi for an unresolved love to leak out. Questioning whether his friendship with Eva had confused my judgement. I knew I had a tendency for disorderly conduct, just to see what happened. I knew the idea was absurd, inappropriate. A sign of my endless capacity to do dumb things. But I did it. Driven by only god knows what. One afternoon, I put on a pair of light green corduroy lederhosen, placed my mother's fake camel-fur knee boots in a carrier bag, put them on just before I got off the train to economise on the hurt, and visited him. I expected a comment, a story, my mother's name dropped casually in the conversation. I found myself crossing and uncrossing my legs several times as if my lower body had taken a life of its own. I was trying to direct his gaze towards my mother's boots. The fake camel-fur boots were met with supreme indifference. My father was playing Scrabble with Eva and then we watched *Gone with the Wind*. But then when I left El Refugio that evening, my father greeted me goodbye with what sounded like a smooth chat-up postponement. He whispered to me: *hasta la vista, baby*. Then later that evening I started wondering whether his remark was provoked by the lederhosen I was wearing rather than my mother's fake camel-fur knee boots: I shouldn't have worn the light green lederhosen! Back to square one, I thought.

The snowing dream

During those crisp, luminous days, while I cleared my father's house, I became aware of the furniture's fuzzy presence, the austere still-life forever on the wall. It was as if I was witnessing the beginning of a haunting process, a rearrangement of molecules that superimposed a hazy layer of resistance onto the ever familiar surroundings. I found the ghosts at my father's flat difficult to share the space with, especially at night, with the darkness. Except for my father and my cousin Antonio, except for my love of the language, I had more or less severed all contact with the place where I was brought up. Hadn't been in touch with my friends there. Felt strange about being there. Had no sense of purpose when I was there. It wasn't so much that I had severed all contact with my friends, but that there was this gap that separated me from them. Time-space separated me from them. I still had school friends. Deep down I was attached to them, but I only saw them briefly during my stays. I saw any attachment to the past as nostalgia. Nostalgia, what a dirty word! The past was something I didn't have time for. Too busy immersing myself in a sheer present, in the next adventure, too busy to realise fragments from the past forever re-organise your present asking for acknowledgement, soliciting a revision.

Revel in the ephemeral, that's what I used to do.

I saw my father, I saw my solitude, I saw my cousin Antonio. Seeing Antonio rescued me from the ghosts at my father's flat, from myself. I started hanging out with him in the evenings, staying overnight at his place. Antonio was a few years older than me, his black straight hair hung down to his chest, he was studying cartoon animation, his flat was full of empty bottles of rum, blurred mementoes of intoxication altered by the dry dripping wax left by melting candles. Together we in-

creased the rum bottle collection. Jokes. Our friendship was
mainly based on that, humour. Everything can be lightened
up into a joke. I needed that at the time, the lightness. Antonio gave me lightness. He loved flea markets, bazaars, second-hand clothes, the traces of life on objects, the possibility of bargains, the chaotic display of sacrificed goods. So did
I. One morning we went to El Rastro, the main second-hand
market, good junk, bad junk. He was looking for an old
leather jacket, while I found myself looking for my mother's boots, Jeanne Moreau's boots. We walked. We stopped.
We separated. We met again. Walking around these sacrificed
goods you created an intimate map where you could get lost,
a map with landmarks created by involuntary objects, a broken vase, a legless doll, a German edition of Mallarmé's poetry next to a tiny plastic dinosaur, then all these spaces of
disconnection, mini wastelands where objects failed to trigger anything except for the delayed sadness that utter apathy
transmits. Amongst all the colourful and neutral trash, Antonio found an old leather jacket. A pilot's jacket. As fashions
were endlessly recycled in a dizzying whirlpool to trick you
into a mirage of change, his theory was you only had to own
a few trousers and shirts from a handful of periods to look
forever updated.

Some of my father's polyester suits and shirts were now
the last retro fashion. We went to my place. We ran up to the
loft. We went through my father's suits. While I was tinkering
with an old radio, finally tuning into a mystifying Arab station, Antonio tried on a few suits including a navy blue stripy
one that looked as if tailored for him. It was strange seeing
him with my father's stripy suit on, it was strange seeing his
high rib cage partly covered by his long, black, straight hair
when he took his top off to try on a shirt. The Arabic song
brought with it the fake camel-fur knee boots. I showed him
some of my mother's shoes, a green pair with 'comma' heels,
a deep-throated shoe with a 7-inch heel, then the fake camel-

fur knee boots. He touched them, he loved them, he jokingly kissed their aura. They're the most extraordinary boots I've ever seen, he said. I slipped the boots on, felt the pressure on my calves transferring all my blood upwards. We spun around and around to the Arabic singing until we fell exhausted against a beam. Then we did everything everywhere.

Everything.

The following morning we behaved as if nothing had happened, as if what had happened had happened on the other side of the mirror. Antonio took the suits he wanted. Other things we took to the Red Cross. But I kept all the boxes with my mother's shoes, Nina Chiavelli's shoes, I couldn't possibly part with them, with my strange inheritance.

There was a tacit agreement that what had happened between us belonged to the set of things that only happen once. Throughout, I had neglected the accumulation of things piling up in London. Mary Jane was opening my post, answering calls for me, sorting out bills, the rent. DHL deliveries to Mary Jane containing documents signed by me were proving expensive. I had faxed Mary Jane a page with a few samples of my signature so that she could sign things on my behalf. Had felt odd about that. Somebody else forging my signature with my permission. There were things for which I had to be there, my presence was needed there, filling in forms, cashing cheques, problems with the bank better solved in person, the bureaucratic trail that follows everyone like a shadow from hell.

Then one day Mary Jane's call shocked me out of my torpor. El Refugio had had over me an anaesthetising effect mixed with a real but quiet concern towards these people who shed memories on their way to paradise. We have to move out, she said. The housing market is booming obscene, Mr. Bloodsucker wants to sell the flat, we either pay a substantial rent increase or we're out, he's given us a month's notice, she said. Then she said that she had finally dumped the Pennsylvanian guy, he was a rat, she was now seeing a beautiful boy, Sam, she was also producing new work, she couldn't wait for me to see it, she said. She didn't know how to say she'd rather I came straight away. But then she talked at length about the mountain of things piling up, my things.

Slowly, my gaze changed mode during the following days. I started seeing everything as more distant, my surroundings started fading, as if I was already somewhere else. My new gaze embodied this process. I was slowly absorbing the fact that I should make a move, say goodbye, unconsciously digesting the possibility that perhaps this would be the last time I saw my father. My father was busy with Eva. Or that's the way I deluded myself that he was fine. He was fine, the doctors and nurses said, he was fine.

Somehow, I restrained a tear when I said goodbye to him. I said to him, *hasta la vista, baby*. It was a way of lightening the moment. But he didn't react. Some of the people at El Refugio hugged me goodbye stroking my hair, stroking my cheek. Others were amiable too. But I knew that some of them didn't know that I was the same person who had played Scrabble with them the day before. For them, I was forever a kind new face that left no indentation on their minds. The days before my departure had a strange taste. That's when I saw them all naked, some time during the days before my departure, I had this strangely familiar dream. It was snowing gently. It was a luminous day. Eva was the first to take her clothes off, in the living room, in front of everybody. Others started doing the same, uninhibited, indifferent to their bodies. Others went into their bedrooms. I saw them all naked, with their beautiful shrivelled bodies walking unaware around the living room, being tactile with each other. Then this couple of old women came towards me, invited me to dance, I could see the stains, the freckles, stitches on their stomachs, scars that spoke about the physical memory of flesh, time written on their bodies, there was a beauty about this time, about its folds. I saw my future in those bodies. I became aware of the difference, of my unwritten body. It only had a few, gentle stretch marks, the effect of gravity wasn't quite there yet. The old women pushed me towards the others, who had gathered in an amorphous circle. I looked for my father. He was nowhere to be seen. He was probably in his room. He was glaringly absent. Dr. Alvarez and a nurse came with blankets, reminded them they could catch a cold. They all laughed, they had relished their nudity spell thoroughly. The amorphous circle of naked bodies now covered by blankets broke apart. Dr. Alvarez explained. It wasn't the first time this had happened. Old-age-related illnesses could affect the inhibition centre in the brain, some of them did things like that, one of them would now and again urinate in the corridor, then somehow realise what he had done. Then Dr. Alvarez left with Eva, they were both naked, they were holding hands, walking slowly on the snow-carpeted road towards the grapefruit trees, admiring the sheer whiteness, oblivious to the ice in the air, admiring the hypnotising snowflakes.

My cousin Antonio, that dream, my father, my gaze underwent a further change, reality was definitely elsewhere, I had to finish my art degree, it was time for me to go.

I couldn't throw away, give away, all these shoes, Nina Chiavelli's shoes, my father's sentimental museum, my mother's shoes. I counted them. Ninety-five pairs, ninety-five different identities, ninety-five stories. I didn't know where to store them, couldn't choose a few, forget about the rest, most of them were meaningful in some kind of way. The truth is I couldn't part with them. I wanted to keep them. I wanted to revel in such a splendid collection. The truth is when I first saw them in the loft, I knew I would take them with me. Was I stealing from my father, from my parents? Was I being voyeuristic over their ineffable secret? I had told my cousin Antonio about the shoes, my mother's shoes. I didn't want

him to store them for me. I hadn't told him about my father hugging one of my mother's boots in his sleep, the boots
that looked like Jeanne Moreau's. He had asked no questions.
Now he was taking me to the airport with all these boxes full
of shoes. I barely had any personal luggage. The shoes didn't
weigh that much. It was the volume. Three large cardboard
boxes full of exquisite shoes. I wrote my name and address
on all of them. Put the warning label 'fragile' on all of them.
Explained to the navy-blue-uniformed creature at the counter that they were my inheritance, my mother's personal belongings. The hostess-like attendant consulted with another
navy-blue-uniformed woman, she smiled, the flight's luggage
boot was half empty. I put the boxes on the conveyor belt
and watched them go through the rubber tussled door into
their journey, then dishevelled Antonio's hair as if I was going to see him the following day. Not sure where I was while
the X-ray monitor scanned the unrecognisable contents of
my handbag, no tumours, no cancers, only black and white
translucent volumes that the security guard had been trained
to recognise.

Leather-bound Stories

Guilt has always accompanied me through customs, as if in the contents of my travelling bags, undeclarable dreams could be detected. But this time I had the boxes. There was nothing illegal about my mother's shoes. Perhaps the quantity was unusual. I waited at the pick-up point. The immense, truncated zero made out of rubber was still, as if waiting for the last passengers to arrive. Then the slow-motion movement. The parade of almost identical-looking baggage. I watched the dark coloured bags circulating on the conveyor belt, like so many burdens people carry through life. I looked at expensive looking luggage being picked up by relieved travellers, my eyes fixed on the luggage flap, the stark fluorescent atmosphere adhering to my person like an offensive aura. I watched a dark green suitcase going round and round, unclaimed, suspicious, redundant. The last one. My travelling bag and boxes hadn't turned up. I still waited for a bit. I waited till the carousel stopped. Then complained to an airport worker who then disappeared behind a rubber door. When he finally reappeared he was carrying my travelling bag and boxes on a trolley. But then at customs I was stopped. A couple of customs officials invited me to a small room, their neutral faces betraying self-congratulatory restraint. My mother's shoes, Nina Chiavelli's shoes had been intercepted. I saw a trained dog sniffing the boxes, somebody touching them, probably laughing at them. I loathed the thought. I knew that crawling would be my only way out. I crawled. I explained, restraining my blood from rushing to my face. I didn't belong to the second-hand trade, or any trade at all for that matter. They were vintage shoes, they had belonged to my deceased mother, they were a token to remember her by. I scanned their faces for invisible laughter. They asked for credentials.

Were they looking for sweat as an indicator of lying? I said they were just shoes. I smiled. Credentials? What credentials? Then I followed them to an aside where the shoes were being searched. The custom officials went away, talked to each other. I waited. When they came back, they asked me to pack the shoes and go away. They had left everything in a mess. As I was packing, unable to release my anger lest they decided to carry on with their game of self-righteousness, I realised that a generous amount of sublimated sadism was in-built in so many professions, a therapeutic bonus just as valuable as a company car.

I took a trolley, the cardboard boxes completely blocking my view. I went through the car-rental companies, the exchange bureaux that led you into the totalitarian paradise of ubiquitous High-Street shops. I had to leave the trolley at the escalators that led to the train's platform, didn't see any lifts, wondered how disabled people managed, perhaps they just didn't travel. A gentleman helped me with the boxes on the escalators, probably wondering what this foolish young lady was doing with such cumbersome luggage. He helped me put the boxes into the train, then ran to a different carriage, as if weary of further human contact. He had been kind, but I was now in the land of non-eye-contact, where strangers had more or less forgotten to smile, where people unwittingly exhibited their misery in public spaces, so much anger and frustration, so much worry spelt out in those exhausted faces.

Battersea Power Station has always filled me with a strange joy. A feeling of being home. A feeling slightly polluted now by the knowledge that it once poisoned the city with lethal fumes, that these fumes killed people. But I didn't know this at the time. I celebrated the building. Then the joy subsided, I started regretting all these boxes, my mother's shoes, when an unusually stout taxi driver told me that they would cover the back window, it's dangerous, he said. A mini-cab came to my rescue. As usual, I gave precise instructions as to my address. He helped to take the boxes out of the cab onto the pavement, then I had to leave everything on the drive and carry one box at a time down an alleyway to the side front door, worrying someone would steal the boxes I had left unattended for a few seconds. Mary Jane opened the door, the cordless telephone adhering to her ear, tipsy.

I left the boxes on the landing, waiting for Mary Jane to finish her intoxicated call, surprised that she didn't hang up straight away, she was talking to Sam. The flat looked so different. It had just been painted, it looked so bare, I hadn't seen Mary Jane for so long. We sat around the kitchen table, an unrelated and unopened Chinese pot noodle soup presiding over our conversation. The boxes? My parents' inheritance, I said. My father? Fine, fine. I didn't want to contaminate the air with bleak thoughts. So many things have happened, she said. She said that she had done a lot of work to the flat, and now we have to bloody move out, she said. She had already found another flat. The notes of anger in her voice changed to notes of pleasure as she spoke about Sam. She wanted me to meet him. He's so beautiful, he's ten years younger than me, rum-coloured hair, brandy-coloured eyes, caffè latte skin, espresso heart, macchiato mind, she said. He had been disturbed as a child, his mind revealed the traces of the disturbance, he was strange, he was weeeird, these were the kind of things that inspired her, to be shocked into a different reality, his skin was silk. She tumbled against the cardboard boxes, then against her room's door. This guy, Sam, he was a hypnotherapist and a sculptor, more of a hypnotherapist of late. Then she talked about her work, her work which was her life.

Mary Jane had converted her bedroom, which was quite big, into a studio. She had started to collect blue and pink baby objects and arrange them in a way that refreshed the gaze. She was fascinated by the soft shapes, the gentle colours. Seduced by the utopian lie they represented. In the way she had arranged some rattles, you could see a methodical mind, a ritualist. The sense of ritual was somehow encoded in her work. Baby toys are so important, they're the first objects we have a binding relationship to, the first objects of intensity, she said. I pointed my index at a pristine bib on the wall, said it was dead, it was too clean, it lacked the milky smell babies ooze out. That's precisely what I like about it, she said.

Looking at a pale blue rattle that she had placed in one corner of her room, I thought about the traumatic experience she had had recently. She had blamed the large quantities of vodka she was drinking for the consistently negative pregnancy tests. I wondered whether her new work was a way of mastering trauma, dissolving it. She had abandoned the Pennsylvanian guy after discovering that he was a married man. He had just forgotten to tell her that he was married, with four children from four different marriages on three different continents. He couldn't possibly tell her that he was on a mission to fertilise as many eggs as possible from as many countries as possible. Out. She had deleted him from her life. Never told him about the pregnancy, about the way it had gone undetected for months, about the sudden miscarriage. Her new work, all these baby toys, had probably emerged to conceal the confusing nightmare the miscarriage had entailed. She never talked about it those days, about the miscarriage. She was immersed in her work. I walked around her studio, around her obsession. Some of the cute bunnies were in pristine condition. Others were dirty, brutalised, battered victims of a pathetic violence. I loved these things. After so many years, I still have a fond memory of them.

Being back in London always created a two-day time warp resembling some kind of dizzy objectivity. The post, bills, bureaucratic nightmares, that was also part of being back. Sam stayed in a few nights, rum-coloured hair, brandy-coloured eyes, caffè latte skin. He was beautiful, he was crazy, there was a strange violence in his eyes. He would flirt with me, I would smile, and Mary Jane would pretend to be jealous. Mary Jane

was going out a lot. With Sam. And when she was in, instead
of packing up, sorting things out, she would sit in the maze
she had created for herself drawing simplified cute bunnies
while listening to the obsessional compositions of Michael
Nyman. Sam must have reinforced in her mind these ideas
that she was already toying with, ideas about regression, finding inspiration through regression and play. Surrounded by
all these baby toys, playing with them in ceremonial manner,
Mary Jane had also started using baby talk. She had always
been a big kid, it's never too late to have a happy childhood,
she would say. It was during those days that I realised the
extent to which she had been absorbed by Sam while I was
away. It was also during those days that a thought kept going
through my head: whether Sam had hypnotised her and left
her semi-stuck in some amorphous childhood zone.

I had already cleared my father's flat, clearing my own flat
was much simpler. Still, no matter how detached my attitude, it was hard not to stop, reread some old letters, browse
through old art books I had forgotten, wonder at something
I didn't quite recognise, reflect on why I kept some broken
things of no use whatsoever, whether I was attached to their
interesting texture, their hidden meaning. Like my father, I
had this tendency to hoard, to keep scraps of paper, newspaper articles, old leaflets. I suppose I kept these things just in
case, then on a regular basis threw some of them away.

In a way, Mary Jane was the opposite, she had become a
minimalist with things, with space. The space she had created was clinical. The few objects that she now possessed shone
with all the energy of the empty space. It was the empty space
that gave them an aura. In my absence, she had turned the
flat into a secret gallery for nobody to see. The baby toys,
manufactured and anonymous, with no trace of the hand
but with their aura of a fabricating mind, had acquired a tal-
ismanic presence due to their display as sacred objects displaced from playland.

I was fascinated by the strange power that emanated from these baby toys. Mary Jane became fascinated by my mother's shoes. Swell. Mighty swell. Weird. Over the following days, I removed the cardboard boxes from the entrance, as they were almost blocking the front door. There was no question of putting them in Mary Jane's room, even if it was almost empty. That's the way she was with her space. It was a shrine. So I took the boxes upstairs and piled them up in a corner of my room. It was then that I showed her all of them.

Maybe we won't have to move out . . . Did you know that medieval people used to hide old ugly shoes in their house to ward evil off? she said. No, I didn't know. I was aware that some of my mother's shoes were quite vulgar. And I liked that. I felt drawn to this vulgarity that made me uneasy, made me muse on matters of taste. I persuaded myself I liked them. Vulgarity was the great outsider, ornament was considered vulgar, at least in the circles I moved in where the in-look was restrained and minimal. And yet there was something truthful in vulgarity, a loss of restraint, an histrionic irony, a nightmare of manic excess. Mary Jane quite liked them in that way too. Like me, she had barely ever worn high-heels, we wore trainers, flat shoes, platforms, Dr. Martens, but not stylised stilettos, those belonged to a different generation, the ladies, our mothers. Like everything, they were bound to come back, but at the time high-heels were a no-no, hard time for shoe fetishists, they were considered cheesy, tacky, vulgar. Vulgar? What was vulgarity? Wasn't it a prejudice conjured up by a given tribe, at a given time, in a given place, so as to belittle others, like so many other prejudices?

The flat Mary Jane had found was in Old Street, ordinary rented accommodation, practical and lacklustre. It was smaller than the previous place, especially my room. I didn't know that I was going to wind up living in a room even smaller than the previous one. As new buildings weren't built, living space had become a real problem in this city, most people we knew living in ridiculously small places, matchboxes, spacious toilets. We had been looking for a flat with storage space, with a loft, but the price went up with every square millimetre, with every inch. There was something obscene about the prices. They were unreal. Sanctioned theft. It was the mystery of value, something that I was about to discover. We lived a couple of months without unpacking, surrounded by travelling bags, suitcases and cardboard boxes. I had put my mother's shoes, the cardboard boxes, in my bedroom. They took up most of the space, so I decided to build a continuous shelf near the ceiling and display some of the new shoes there as if they were books, leather-bound stories.

Mary Jane occasionally bought baby toys, placed them on the wall, stared at them for hours on end. She said that she was trying to find the mental point where things ceased to be perceived as contradictions. She was trying to get an exhibition with no luck. She was suffering. She would overwhelm my ear, Sam's ear. How can you approach gallery directors if they create a no-go area around them when in public, if they never answer letters or proposals, if they never answer the telephone or return calls? How can you approach them if they're unapproachable? A few young artists were emerging as big names, media events that had been orchestrated for maximum impact by almighty agents and their entourage, money, money, money. But didn't we know that, hadn't it been like that all through, wasn't art always, at least the art that was promoted, no matter how interesting, intimately related to the smell of money? If we knew it, we had forgotten it.

Sam's right, any good artist can be picked up and promoted into an omnipresent star. It's all about money, money shouts, money seduces all the media, it's all a question of money. And power, it's also all about power. I listened to Mary Jane. It was shocking for her, for Sam, for me, to realise that it wasn't about the work, it was about a combination of the right circumstances, who you knew, where you were, who your friends were. That's it, Sam would say, it's about a handful of BLEEP, a BLEEP handful of ambitious lepers deciding what's BLEEP in, what's BLEEP out. It's about BLEEP knowing how to BLEEP say BLEEP 'dahling-dahling'. It's about BLEEP being at the BLEEP right place at the BLEEP right time with the BLEEP right people with the BLEEP right attitude, it's about BLEEEP BLEEEEP BLEEEEEP psychopaths … BLEEEEEEEEP, Sam would say.

Mary Jane revelled in Sam's sense of fair play. He had had hideous experiences with a few gallerists. They owed him money. They treated him like a nobody. And one of them stole his ideas. Therefore he wanted to at least shoot down a couple of them. Put the trigger against their temple, look menacingly into their eyes and shout: You enjoy being a psychopath, don't you?

Sam regularly fuelled Mary Jane's anger. I understood the anger. But at the time, I didn't understand that so much anger had pain as its source. It was Sam and Mary Jane against everything, Mary Jane and Sam caught up in an antediluvian duel against institutionalised injustice. That's when I knew Mary Jane, at the centre of a painful rite of passage. Her life was dominated by a series of near misses. Being at the right place at the wrong time, meeting the right person at the wrong time, meeting the wrong people at the right place, being at the wrong place at the wrong time with the wrong people. In the rule of variables, everything happened out of joint, bad timing predominated. Perhaps that was the norm, for so many people, general bad timing. Was art about that, about timing? The right people? The wrong people? Seeing other artist's work being elevated into stardom, had an unexpected violent effect on Mary Jane's psyche. Anger, furious anger. And envy. But envy isn't the right word, it was more like a sense of wrong. It was wrong. She believed in a system based on merit, on originality. She became suspicious of successful artists who were the same age as her, angry. She was devoured by this anger. She would talk about it incessantly. She would see her energy deflating a bit more with each new rejection, each new rejection took at least two to three weeks to absorb, her calls were never returned, her proposals met with silence, these people had no manners, indifference was their deadly weapon, deadening aloofness their claim to supremacy. Magazines and newspapers regularly featured glamorous articles about a handful of artists purely made visible by money's magic wand, thus creating and shooting up in turn the value of the work. That triggered her fury every time, the media ubiquity of these artists. All these art articles were mere advertising for wealthy clients. She was mad. She knew that she wasn't alone. Thousands of artists were thrown into the same abysmal pit every year, thousands of artists suffered the sheer irregularity of the endless fall.

Everything's going to be fine, I know it, Mary Jane used to say.

Mary Jane was becoming desperate, bitter, dejected, insecure, slowly, progressively, increasingly. But then you weren't supposed to show desperation. You were supposed to pretend everything was fine, you were on top of things, you were in control. Control. Mary Jane began to lose control. She couldn't hide the desperation, bitterness, anger. She couldn't hide her contempt towards the decision-makers, those who decided what to push, what to ignore, basing their judgements on their arbitrary likes or dislikes, like spoilt brats ruling a small model of the world with the manipulating vision of a tyrant that has learnt the necessity of being soft-spoken, amiable, courteous. All these cannibalised Mary Jane's energy. She was convinced that they survived through the cannibalisation of other people's energy, that they revelled in provoking dejection through indifference. This is what Mary Jane was repeatedly saying these days. These thoughts had colonised a part of her head, at the expense of other neural networks. She was obsessed, her anger and bitterness were taking the lead. And it was a lead to nowhere. She was becoming more and more resentful, the unwilling host of a neurosis made out of layers of enthusiastic rejections, mounting problems, the ensuing frustration, impotence, the realisation that certain things were perfectly beyond her.

I wasn't aware at the time, but there was a level of sinkage around me that was going to leave its mark. Mary Jane hovered between her baby toys, Sam's devotion and the screeching cry of being encroached upon by the social. The social infiltrated everything, indifferent to its demolishing force, mimicking the indifference of the demonic forces of nature, she said. I felt more and more distant from art. But somehow I didn't know how to tell Mary Jane. I wrote. These stories I had broken into fragments and then into further fragments became aphorisms. I kept writing contradictory aphorisms in an orgiastic celebration of chaos, that was what I was going to show for my final year at the Slade. If an aphorism was a point of sense, taken together, my aphorisms were always a counterpoint where I didn't dream of gathering the whole world at one point in space but of escaping its immensity through tiny gestures that cancelled each other out. Yet Mary Jane insisted on me being an artist, she didn't want to be alone, she said that I should show Nina Chiavelli's shoes, my mother's shoes, for my final year show. After all they were an amazing objet trouvé, a ready-made that spoke about defying the gravity of the earth, an amazing riot of colours. Where these shoes secret entrances to another realm? What if the sexual world they promised really transcended the obsolete body? She said things like that to persuade me, to draw me back into the orbit of art, her orbit.

My mother's shoes had after all become my companions,

instilling in me a riddle by proxy. In the past, I had thought of writing the story of my life through all the memorable shoes I had worn. I knew that every pair of shoes I had worn represented a phase of my life, that I could retrieve my life through them. I never followed the idea, never even wrote a line about it. It was one of those slivers of thought that don't leave enough of an imprint on you. Perhaps it was related to forgotten memories. And now, all these leather-bound stories on top of the continuous shelf, my mother's new shoes, Nina Chiavelli's shoes, scrutinised me with tacit expectations. But I couldn't reconstruct my mother's life through her shoes. Those stories were buried with her, with the demolition of my father's memory paths where every pair had probably conjured up an after-image of my mother's face in his mind. If one thing was certain, it was that while Franco's new order paralysed the country's air, my parents had inhabited their secret passion in the privacy of their home.

I can hear music now.

The countless steps, the long long strides.

Cha cha cha.

Tap tap tap.

Steps, steps, steps, twist and shout, rock and then the pop ballads.

Some of these shoes must have crossed countless bridges in Venice, become lost in writhing mazes, rushed down the narrow steps of Piazza Spagna, rested by a cinematic fountain in a forgotten city, all of them traced my mother's private map. I could see some of them had been worn for a special occasion and never again. I could picture an elegant party full of effervescence and postponed private dramas. My mother's feet had been inside these shoes, with their sweat, their varnished or unvarnished nails, she had probably had bunions, her ankles had probably bled grazed by new shoes, almost certainly the blisters, the plasters, the calluses. These shoes had enveloped my mother's feet, housing a forbidden impulse. Perhaps their spiky heels had been used in painful rituals, perhaps my mother had walked on my father's stomach, inserted them in body holes, my mother an absolute dominatrix subjugating my father with her patent high-heel boots. Or was it the other way round? My mother having to endure my father's compulsion, fed up of having to wear them in bed, feeling slightly ambivalent about my father's obsession, sometimes feeling that he was immutable in his disposition, then resigned to boredom until one day she threw a spiky shoe at him with all the violence of the world. I could picture these scenarios. I wondered whether they were blurred intimations of forgotten memories. Ninety-five pairs of shoes, ninety-five stories, all these stories put together probably didn't make any sense, they probably ran in all directions, contradicting each other, cancelling each other out, like all the voices of the world, telling opposing tales of simplicity, baroqueness, elegance, vulgarity, intensity, humour, restraint, eccentricity, blandness, softness, status, playfulness, boredom, fragility, plainness, naturalness, sensuousness, desire, function, rebellion, perverse pleasure in conformity, but perhaps we had to learn to live with that, with the ultimate lack of sense, with all the voices.

I liked my mother's shoes placed on the continuous shelf so close to the bedroom's ceiling, all these colours and textures, all these shapes, I liked the fact that they were disturbing. But at some point their presence became onerous. It was somebody else's story, my mother's story encroaching upon my life. Encroaching. All these shoes watching me from far above, becoming blurred at night, guarding my sleep like potential incubi, witnessing my love-making to strangers that I was picking up in my dreams, judging me. In addition, there were all these nights when the light bulb in my bedroom started flickering in presage of horror movie stuff. It flickered while making an unnerving, low-level insect noise. I hadn't bothered to put up a lampshade, so there was just this bare light bulb, sad, minimal. And whenever I switched the light off at night the light bulb flickered now and again for half an hour or so projecting gleams of light on my mother's shoes that turned them into unsettling manifestations of something grotesque. Dodgy electrics, this place is going to explode one of these days, Mary Jane said. Have you tried tightening the light bulb? I tightened the light bulb, but the flickering continued. I decided to act. I took some pictures of the shoes, then got a ladder, took all the shoes down, put all the shoes back into the shoeboxes, rather had them there, muted, inside the shoeboxes, than looking at me every night of my life. The flickering subdued, probably a coincidence. In any case, I soon had to pack up all of my mother's shoes, for two months afterwards we were on the move again.

There is a well-known rule in London where you have to move at least five times before you find a place you can call home. But at the time, we didn't know that. We were working hard for our degree shows. While Mary Jane made a model of her show in a shoebox, I found myself stacking some of my mother's shoeboxes upright, so they made an abstract geometrical pattern made out of colourful rectangles of different sizes and depth. I stacked them into three layers and tied them all up with rope. Then ended up making some straps, so the new creature could easily be carried like a rucksack. I put it outside in the landing, as there was no room in the flat, a portable sculpture made out of colourful shoeboxes. Mary Jane lifted it on to her back and walked around the flat, looking like a chic tramp stranded on the wrong film-set. Why don't you show this? This or your mother's shoes, she said. That's a good idea, it's like recycling modernism, a colourful cardboard grill, I said. And yet, when our final year show came, Mary Jane showed her battered toys, whilst I stencilled a series of floating aphorisms on the staircase of the Slade School of Fine Art:

*Never try to organise an orgy when
you have the hiccups: it doesn't work.*

*It's better to live life like a thriller
than like a theorem.*

*It's difficult to see what's inside one.
You need an endoscope, an outside
screen, and an expert.*

Mary Jane got a well-deserved first and I got a 2.1. But the relief of finishing our art degrees was short-lived. Capitalism's violence was besieging our lives. It was an initiation into the adult world, a violently red bill telling us to forget about our dreams. Again, with property prices on the rise, the new landlord, who happen to live on the floor below us, tried to put up the rent an amount beyond reason, then decided to terminate the contract, to seize the moment, it was a good time to sell, the lords of the land were going insane. Needless to say, we didn't have any rights, any anything. That's what we found out. That's what the contract meant. And when we even didn't get our deposit back under the unbelievable accusation that we had been urinating in one corner of the room, ruining the ceiling underneath, we couldn't believe there was nothing we could do.

Nothing.

We spent days dreaming of burning the landlord's house down, of throwing a brick through one of its windows. But with cameras increasingly everywhere, we knew we could end up much worse off. The landlord, an old gambling bastard, had simply gambled away our deposit while waiting for the big shot. He knew the law was with him. We didn't know that, the way things are. We started flat-hunting again. Looked at all these indescribably sad places, black rain filling the hours. We even found a family who wanted to rent us their pent shiplap shed as a double room. And we even considered it for a second.

Urinating in one corner of the room? Before we moved out, Mary Jane had an idea, her idea of fun. She went out and came back with an extra large fish. What the hell is *that*? I said looking at its haunting eye. Don't know, it was the cheapest at the fishmongers, she said. We bided our time. And when we saw the landlord leaving for his habitual trip to the betting shop, we removed one of the wood planks from the floor, buried in the dirt the large fish and carefully nailed back the

plank. That'll show Mr. Bloodsucker II, urine smell, but of
the fishy type, Mary Jane manically said raising her hand for
a high-five.

We closed the door quietly.

We left the fish to work its voodoo.

We went separate ways.

Mary Jane went to live with Sam, to the outskirts. She said
that she preferred that, the proximity to the motorway, to the
car parks, to a gigantic shopping centre where you could walk
for a whole day without running into the same shops. Eventually, I found a hole in a wall in a startlingly drab area called
Cricklewood, a place in a council block, sub-letting from a
guy who had fled to the Sahara desert to walk its dunes naked.
I was lured by the cheap rent, by the fact that it was on the
seventeenth floor. I knew the way concrete blocks were perceived in this country, I didn't have a problem with concrete,
although it was strange that ethnic minorities, ex-convicts,
single mothers, the disabled and the intellectual underclass
had all been put together in one concrete point in space.

I had to do two trips to move all my stuff, as the portable
pile I had made with some of my mother's colourful shoeboxes didn't fit in the taxi. On the second trip, I put my mother's
strange inheritance on my back and walked across London
guided by the Telecom Tower. It was good that it could be
carried like a rucksack. I walked through Regent's Park, then
Primrose Hill, looking at the grass, smelling the ground, relishing the fresh air, thinking about my unusual baggage, unaware that my mother's shoes were biding their time to spring
into action. Strollers looked at me in amazement, probably
wondering whether I was a new urban species. The colourful cardboard pile on my back was like a rectangular upright
carapace, an outlandish portable home, I probably looked
like mutant tramp. I looked ahead, thinking of refugees with
their bundles moving to another country, to another possible hell. I knew it couldn't be compared. Ultimately, once you

got over the compassion, that's what these documentaries infinitely paraded on TV remind you of, that things could be
infinitely worse, that you should consider yourself privileged,
after all you had been given a free ticket to an immense shopping centre. But being uprooted by the property war, was a
fate that had all the signs of ruthless displacement. I pressed
ahead, that's the only thing you could do: press ahead.

Hole sweet hole. I tried to convert the hole into an inert box in order to transform it. A new coat of paint seems to
erase the presence of previous occupants, but the wallpaper
had to be removed, the walls sanded a bit, work, time, like
everything. The place was unfurnished except for a double
bed. And except for the sad wallpaper and a picture of a child
in a cheap golden frame, there were no other traces of the
previous occupants. It was strange that my landlord should
leave a picture of a child behind. This time, I took forever to
unpack, as if ready for the next move, reluctant to do what
seemed fated to be soon undone, just eager to disinfect the
walls, to remove the previous occupant's dead cells, their in-
vasive presence. In a way, I only needed a small room to work
in, a sort of spacious toilet. But my possessions, together with
my mother's shoes, barely fitted in this self-contained flat. It
was like sleeping in a storage room, entrapped by the muted
existence of packed things.

I welcomed frugality. Not unpacking made me resource-
ful, I was better off with this new frugality. Except that I often bumped into the portable sculpture made out of my
mother's colourful shoeboxes, the other cardboard boxes full
of shoes were in the way, the door didn't open fully, there
were things behind it, I couldn't jump into the bed by the
sides, as one side was cluttered with my things, the other side,
just a few centimetres from the wall. A self-contained flat,
that was a luxury for a young person. But the room was a
tiny low ceilinged room. These low ceilings weren't designed
for tall people like me, I couldn't quite stretch my arms, my

head was far too close to the ceilings, I had to shrink a bit to go through doors. And then I had to jump into bed from the end of the bed. Sometimes it was just plain difficult to just to get into bed, its base being one of those drab fabric covered rectangles that prevent you from putting anything underneath. In order to save space, I bought a laptop. It became an extension of myself. It was one of the first laptops, the latest novelty, the green liquid crystal screen, a killer to the eyes, the first generation of portable PCs to only weigh five kilos! I learned to balance it on my legs, on my knees. Occasionally, I used it on the kitchen table, which was usually covered by dirty plates. In the previous place it had been worse in terms of the landlord's ominous furniture, but then, there was more space.

At some point, it dawned on me that I was living in a shoebox.

I was surrounded by all these shoeboxes which in turn were in a larger shoebox which in turn was inside a behemoth vertical shoebox made out of five shoeboxes per floor, each floor being in turn a huge shoebox. The splendid aerial view of the city was the only redeeming thing about the shoebox where I lived. I spent hours on end looking out of the window, experiencing the variable light, admiring the evening, hypnotised by the shimmering spectacle of darkness and lit windows, puzzled by the simplified ground perspective offered by dizzying height, mesmerised by a couple of slow-moving red cranes that presided over the whole view as if they were gigantic flamingos from the future.

Mary Jane's molecules had become enmeshed with Sam's. She rarely rang me. And when I rang her, Sam always answered. She's unavailable, he would say. Unavailable? It was a sign of Mary Jane's new strangeness. She was paling away. She once came to see me, stared at me in a strange way, took out her sketch book, drew cute animals, then looked forever out of the window into the immensity of the sky, all this in si-

lence. I didn't mind that, the silence, but this time there was
tension in this silence, a tension that I chose to ignore. I was
busy ruminating on aphorisms, pondering what to do with
my life, writing letters to my father in which I pretended that
everything was fine. Mary Jane and I had always allowed each
other to be lost in thought, to inhabit our respective worlds. I
admired her for her zeal. It motivated me. But I failed to see
that she didn't look at things anymore, she stared, her gaze had
become a point of disturbed intensity. It was only afterwards
that I realised the craziness of her look. I initially interpret-
ed it as a sign of creative frenzy, her stare was intense because
she was producing intense work.

I was producing intense work too, writing aphorisms in
my diary, then typing them up on my new laptop. I realised
one thing was 'work' and another thing 'getting a job.' After
finishing my art degree and moving into the new shoebox,
there was this void where I realised I had never thought about
getting a job. A job? What kind of job? I needed a break. Visit friends in California, Berlin, wherever. I had to visit my father first, though. I went to visit him. I knew that I could
stay at Antonio's flat, even if he wouldn't be there, and that
the heat would be sweltering. But I didn't expect my whole
being to be suddenly pushed back into first gear. I had forgotten about the somnolence, the lethargy, the solid block
of unforgiving heat. Sunstroke particles invaded everything.
Everything was liquid and dry at once. The streets were melting, the land, cracked beyond deliverance. Fortunately, El
Refugio had air-conditioning, and I spent the days holed up
there, watching inane TV programmes with my father. He
didn't talk about the war or anarchism anymore. He had been
such a feisty man and now I smelled fear in him, but it was a
fear coming from within rather than without. They say with
old age you become like a child, he said. Sometimes I just
feel like skipping, he said. Well, skip, I said. I'm becoming
touched in the head, *tururú*, he said. Tururú was a word that

I hadn't heard for ages and it just made me laugh. Quack, quack, quack, he started quacking, to make me laugh. Moo moo. We exploded into chuckles. He just couldn't stop laughing and I couldn't stop laughing at his laughter and he couldn't stop laughing at mine.

Never take yourself too seriously, he said, knowing that I didn't. He said it in such a serious way, though, that something cracked up within me. I was too young to understand, I didn't want to understand, I understood. Promise? he said. And I didn't say anything.

Then, there was this time when he talked about a girl-friend from before he married, a secretary. And when I asked him what she looked like, he just replied that she wore the most extraordinary pink pumps he had ever seen. I felt as if I had heard something that I shouldn't have heard and then wondered whether all his memories of affects were consistently displaced into footwear. And then, a few weeks later, I saw something that I shouldn't have seen: I saw him looking at Eva sitting on the armchair opposite him. He was looking at her green velvet slippers. They were a sensuous Christmas green. I would have sworn that I had seen those green velvet slippers amongst my mother's shoes. Eva had one leg crossed over the other, she was dangling her slipper, slipping her heel from it and letting it dangle from her toes. He was happy, my father, watching Eva swing her foot, so that the green slipper also swung. I caught a glimpse of his mesmerised gaze connected to the slipper by an invisible lasso. I closed my eyes, I blushed, but the image had already entered my head.

El Refugio was an unsettling space. It made me hear things I didn't want to hear, see things I didn't want to see, it made me feel too vulnerable, too close to mortality and I welcomed Mary Jane's unexpected call, even if it seemed that she only missed me when I was away. Sam's gone to Dublin for a few weeks, something to do with an inheritance, she said. This gallery, Solo gallery, had shown interest in her work, suggested that maybe she could do an exhibition, maybe she knew another artist whose work would complement hers. Maybe I could show with her? I said that I was looking after my dad, I couldn't be further away from 'art.' You know that only art can rescue you from yourself, she said.

Mary Jane was ringing me from a free phone in a squat. She started ringing me every other day. She was just enjoying the free phone ride and of course the only thing that made sense was to make long long calls abroad. She also started talking to my father, absurd conversations made out of single words and laughter that had a salutary effect upon him and eased the numbing hours, days and weeks at El Refugio.

We met up a few days after my return. She seemed back to normal. She came round with a bottle of wine and gave me a small pink helicopter wrapped in cellophane that I still keep. Welcome back to the loop, she said. I made some popcorn. We watched the corn exploding into whiteness against the saucepan's transparent lid, first slowly, then manically, like a private spectacle of contained fireworks. That's my idea of beauty, she said. Something domestic and ordinary and yet quite special.

She then tried to persuade me to show my mother's shoes, Nina Chiavelli's shoes, with her. I didn't know how to tell her that I was losing interest in art, I wasn't an artist anymore, I had grown weary of my mother's shoes. But does that matter? Aren't you supposed to flow with things? We visited the gallery, a white cube run by an opaque, cropped-hair blonde whose laconic manner echoed the minimalist space. They were interesting, my mother's shoes, they wanted to show them, the laconic gallerist asked me to write a statement on my work, two pages or so, no rush, the show would be in seven months or so.

I retreated.

I mused.

I finally got a few books on shoes, on fetishism. I read. I

was assaulted by the penis nightmare, a lurid incursion into psychoanalytical fetishism that would eventually pay off in the form of ghostwriting.

The penis nightmare

Most people inherit a nebulous jumble of experiences from their parents. Exquisite skills, useful traits, then a considerable viscose amount of unwanted stuff. Some people inherit fear from their parents, an erratic insecurity follows them like a curse. Some people inherit carelessness, others are their blind spot. I inherited the riddle of a word, 'fetish,' a paradox, fetishism.

Fetish: a word loaded with unconscious radiance?

There was a time when the word 'amulet,' the word 'charm,' the word 'talisman' were invested with a similar aura. Words age and lose in luminosity. The word 'fetish' still has a raw quality to it, it still speaks of the untamed, perhaps of the untameable, at a time when domestication can be seen as a curse, perhaps a necessary curse sometimes, but a necessity that speaks of loss, of compromise. An untamed, an untameable re-packaged now through consumerism. But . . . hadn't that connection been there for quite a while now? Untamed? Untameable? It was probably the other way round. A real fetish tamed people into compulsion. A real fetish was simply another kind of compromise, a rare compromise. Or at least, that's what I found out when I tried to spawn some writing for the gallery on my mother's exquisite shoes, Nina Chiavelli's shoes. To begin with though, I gazed entranced for a few days at a white sheet of paper, a strenuous exercise that required long breaks every twenty minutes and put me in touch with my unlimited capacity for procrastination.

During that intense white sheet staring phase, my neighbour, Pearl, a big girly woman who I had nodded to in the lift, knocked on my door. She invited me round to her place for a cuppa tea. She was big at the top, but her legs were quite long and thin, as her tartan miniskirt revealed. Her hands

were covered by gigantic rings, like gold finger asteroids: Pearl
was undoubtedly a precursor of bling. I went to her place, just
ten minutes, I told myself. It was impeccable. It was always
impeccable, which lead me to diagnose some kind of intractable neurosis. She had a collection of pigs, pigs everywhere, re-
clining pigs, a pig doing a headstand, a dancing pig, a sleeping pig, a pig in the Buddha position and another one doing
a somersault. Also, a few exotic plants which, she confided
to me, her ex-husband had nicked from Kenwood House, in
Hampstead Heath. She was epileptic, that's how she got her
council flat, the epilepsy had disappeared now, just like that,
out of the blue, maybe it was the divorce, no comments, it
was so difficult to find somebody at her age, it was like becoming a virgin again, thirty-five, she was. Thirty-five wasn't
that old! I said. She was into clubbing, maybe we could go
clubbing together? I wasn't into clubbing, definitely I wasn't.
She started rolling a joint. I said maybe another day, maybe
later, I had to get on with some work.

I went back to my flat and stared at my mother's high
heels, focusing on her absurd deep-throated shoes with a
7-inch heel. I thought about Pearl's collection of pigs and
then, about her gigantic rings. I couldn't concentrate. The following day, I ended up at the local library, walls of knowledge, enthusiastic students, the unemployed and angelic
souls. Then I went to Queen Mary's library, made photocopies and borrowed a few books. My world became a world
of printed matter. I started reading about fetishism. I soon
became acquainted with Sigmund F.'s theory and soon dis-
missed it as nonsense, a peculiar delirium from what must
have been a troubled mind. But it was the main point of departure for writers talking about this subject. Sigmund F.
claimed that initially all male infants believed their mother
had a penis exactly like theirs. They all desired their mother, saw their father as a rival. One day they saw their mother naked and were shocked at discovering that she had an

inverted triangle of hair but no penis. They panicked, they
were terrified by the sight. It must have been cut off, their father must have done it, they were next on the list for desir-
ing their mother so much. Their father was going to cripple
them. Then, when the fear subsided, those who couldn't give
up their belief in the female penis found a solution: the fetish,
a high-heel shoe. The high heel endowed the woman with the
penis she didn't have. It became a substitute for something
that didn't exist: the maternal penis. It became a memorial to
castration anxiety as well as a magical protection against such
fate. And the girls? Women fetishists? Well, according to Sigmund F., girls, simply didn't have genitals. Puzzled, I stared
at a white sheet of paper for a few hours.

Pearl knocked on my door the following evening or the
one after and I answered it hoping that it wouldn't become
a habit on her part. My flat was a pigsty. Paperwork everywhere. I tried to vanish the mess by saying that it was the
rightful place for her collection of pigs. I said that I was working, that's why the flat was in such a mess. Fancy a smoke? she
said. She sat on the sofa covered by photocopies. Hadn't she
heard me? I was working!

OK, I said.

It was pretty strong, the stuff she smoked. What are you
working on? Never mind, I said. I said that I was going to have
a show, that she was invited, but she replied that art wasn't
her kind of thing. Then I said that I was working on fetishism. Oh, kinky stuff, she said, while rolling another joint, I've
done a lot of that, not for a while now though. Are you into
kinky stuff? she asked. I said that I had this boyfriend with a
fetish for minimalist pubic hair and I loved shaving it, just
leaving a minimal line. I know what you mean, she giggled.
Then I said that I was just reading about a hushed cabinet at
the British Museum replete with penises from public statues,
quite a few knocked off by scandalised Victorian puritans.
There were a lot of missing cocks in the world, so many neu-

tered statues. Perhaps there were hushed cabinets replete with penises from statues hidden in the back rooms of museums all over the world! She giggled again and while she giggled I thought that perhaps there was one in sickly sweet Vienna, that perhaps Sigmund F. saw this cabinet, that that one was his internal cabinet. What's this stuff, I said, it's pretty strong. I don't know, skunk, my dealer gives me the strongest. Shall I get you some? I said that I didn't smoke usually, that I was going to bed. Pearl left a chunk of skunk on the table, even though I repeatedly told her to take it with her, then giggled again and left.

A palpable state of altered consciousness floated around the flat, lingering on the chaos of clothes, photocopies and ashtrays. I cleared the living room hoping that that would de-clutter my own neural networks. I went back to the photocopies and flicked through them, wondering whether my father felt somewhere in his head that my mother's stilettos were a memorial for the penis that she didn't have. I tried to imagine him in such scenario, but my father had no father to be afraid of, he was illegitimate, that was his mother's scandal. The sighting of his mother's inverted triangle of hair was also hypothetical . . .

I rang Mary Jane. She hadn't started on the writing for the gallery, that was aeons away and she didn't know what to say anyway, she was going to get Sam to do it for her. Maybe you can talk about post-modern puerility? That will go down well, I said. We talked about this and that, about my new neighbour. Then I told her about Sigmund F.'s theory. She could perfectly understand castration anxiety in guilty adults, she said. With the Pennsylvanian guy, she had *definitely* felt like chopping off his balls. And she was sure that her voodoo intonation when she last talked to him had fully conveyed her curse. Wolves deserved that. Guilty men deserved that. But castration anxiety in children? As a universal experience? She then talked about baby toys, fluffy toys, teddy bears, the realm of the sexually muted. First toys introduced children to this kind of realm, a completely sexually muted world, then later, we were introduced to gendered toys, toys where difference was inscribed anywhere but in the pudenda, she said. Children then became all too aware of differences, as embodied by saying mum and dad, as embodied by women's breasts, long hair, signs of femininity the father lacked, she said. Wouldn't a boy wonder at his father's lack of breasts? Wouldn't a boy wonder at his mother's lack of beard stubble, her smooth cheeks? What about gay men's fetishes? How could their fetish substitute a penis if their object of desire was already furnished with one? And how did humankind manage to reproduce itself for thousands of years if the sight of pussy was so traumatic for men? That's a good question, it's usually the opposite, isn't it? I said. *Definitely*, she said.

For about three weeks, I didn't write anything, but the penis nightmare had begun, the penis virus, the largest cabinet in the world replete with mutilated genitalia. I could never quite believe that Sigmund F.'s assertion that all men suffered from castration anxiety could be taken seriously by so many writers. And that's what he related fetishism to. Sigmund F.'s strange theory was a seminal slip of the pen, an orgy of serial violence that had generated volumes and volumes on the subject. I browsed through the books that I had borrowed. How could a man born almost a hundred and fifty years ago be taken so seriously when so many things had happened since? I agreed that his theory was bizarre. But then I thought that I didn't know about children, I wasn't a psychoanalyst, if so many writers were taking it seriously, perhaps there was something that justified their endeavours. I became more and more disconcerted at not finding alternatives to it. I wanted to write something good about Nina Chiavelli's shoes, my father's sentimental museum. But Sigmund F.'s theory was what most writers writing about fetishism wrote about, especially those entertaining castration worries. Many of them referred to it unflinchingly as if it was a fact, others fiercely criticised it, altered it, extended it, but none of them came up with something radically different. Many took castration anxiety as a universal foundation of human subjectivity, others reversed it to say that it was the mother who was feared as a castrator. Undoubtedly, all of them were rehearsing their own psychodramas.

I read. And read. And read. I would turn a page carefully, and then there they would be, all these mutilated testicles and cocks and inexistent vaginas jumping out at me, all these vagina and penis snatchers brandishing their swords, all these blood and guts sanitised by the use of psychoanalytical jargon. After reading pages and pages of the same stuff, I realised what I already knew, what everybody already knew: there was little that could justify castration anxiety as universal. Only Sigmund F.'s eagerness to fill in the gaps of his Oedipus complex, to put a Jewish father at the centre of the beginning of times, a circumcising father, to make of his trauma a myth of origins.

Of course the theory was of its time, everything is of its time. Of course it was a gem of bizarre misanthropy to claim that women's genitals didn't exist because they folded in on the inside rather than hang out on the outside. Sigmund F.'s theory was completely embedded in his time, the history of his time, the culture of his time. But not only that, he was consistently insulting, his words betrayed hatred, contempt, triumphant contempt towards women. In the name of what he wished to be science, in the name of what he wished to be fact, he repeatedly spat out insults to women in an orgy of ritualised violence. Where did this triumphant contempt come from? Had he won a war? After the deed, triumphant contempt. Sigmund F. did that, physically mutilated half the planet.

Sigmund F., a mad gynaecologist who used his rusty fountain pen in a symbolic scenario of triumphant mutilations.

An intellectual fiend set on the extermination of female genitalia!

An army of angry young women had retaliated. But there was a a delay of more than sixty years. Female Assignment: counter-offensive. As if shooting at a dead adversary was a way of avenging half the planet from a hundred million years of male domination! But of course, how could that not be? When women had been completely absent from all the theories of the modern state, from the social contract to most cultural practices for millions of years? When a phantom history had rendered visible all the abominable debris? Women had been gagged for a long long time, the gag had begun to hurt. It was a monumental mutilation of history, of life, of personal stories, personal loss for centuries, for everybody. The absence of women from history gleamed with the ghostly energy of the return of the repressed, a spectre had attained a critical mass. It had created an immense female phantom limb, a phantom muzzle had appeared on the threshold of the twentieth century, ripe with time, so dense in its invisibility that it exuded all the shattering energy of a personal vendetta, a long-gestated vendetta that extended to the end of the twentieth century.

I spent days and days trying to unravel those writings, strange days.

Thinking that all the articles that I was reading were part of this female vendetta, one of those strange days I smoked some of the skunk that Pearl had left on my table and then went to the British Library. I wondered whether it showed that I was out of orbit but everybody was immersed in an atmosphere of sheer concentration. I ordered a few of these vicious and arid books populated by the Sisters of the Feminist Liberation Army and savoured all these female wrestlers engaged in a duel that perpetuated on the page a spree of atrocities. In the mist of the battle, I noticed machetes lurking between the volumes that went on upwards to infinity. The

female penis! I laughed out aloud, receiving a few sideways
glances from other readers. The image of a dominatrix with
a strap-on-penis flashed through my mind. I started giggling
mentally at Sigmund F.'s universal concept of castration anxiety. I began to like the way it sounded. The way it compacted
sex, violence and fear in a couple of words like a contemporary Hollywood blockbuster, a great horror movie title. The
way it condensed feared brutality and implied vulnerability.
I thought of the elation that he must have experienced when
conceiving the term. It was the kind of term that would seduce speculative minds. The term stretched itself in so many
directions. It pointed to the fear of mutilation, the fear of loss
of body integrity, a fear experienced in a minute way by anyone while cutting a difficult vegetable with a beautifully sharp
knife. I should think that that fear must be universal, the fear
of your body being brutally cut. Except for those who are into
self-mutilation. Or those cultures where mutilation is part of
belonging to a group, like circumcision. And then, if he must
have felt elated about the way castration anxiety sounded, the
theory that he built around it allowed him to sublimate his
own sadism. But it wasn't supposed to be fiction, he was writing. He wasn't Sade articulating dark games from a luxurious
prison. He was a lucid and brilliant horror writer who wanted
to sound like a scientist putting forward his mad vision as the
founding principle of human subjectivity.

The British Library became a dissection room while I conjured up former lovers, one-night stands, it was a large but
finite number, I conjured them up in search for castration
anxiety, but found no such thing. Au contraire, I found a sur-
plus of eagerness and a sudden monomaniacal intensity in
their dogged gaze, as if all their being was possessed by a single thought. I couldn't remember some faces, the colour of
some of my lovers' eyes, but I remembered the zeal, the occasional trembling, the humour, the gentle, rough movements,
the orgasmic brutality, the unalloyed sensuality, the vertigi-

nous dance. I then vaguely remembered an impotent guy who was having Lacanian therapy, but that was an exception. Perhaps some individuals did experience castration anxiety, but you could hardly hold it as a founding principle of human subjectivity. Separation anxiety would have sounded so limp in comparison. The devil always gets the best tunes. To speak of a memorial to separation was to speak of the mother, the all powerful presence of the mother. But girls had been deleted from the equation, after all they didn't have what it took. And that was what was at stake.

I noticed that bleeding penises and vaginas were appearing on the British Library walls, hanging from the blue and golden dome like stalactites as in a macabre film-set. I decided to ignore it but then I noticed for the first time the blue-eyed librarian's plaster on his index finger, an indelible proof that he had been bitten by a vagina dentata. I stared at the books on my desk realising for the first time the profound ugliness of all this writing splattered with maimed genitalia. Real hatred, real violence coming from all sides, lavishly bespattered on the bookshelves. So much anger, I couldn't tune in with this type of anger. And yet, somewhere, I needed to solve this riddle, somewhere I'd become infected by this highly contagious virus. Penis. Penis. Penis. Phallocentric order. Phallicised women. Phallic envy. Penis envy. Phallic economy of fetishism. Phallic accessories. Phallic men. Phallic women. Women as castrators. Women as castrated. Fathers as castrators. Mothers as castrated. Castrating mothers. Castrating castration theories where everybody became part of a monstrous chain that resulted in an abominable world of crushed sexualities. I entered the casualties unit of psychoanalytical fetishism. I wanted to find ideas that didn't depart from a fundamental violence. I read. And read. And read. Every page contained the word 'penis' innumerable times, the word 'phallo' innumerable times. I started coughing, I became choked. Suffocated with so many penises. Undoubtedly, Sigmund F. had inoculated a virus into history, the penis virus. Undoubtedly, he had generated the longest deep throat in history. Subjugated sons and sisters to a seminal fellatio in the name of the lost father, the murdered father, a Jewish father who circumcised his sons. Sigmund F. had created a penis epidemic. I could see female snipers carrying sub-machine guns shooting from all angles, reaching climatic levels of apocalyptic heinousness. I read. And read. And read. There was only hatred in those sabre-cut pages, it was contagious this hatred. It was implacable. The problem wasn't so much the reality of castration anxiety and whether it was symbolic, whether the phallus was an emblem of a desire that could never be attained. The problem was that power was forever aligned with the almighty penis. The problem was with the words, the associations, those words to describe reality partly created it, perpetuated it.

But what did all this have to do with my mother's shoes? I had become infected by the whole thing, the whole choking thing. If every experience transforms us, I abandoned all this reading with a fractured smile and a damaged head. In creating this laboratory virus, Sigmund F. was probably attempting to suffocate the emergence of a different immunological system, for he had always been interested in illness, not in health. Time, I had wasted so much. I crumpled all the sheets of paper with notes I had taken, left them on an empty desk and looked at them. There they were, all these useless jottings, crumpled into shapes that had no names as yet, shapes that were creased, folded, full of crevices and grooves coming from the hidden core. I looked at the play of light and shadow, looked at the crumpled sheets of paper realising that they embodied not only my anger and my ignorance, but also the end of a nightmare. I threw all the paper into the bin. It was difficult to move. The floor was covered with fallen penises and inexistent vaginas, blood spilling out of every gash. I left the library's angelic souls, its blue-eyed librarian

with a plaster on his index finger and the smell of warm human blood. As I went down, I noticed a few unburied penises
rotting in the monumental staircase, flies buzzing over them.
I went to Queen Mary's library and placed all the books I had
been reading in the Horror section next to Lovecraft and the
biography of Nilsen. I woke up from the nightmare at home
and had an eternal shower while having lurid fantasies about
the blue-eyed librarian. Then, once cleansed from all the bol-
locks I'd just read, I sat down nibbling at a chocolate bar and
finally wrote a piece for the gallery.

Pearl knocked on my door that evening: fancy a smoke?
Yeah, OK, I said. You looked so tired, she said. I'm knack-
ered, today it's been a complete cock-up, I said. What was
the cock-up about? Never mind, I said. I fetched two cans
of beer from the fridge and we drank them while Pearl told
me about her epilepsy, how it had been so bad, how she had
so many seizures during college, she had to give it up. Then
she giggled, went into her flat and came back with some cocaine. That's what she liked, to get really stoned out of her
head, she said. I hadn't taken cocaine for years. I dreaded the
prospect of her coming round every so often with an arsenal
of drugs. I said that I didn't take anything, this was an exception, I had always liked cocaine, I said. Oh, I'm seeing my
dealer tomorrow, I'm going to Paris this week, she said. Shall
we go to the pub? she asked. I said I had been out and about
all day, no way, I said. I'm a pig, she said, showing me one of
her gold rings which was in the shape of a recumbent piglet:
hard-working, gullible and obstinate.

Pearl left around 1:00 AM. I stayed up all night. It was
oh so quiet. As if I was the only human being awake in the
whole world. Enveloped by an alien lucidity, I wrote a short
story while the darkness outside acquired density. I wrote in
English, in one go. It was strange writing in English. Maybe it was a sign that I was reconciling myself with the English language:

A tale about an extraordinary mind whose face is printed on Austrian bank notes

Sigmund F., a nineteenth century Jewish man shell-shocked by circumcision. Perhaps he witnessed the terror in his sons' eyes when they had that little snip, when his relatives had it, he had forgotten the messiness of that little snip he himself had had, was rehearsing endlessly that trauma through writing, through transference, the female body a site for that traumatic transference.

Or Sigmund F., a dysmorphic, perhaps an inverted dysmorphic by proxy. Dysmorphics, a problem related to body perception.

Or Sigmund F., a sublimated part-time butcher.

One morning, Sigmund F. opened a newspaper and saw the haunting picture of Alessandro Moreschi, the last castrato. It was 1922. The last castrato had died. He vividly recalled the headlines from when castration was banned back in 1903. Castration before puberty preserved a treble voice in men. The headlines had generated a general outrage at such practice, a sudden fear of loss of body integrity. And he had been strangely affected by this most brutal of acts. Apparently, the castrating practice had originated at the Vatican in the sixteenth century to compensate for the absence of women's voices in the choirs. Thus castration and the absence of women in history was from the onset tragically linked. Sigmund F. had a record by Alessandro Moreschi. He played the record that morning. Disturbed by the castrato's voice, he stopped it halfway through. An angel passed. The female angel of history. But he was blinkered to certain angels. A few years later, in 1927, he wrote his theory about fetishism. Enveloped by the bliss of closure, the week Sigmund F. finished his perverse theory, he sat as usual at his desk

covered with Egyptian and Greek figurines, his hands
between his legs. Puzzled, he scribbled down: Why does
woman resent man so deeply? Confused he repeated it
out aloud: Why does woman resent man so deeply?
That very same week Sigmund F. had that recurrent
nightmare that he would forget as soon as he opened
his eyes: he had become a foetus again, a gigantic breast
was loose on the streets threatening to invade the planet
and a stuffed bird on the wall strangely reminded him
his mother was not feeling quite right that day.

The dehumanisation of artists

The indescribable weather continued. Suffocated by my readings, having nightmares about realistic, tiny penises made out of raw beef, I began to look at the cardboard boxes around me with comical disgust. Was I surrounded by boxes full of penis substitutes? Wasn't it the case that high-heels were androgynous objects, a beautiful example of the optical unconscious translated into matter, moreover animal skin transfigured into the elegant and sensuous straitjacket of culture? Undoubtedly, some of these shoes, my mother's shoes, were quite vulgar. I liked this vulgarity in terms of its convulsive beauty. But the fact was that I had never looked at these shoes as shoes. The fact was that I saw high-heels, not as shoes, but as sculptures. I had rarely worn high-heels myself, put off by the limitations they entailed in terms of movement, by the pain. I had now and again worn platforms. Platforms also displaced anatomically the centre of gravity forward, creating a lengthening effect of the body, but the lengthening effect wasn't quite the same, minimal contact with the earth was lost and as objects they were not androgynous.

Italy, the land of shoes, it had been written on its geography, an obvious high-heel boot. As part of my curiosity I wrote a letter to my mother's sister in Italy, zia Carla. I had never thought of her as an aunt, I barely knew her, all I knew was that she was a bit stern, a bit of a snob. My mother, the black sheep of the family, who had married a night porter, my father, that's how my aunt perceived my mother. An Italian dictionary helped me with the letter, my written Italian was a bit rusty, I wanted her to take my words seriously. I didn't tell her that my father was in a care home, I told her about the shoe bounty I had found in the loft, told her I was doing an exhibition, then asked her if she knew anything about all these shoes, her sister's shoes, *la incredibile collezione di scarpe della mia mama, sua sorella*. I wanted to know before the exhibition. I had agreed to share the exhibition with Mary Jane. Saw it more as Mary Jane's exhibition. Was glad to see her positively energised. Her psychotic stare had lost intensity. It now emanated euphoria. Sheer exhilaration. I was charged by her exhilaration. Intrigued by her collection of thumb sucking substitutes, teething objects, objects that inhabited the border between the inside and the outside, the first possessions treasured by babies. She was intoxicated while preparing her show. She would display all her baby soothers, all her baby toys. Me, the adult toys, my mother's shoes. In a way, they were all adult toys, the kind of toys some adults become fixated upon.

Some of the shoes had gathered a bit of dust. I bought an ostrich feather duster. Carefully dusted them. Then thought shoes were usually brushed, not dusted and brushed them carefully. I didn't know whether to show them scattered all over the floor as if waiting for the emergence of order, in a circular whirlpool that hypnotised you towards the void, in a rigorous formal taxonomy arranged by tonal relations, arranged by shape, whether to organise them in groups of sense branching out from pristine to worn, from perversity to modesty, from beauty to horror, in a linear way with a beginning, a middle and an end, in such a way that they would delicately contradict each other, just display one pair in the middle of the room and push to a corner all the rest or display them against the skirting-board one after the other according to a chance logic that made the gaze jump in unexpected and personal ways. I didn't know whether to call them 'Specular couples,' 'Elegant animals' or 'Leather-bound Stories.' Mary Jane wanted me to call them '25% Protrusion' after the fact that high-heels make your buttocks protrude 25% mimicking the vertical posture typical during female arousal. We thought of crazy titles. She decided she would call her toys 'Things of Initiation'. She decided she would do the show under a pseudonym, she didn't believe in authorship, she chose Lala French. It would be amusing, the gallerists calling her Lala, strangers calling her Lala at the opening, and her slight delay in turning round, in responding. But then, the gallery rang saying Mary Jane should remove the brutalised baby toys, she should only show the pristine ones. It was ridiculous. Mary Jane refused to remove the dirty toys. New, polished, slick, clean, that was the law at the time, anything that didn't comply with the law was censored. It didn't make any sense. The whole thing came to some kind of impasse. Mary Jane said she wouldn't do the show. I didn't want to do it if she didn't. But then, she insisted I should do it, they didn't have anything against my mother's shoes, they were acceptable, even the slightly worn ones, they were relatively easy objects.

A shoe swarm about to attack you.

A shoe explosion.

A shoe-web.

I was still toying with ideas as to how to show my mother's shoes. An explosion. To recreate an explosion with shoes thrown violently against the ceiling, the walls, the corners. In order to recreate it realistically, I would have to damage my mother's shoes. That's what I wanted to do though, an explosion.

To my surprise, the gallery was into the idea. I chose the stilettos that I disliked, the dullest ones and the pink pair that was revoltingly girly. I started disfiguring them. I chose seven pairs. Cut six shoes into pieces and burnt them here and there with a lighter and then I put them under the grill. The other eight shoes I bunged in the oven and carbonised them to different degrees. Some of them had grown charred bubbles. There were also droplets of melted plastic in the oven tray. And the pink pair that was revoltingly girly had disintegrated.

Energised by these small acts of violence, I loaded my mother's shoes without the shoe boxes into a minicab and once in the gallery, quickly started thinking up the show. I wanted the shoes to capture both motion and stillness. I looked at the white room as if it was a white page. I hung some of my mother's shoes with nylon thread as if they truly defied gravity. I stuck the carbonised ones to the ceiling, to the walls, was given permission to break a window and scattered the lacerated and torn ones on the other walls. I created the impression of a chaos of shoes, a few trashed and seared, others floating in mid-air, as if the explosion had been frozen two seconds after it happened. In the whiteness of the room … you could experience a psychological state of panic.

Acidic wine, friends, acquaintances, desperados, posers, strangers and polite enemies. How nice to have an enemy, someone specific to hate Mary Jane would say. I had started to see commercial gallery openings through Mary Jane's eyes. Artists who believed in art, friends, but then also debutantes and posh psychopaths who had the money to run galleries, completely out of touch with the tough side of things, beautifully lobotomised by this ignorance, with pathetic little problems, who had seen the tough side of things as tourists, on TV, how fascinating to live in a council flat next to real squalor, entertaining stories to tell at posh dinner parties, these were the people Mary Jane was supposed to get on with. Some of them were OK, they were innocent of their game. But some of them sported an arrogance that made them all the more indigestible.

Mary Jane called them 'snootos'. I know what they're like, I've gone to school with them, they swan around as if they were a superior race, she said. To be a snob is to waste one's life in supreme pettiness, she said. Get real, you only live once, that's what I'd love to shout at them.

Mary Jane didn't want to know them, she couldn't stand snobs. She saw commercial gallery openings as celebrations of the false self, she couldn't become a false self. Sometimes there was a benign atmosphere, but sometimes the lack of ox-

ygen, oxygen rarefied by the voracious energy of ambition, ri-
valry, envy. Maybe we were too young. Too receptive to the
aggression in the air. To the competitive ruthless spirit. Artists who believe in art? Me, me, me, me, me, ascending in a
manic spiral towards the ceiling, then descending, flattening
everything out, a viscosity in the air poisoning people, people who would have shot their mother, their father, for their
work's sake, so many people treading on each other, so much
violence in the air. I suppose it was the situation that created
this cannibal ambience, artists inhabited a perpetually fragile
situation, no guarantees, sometimes recognition, sometimes
not, most times not, sometimes money, sometimes nothing,
most times nothing, the hierarchy of the art world replicated
the world as a mass sacrifice pit.

Names, names, name-makers and name-lickers, to lick a
name, look at them, you can't even look at them, your gaze
bounces back, Mary Jane would say.

The harsh wine would soften the barriers. But still, there
would be a few creatures with invisible orthopaedic collars,
people who had mastered the art of subtly turning away when
they sensed the presence of possible undesirables, beings
whose thirst for power created a hard aura of self-importance
which made Mary Jane feel like she would never ever ever
ever get anywhere. They adore wringing others around their
deadening fingers, gently abuse their power to sublimate their
sadism, she said. If I want to get anywhere with my art, these
are the people I'm supposed to get on with, the invisible orthopaedic collar sect, a bunch of snobs unashamed of exhibiting their stuck-up symptoms, she said. Not all of them
were like that. But there was a game they played that became contagious. The blanking game. Barbaric as it was, it
was a practice that everybody ended up more or less playing
at some point. It consisted of nobodifying others through a
permanent non-eye contact until the person felt completely invisible. It was a non-rapport that told you: you don't ex-

ist. Perhaps it was played out of insecurity, perhaps out of a pathological sense of superiority rooted in a pervasive feeling of worthlessness. It definitely had to do with status, denying others the status of visibility while only acknowledging those who could forward their career. With all probability, it functioned as a chain reaction. Somebody blanked somebody who blanked somebody in turn who in turn blanked somebody ab aeternum.

We were too young, we were shocked at the way the world worked.

Blanking.

Nobodifying.

Shocked.

Mary Jane finally agreed not to show the brutalised toys, she would only show the new ones, a different kind of trauma, the trauma of the new, the trauma of the aseptic, her hope was that at a later stage she could show the brutalised ones. And when she was offered to show the brutalised ones, she said no, she had changed her mind, she wanted to explore the trauma of the new. She wanted the baby toys to convey a surgically icy mood.

The night of the opening Mary Jane smiled awkward smiles. She would usually look at me, look at that lot there, so perfectly superior, that's what Mary Jane's complicit glance at me usually meant. The problem was that Mary Jane actually believed in art, in the work itself, she didn't want to realise that it was the possibility of money which vitiated everything, including art. At that time, I hadn't realised either. But the night of the opening Mary Jane's complicit glance meant something different. That night, Mary Jane was diffusing her hurt. She had put her bitterness aside. It was her night. Artists were complimenting her work, even if it had been pushed to the back of a room in a tiny space. In any case, hardly any superior beings had turned up. It was a small gallery, it was mainly artists, artists exchanging similar delusions of grandeur, confessions of helplessness, relaxing, being themselves.

Mesmerising, magical, beautiful, I heard and overheard compliments of this sort.

My mother's shoes, which I finally called 'Leather-bound Stories' were exploded all over a medium-sized room. It was mainly Mary Jane's friends who were interested, violence-addicted men. A well-known gallerist walked in halfway through the show tensing up the air with her blonde ponytail, her frigid eyes, her crimson lipstick, her severe stance. This superior being glanced at the exploded shoes as if she saw explosions of objects all the time and walked off. Then she was lost an unusually long time on Mary Jane's fragments from infant reality. Most of the exhibits were the kind of objects that are sucked and cuddled by babies, loved objects. But in the cold atmosphere of the gallery they seemed to oscillate between affection and utter detachment, their auras were cold auras, yet they were imbued with a strange power. Mary Jane had chosen the objects carefully. They were all pale pink and blue, not primary red, blue, yellow, the current garish but warm baby toys. And when taken out of their supposed context, these objects seemed to lose their friendliness. How could such objects have ever been seen as reassuring? Considered loveable? They were objects to be handled by caring humans babbling away absurdities, not to be displayed on immense empty white walls as enigmatic power objects. The superior being gave Mary Jane her card. She loved her work, so beautifully cold, so traumatically poised. Suddenly Mary Jane was ready to sell her soul to what she used to call the 'taste Nazis.' The woman spoke about the possibility of shows in Los Angeles, in Milan, in Düsseldorf, then she left. Mary Jane's ego levitated. She was going to have a break. She was drunk, she started to cry. Everybody had left for the pub. We glided on the streets towards the pub. Mary Jane had been chosen. She was that little bit nearer to her dream, to be able to do her work.

The next few days we popped in the gallery to show our faces, to see whether there was any interest, to take transparencies of the work. Mary Jane's superior being would be ringing within the next couple of weeks. Knowing Mary Jane, I knew she would be answering the telephone all the time, hair raised, then disconcerted, no, not this time, the superior woman never called, was always unavailable when Mary Jane rang her, yet again, same game. I told Mary Jane the most difficult thing in life was to learn not to expect.

Words, so easy to utter.

Then, a few days before the exhibition closed down, I got this call from the gallery. A curator was interested in touring 'Leather-bound Stories,' but they were only interested in the shoes as historical artefacts, not in the explosion *per se*. The curator was from a shoe museum in Toronto. I didn't know shoe museums existed, but they do. Thus my mother's shoes, Nina Chiavelli's shoes, started their comings and goings, a two-year tour during which I went to Almería to visit my father five, four times, while my mother's shoes travelled the world. Stilettos were not neutral fragments, they were objects invested with libidinal splendour. Some English critics wrote rigorous castration anxiety rubbish about my mother's shoes, others wrote about 'quasi-objects,' others about the truth each pair embodied, about the world being made up of so many truths. In Milan, a critic wrote about the sheer cultural diversity of 'Leather-bound Stories,' about the fact that although so many were made there, in Italy, these shoes pointed to so many directions, to the north, to the south, to the west, to the east, there were sandals of Native American origin, wooden sandals, Moroccan sandals, Dutch wooden clogs with flowers painted on them, the traditional Scottish shoe with laces, British plastic flip-flops, Spanish espadrilles, moccasins, cowboy boots, eastern mules. In Frankfurt, a critic mentioned the mountains of shoes in Auschwitz, the fact that no shoe poetry could be written after these mountains of sorrow.

In Paris, an Yves Klein blue pair went missing and was recovered thanks to modern surveillance. The gallerists hinted at the identity of the thief, an art critic who had written a meticulous review where the obscure terminology revealed the riddling recesses of a mind chronically lost.

In Toronto, 'Leather-bound Stories' was shown next to a hair-raising show about the Chinese regional variations of Lotus shoes. The Lotus shoes show broke my heart. I did know about Lotus feet, about Chinese foot-binding, the minute size of the shoes, the deformation of the feet, but I had never quite understood their actual size, the utter immobility they implied, I had never actually seen them before. I had never quite taken in that these Lotus shoes, made out of silk or cheaper fabrics in the case of the poor, tragically embroidered with flowers and plants symbolising good luck, fertility, longevity, were the foot-size of a four-year-old girl, let's say the size of a small female hand, even smaller. It was only seeing the show that hammered home that these women's revered feet had been brutally shrunken into girl's little feet and utterly misshapen in the process.

Then Nina Chiavelli's shoes encountered a potential buyer in London, while still touring. I got a call from the gallery. An anonymous collector was seriously interested in 'Leather-bound Stories'. I went quiet. I had never thought of selling the shoes. I couldn't say that to the gallery. I couldn't say that I wasn't interested in selling them. How could I sell my mother's shoes, my father's sentimental museum? There was no contract, there was only a verbal agreement. I said that I wanted to meet the Collector, talk to him before a sale was agreed. She would arrange a meeting, the gallerist said, reminding me in a whisper of the forty percent commission they were supposed to keep.

Even if I didn't want to sell my mother's shoes, I was intrigued by the prospect of an art collector's interest in them. I thought of ringing Mary Jane, but I didn't. I had rung her

about the touring exhibition, said I was sorry, I would try
to help her, felt her silence, a silence that had the contours
of disappointment. It had been around those days, the days
that my mother's shoes went on tour, the days that she had
been waiting for a call, that Mary Jane had started talking
about organising her own disappearance. Now she was doing it. The experiment, that's what she called it at first. It was
around the time that 'Leather-bound Stories' were in Frankfurt that Mary Jane decided that she was not going to put
a foot outside her house as long as she could endure it. She
was going to abandon the world. Bye bye, world. Sam would
do the shopping, deal with necessary outings. But she herself
was going to initiate a disappearing action, she didn't want
to be part of this world, she was going to become a runa-
way. I visited her every so often. Other people did as well. She
was quietly angry about 'Leather-bound Stories,' loudly angry
about everything else. I knew that I wasn't an artist anymore.
I knew that it would be an irony if I gained anything doing
nothing, while Mary Jane gained nothing after years of dedicated work. Art was Russian roulette, a racket, another game
to mimic things being out of joint forever. We were still in
the process of learning that. Sometimes the work mattered,
sometimes it didn't, sometimes it was the last thing that mattered.

The Museum of Relevant Moments

I didn't meet the anonymous Collector at the gallery. The anonymous Collector left instructions for his number to be forwarded to me.

A collector, an artist's dream.

A few indecisive days went by. I kept thinking if I could persuade him to buy my aphorisms as works of art, I could rent a bigger flat where I wouldn't be spatially besieged by my possessions. I finally rang him, left a message on his answer-phone, got a call back the following day, met him the day after in Harley Street, a street made out of overpriced doctors, Jaguars and gingko trees. It was the first time that I walked along this street, unaware that it was a self-perpetuating circulatory system of tradition, medical excellence and elitist affluence.

Grand spider lights, grand staircase, the perfect scenario for Cinderella to lose her slipper. As I went up the steps, the words 'posh bastard' came to my head—if my father had taught me anything it was resentment towards the wealthy. I met the Collector at his wife's surgery. His wife was a neurologist specialising in autism. The surgery looked like a swanky office: spacious and swish minimal. Two comfortable chairs, a huge desk, a chair behind the desk, a non-descript water-colour on the wall, a photograph of the Collector on the desk.

I used to be a wanker, the anonymous Collector said with a smirk when I sat at his desk, an introduction that threw me off making my face transpire puzzlement. A banker, he clarified. Futures. But all that is over now, thank god for that, at least the futures part. I'd like to do my bit for the world now, he laughed. I laughed queasily with him, appreciating his honesty but wondering what its purpose was. They used to call me 'The Alligator,' he said, and I looked at the small crocodile embroidered on his jumper thinking that he was good at self-parody and that that was a skill that we should all learn. It's a fake label, he said, part of the thriving Brick Lane counterfeit industry, I bought it myself yesterday. He had an accent that I hadn't quite heard before, as if his mouth was full of misplaced air. He coughed and spat into a Kleenex a blur of green phlegm. I actually saw it in slow motion: green, slimy, disgusting. He apologised, I've got a cold, he said, and coughed again. The Collector, an old man with flowing white hair who still seduced through spirited talk, sparkling piercing blue eyes, a natural charm that cancelled out his shortness, a knotted green silk scarf that pointed to a flirtatious nature and an ambiguous grin that made you forget the world of absolute privilege from which he came.

He tried to seduce me into his world. I thought it was his strategy to make me sell. I was flattered to have a collector at my feet. But then I realised that he was a natural seducer, he would have seduced anybody, regardless of interest. Also, the Collector wasn't just any type of collector. Behind his wife's family there were a few centuries of related collectors. He said that he collected moments, relevant moments. And then, the ignition of empathy. He asked me whether I knew Buñuel, the Spanish surrealist film-maker. When he mentioned Buñuel I knew that it was a case of objective chance. Synchronous chance. Double chance. I think that perhaps we wait all our lives for another chance encounter that will confirm as singular a previous chance encounter. A unique repetition that will dust our lives with a spellbinding trail of purpose. But Buñuel? What did my mother's shoes have to do with Buñuel?

Of course I knew Buñuel, I said. I joked, I said that I could never separate Buñuel's slight squint, his oblique gaze, from the way he looked at things. I knew about Buñuel's disruptions of the real, his long life romance with the irrational, with the problem of sense. Long story, the Collector said. He was fascinated by Omar Sharif and had acquired the dagger and the black Arab robe that Omar Sharif had worn in *Lawrence of Arabia*. I loved that film, I said, the desert, the music, and then all those beautiful men. He grinned, then coughed, then said that he wanted to build a rather personal museum based on his collection, primarily a collection of cinema memorabilia, objects, scenarios that had appeared in more or less well known films, but mainly Buñuel's, that was his main interest, the core of his collection, he was hooked to Buñuel.

Come along, he said. And he opened a side-door in the surgery as if he was about to show me the lateral contents of his mind. The door opened onto a large room with shapes covered by large pieces of grey felt. As I would later learn, he was no stranger to pulling off conjuring tricks. He carefully uncovered one of the amorphous shapes, the central one. The room revealed a huge cross on the wall facing the door. Then he uncovered another one on the left and through the corner of my eye I saw a white wedding dress. I walked towards the cross, looking furtively at the wedding dress on my left that the Collector had just uncovered.

Buñuel.

That is how it all had started, he said. Or almost all. His family had been vaguely related to the Viscounts de Noailles and through a series of avatars they had come to possess the cross covered with hair that appears in *L'Âge d'Or*.

Did I know *L'Âge d'Or*? You see, he said, this cross is both a collective religious object and a hair fetish. The hair is female hair. The hair attached to the cross is an act of brutal sadism, the victimisation of a varied sample of women. It could have been male hair, but the context was Sade's sadism. In any case, the cross already evoked male sacrifice, male masochism as a path to redemption. The film portrayed not just one type of violence, but a variety of violence.

You can't tell that the heads of hair on the cross are female heads of hair, I said. Apparently Buñuel had been unhappy about the way that it wasn't all that clear in the film, the female heads of hair hung flaccid on the cross looking like flaccid horse tails, he said. Buñuel had wanted to hang a notice that shouted: THESE ARE FEMALE HEADS OF HAIR.

Next to each Buñuel memento, there was a framed still from the film where that memento had appeared. I looked at the small black and white film still framed and hung two meters away from the cross. It was strange seeing the black and white picture from this anthropological fetish next to the real thing, which was three-dimensional, in colour and a hundred and twenty-five times bigger.

I looked at the cross again. I thought aloud, my thoughts emerging as I spoke. It was interesting that violence to women had been superimposed onto the initial founding violence of Christianity, making it at least as ancient as Christianity itself. But the brutality implied by the wrenched hair seemed to go back to even earlier times. In fact, the cross looked like some kind of totem, a totem where a double act of sadism was inscribed, fierce tearing out of hair surely preceded the construction of torture devices.

The Collector hadn't seen it that way before, a female Christ tortured in her sexuality, had I been to Torcello?, there was a female Jesus in Torcello, a baby one, sat on Mary's lap. Then he said that he had many other mementoes from Buñuel's films dispersed throughout the world. I listened to him. I said that I would love to see his dispersed collection, said that Buñuel had a special sentimental value to me as well, if he ever carried out his museum dream, I would definitely visit it.

I spun slowly around the whole room. I felt as if I was playing a part in an imaginary plot. I thought that maybe he had Jeanne Moreau's ankle boots, the pair that looked like my mother's. I asked him whilst remembering my gigantic hallucination where Jeanne Moreau's boots became my mother's boots, and he said that he had searched the earth for

them. He had given up, he would never find them, he said. I
thought of telling him that they reminded me of my mother's, but I didn't mention it. I asked him instead whether he
had the piano with the donkeys and ropes from *Un Chien
Andalou*, that image had been so important for art, for instal-
lations, a memorable image born of a cruelty that would be
unacceptable today: the donkeys had been shot for the sake of
this image. The Collector coughed. Then told me in a whisper that at the time they had tried to stuff the donkeys but it
had all gone terribly wrong and the whole thing had been in-
cinerated, that image only existed as an image, not as an embodied fact, as an embodied fact it was lost forever.

Then he spoke about magical invocations. I followed him
and we stopped in front of another shape covered by grey felt.
He removed the fabric. Underneath the felt there was a diagonal stripy box and a tie. He asked me if I remembered the
scene where a woman magically invokes a man through the
ridiculous feminine frills that he was wearing at the beginning
of the film and then adds a diagonal stripy tie. Unfortunately,
the feminine frills had gone missing, unfortunately because
the whole thing was an invocation of an androgynous being,
but here in front of us we had the diagonally striped tie and
the diagonally striped box. After all, that film invoked the diagonal all throughout, as if inhabited by an oblique, transver-
sal logic, not horizontal, not vertical, but diagonal, beyond
black and white oppositions, he said. Buñuel loved magical
invocations through objects, as if objects were a shortcut to
intense memory, he said. Perhaps an invocation was always an
evocation. Then he walked towards the white wedding dress.
There was also a white wedding shoe. There was a label to the
side that said *Viridiana*, 1961. That was useful, for I used to
confuse the titles of Buñuel's films sometimes, didn't even remember whether I had watched that film. Then I realised that
there was a torn corset as well.

I thought that he was going to speak about ritual, but

the Collector explained that the wedding dress referred to an erotic invocation where a middle-aged man, a fetishist of memories, caressed his dead wife's wedding clothes in adoration. The man then proceeded to slide his foot in one of his wife's white wedding shoes, caressed her wedding corset, and tried to put it on but was interrupted. The wedding dress, the wedding shoe, the corset were an erotic invocation connected primarily with absence, with the absence of a cherished person, a cherished deceased wife. These objects clearly spoke about a moment of disavowal, but disavowal of the supreme loss: death, actual physical death. Death, loss, lack, absence, separation, this is what this image spoke about, he said. These objects were a memorial to the supreme loss. A female wedding shoe elevated into a transcendent symbol of death whilst being at the same time a denial of death. Suddenly, a shoe had become a monumentalised sign of mortality, the ultimate separation. That was what the white wedding clothes were about, the youthful innocence that denies the endgame of death. In the hands of a fetishist of memories these clothes became sacred, in the hands of the drunk leper who stole them, put them on and parodied a dance, they had become defaced, an opportunity for carnival, the torn corset captured that moment, a sacred object had become a profane one.

Then he unravelled a razor. It was a historical razor, historical because it was banned in Spain after the film *Viridiana* from 1961, he said laughing. It was a crucifix-razor, very popular in Spain at the time. A crucifix-razor, he smiled. He stroked the blade. In the film it appeared as part of the personal belongings left by the protagonist's deceased father. Another anthropological object, more mortality, more fusion of contraries, a playful paradox, if you like. Do you collect anything? he said. I collect everything, I said, realising as I was saying it that I collected bits of knowledge, knowledge from all fields, from all walks of life.

The Collector said that his collection was made out of relevant moments. He had ended up calling it The Museum of Relevant Moments. He had already chosen a space for his museum, an abandoned convent in Mexico which he wanted to convert. At the moment, the collection was a museum without walls, or rather, a museum with multiple walls. He had bits of his collection in all his houses. They had family houses in Paris, Amsterdam, London and Mexico, but had chosen Mexico, wanted to die in Mexico, that was what he wanted to leave to Mexico.

How did you come by ninety-five pairs of shoes? he said. Here and there . . . car-boot sales, I said, mortified at the sale-question being raised. I was a writer, I wasn't an artist anymore. The exhibition that he had seen was an exception, I said. My friend, Mary Jane Prendergast, had invited me to put something in a show to go with her baby toys, she was an amazing artist, I found her work spellbinding, more interesting than Jeff Koons' or Mike Kelly's, you should see it, I said. 'Leather-bound Stories' had gone on tour, it had all happened beyond me. These shoes were not for sale, I said. Undaunted, the Collector suggested that maybe instead of the whole collection I could just sell a pair. He mentioned an exorbitant figure. Then he handed me a picture of my mother's collection of shoes and pointed to a black pair. This one, the black pair of innocent high-heels with a double strap, he said. They weren't necessarily the best shoes. They weren't the most beautiful ones. I blushed. He said we could forget about the gallery, they didn't need to know about this small sale and then added that he loved what I had written about the shoes for the show, all that stuff about penises and the penis nightmare. Did I know Lecour? Anton Lecour? The notorious French philosopher? he said. I revered Lecour. He created the most beautiful and pristine systems of irrational thought. Lecour was going to write about The Museum of Relevant Moments. Maybe I could write a small preface to Lecour's text?

he said. Me? A complete unknown nobody together with Lecour? I was interested in that, but I wasn't sure about selling a
pair of my mother's shoes. I thought that his suggestion that
I wrote an introduction to Lecour's writing was inextricably
linked to the sale of my mother's shoes. But then if I sold just
a pair of my mother's shoes for the price he offered I wouldn't
need to worry about money for a while. And 'The Museum of
Relevant Moments' was an interesting concept. I wondered
what this guy wanted to do with my mother's shoes. I said
that I would have to think about the shoes, they were still on
tour, but I was definitely interested in the writing, in fetishism. Fetishism? he said. He wasn't sure whether his collection
of relevant moments was entirely about that, he wasn't interested in 'isms'. He then said that he would send me the relevant Buñuel tapes, made a note on his diary and added that
the high-heels with a double strap that he had pointed at in
the photograph reminded him of another pair of shoes that
had appeared in one of Buñuel's films.

As I was descending the grand staircase, drunk with the
high figure the Collector had installed in my head, drunk
with Lecour, confused by this persuasive short man with a
taste for the incongruous, it occurred to me that perhaps he
had known my mother, had had some kind of affair with my
mother, that that was why he wanted her shoe collection so
much, even if it was just a pair.

Anything strang

A museum of relevant moments? My museum of relevant moments was made out of precisely that—moments. A wild instant made out of an intense encounter that could only be lived through the gaze, a starry night where the Milky Way became visible for the first time, a bird singing at dawn, even looking at a ball of dust and fluff. My museum of relevant moments was made out of moments of revelation, it was intangible, the Collector was talking about the tangible, he had sought to possess embodied moments that were relevant for him. I desperately needed the money. These shoes, my mother's shoes, Nina Chiavelli's shoes, just a pair of them could now become my keep. I got informed. Nobody would have paid the sum that the Collector was paying. Unknown actresses' shoes had no value at all. I spoke to Sotheby's. I talked to friends. I rang the Collector. I was told that he was in Amsterdam. I rang Amsterdam. He was still interested, said that I could meet him there, he would pay the expenses. I rang the touring curator and asked her to urgently send me the pair of shoes that the Collector wanted, as my mother's shoes were in Toronto at the time. She was baffled by my request, but did as I told her. The following month I flew to the capital of Holland. We arranged to meet in the Vertigo Café at the Filmmuseum. I was surprised to find him with his wife, Kathy, and his assistant, a French guy of interesting features called Zacharie, an emissary of sensuality who hunted for movie collectables. Kathy was much taller than the Collector, a wrinkled face that insinuated inner beauty. She hadn't had plastic surgery like some rich women do, nor concealed her grey hair with discreet dyes. She had a long silver fringe that covered her blue eyes almost completely. She kept pushing it away every now and again. I looked at her from head to feet, surprised to find that she was wearing delicate silver sandals that matched her silver hair. We walked across Vonderpark towards their house, Kathy's ancestors' house.

'Anything strang.' This dictum summed up Kathy's ancestors' passion for the unclassifiable. Miraculous substances, exotic imports, relics, rarities, automatons, uncanny still-life and then later, African fetishes, subversive objects, surrealist ready-mades, each generation collecting the improbable, a rich anatomy of their gaze, perhaps an anatomy of excess. Kathy showed me some of her family portraits where their fascination with the exceptional, with the anomalous, had been faithfully recorded. Portraits that dated back to the so called Rosicrucian Enlightenment, glossy portraits painted by malicious painters that had mixed the pigments with a shiny trickle of death. She showed me some bits of yellowed handmade paper from that time, some inventories where the listing impulse was at the service of a list of wonders. Showed me her family's collection of wonders, the contents of their Wunderkammern, their curiosity cabinets. Her ancestors' erudite handwriting on fragile yellowed paper discussing natural magic, hermetic philosophy, celebrating anything that defied classification as a wonder of God's creation, letters quoting Francis Bacon affirming that the wondrous provided a novel sense of fact, fragile yellowed letters from wealthy men demanding from merchants 'anything strang,' written like that, spelled without the 'e' at the end, letters talking about meteorites, about Siamese twins. I caressed the old letters. Then realised that Kathy had seen me through the corner of her eye and smiled with complicity so that I wouldn't feel embarrassed.

She showed me more yellowed letters complaining about the increasing vilification of curiosity cabinets, complaining about scholars who considered wonder inconsequential, too popular, increasingly a definite outsider to systems of classification, to systems of taste, to the new scientific revolution and its claims to order, objectivity, rigorous taxonomy. Kathy showed me all these, and yet, her ancestors' fanciful objects had been organised in what appeared to be a rigorous formal taxonomy. Then the Collector handed me a battered 1653 edition by an obscure author called John Bulwer who had been the first to compile a hand alphabet for the deaf. The book was about the honesty of the natural body and condemned the fact that all cultures altered the body artificially. The full title was a mad list that I copied on a scrap of paper: *Man Transform'd: or, The Artificial Changling Historically presented, in the mad and cruell Gallantry, foolish Bravery, ridiculous Beauty, filthy Finesse, and loathsome Loveliness of most Nations, fashioning and altering their Bodies from the mould intended by Nature; With Figures of those Transfigurations To which artificiall and affected Deformations are added, all the Native and Nationall Monstrosities that have appeared to disfigure the Humane Fabrick. With a Vindication of the Regular Beauty and Honesty of Nature.*

This title is crazy, I love it, I said. They used to do that in the seventeenth century, long crazy titles, the Collector said. He then started talking about his museum of multiple walls, how he wanted to unify it under this convent in Mexico before his death. He talked about his nephews, said they had their own lives, that they were not all that interested in cinema memorabilia. Then he referred his fascination with specific cinema memorabilia to Kathy's family's curiosity cabinets, after all, at the time, their contents had also been deemed outside systems of meaning, outside reason. Reason, he repeated, that's what had condemned these curiosity cabinets as irrelevant. Nothing 'universal' could be gleamed from them. As with the exceptional, the irrational. This century had acknowledged the haunting power of the irrational, had been shattered by the irrational, had eventually realised that the irrational had to be contained, not pigeonholed, as it comprised the backstage of our multifarious make-ups, constantly making us face the mesmerising music of disruptive contradictions, meaninglessness, the ineffable. And yet, the irrational was still condemned, anything that stood outside normalised systems of meaning was still condemned.

I listened to him thinking that today so many boundaries had been blurred that almost nothing was exceptional anymore. At least, in the world I inhabited. Then I thought about the mythology of reason, the murders and violence committed in the name of reason.

We walked along a narrow corridor. And then the Collector opened a door that led to a narrow room. The room had only a bed in it, and a window opening onto a garden. On the bed there was an old orthopaedic leg in pristine condition next to some underwear. The conjunction of underwear and orthopaedics pointed to the daily life of those whose bodies were different, whose bodies integrated a manufactured limb to make it whole. To people wearing orthopaedic limbs that must have been a more or less daily sight, sometimes connected to eroticism, sometimes an ordinary image of their existence, after a while losing any of the initial shock-value that it might hold for others.

But the conjunction of underwear and orthopaedics here was supposed to be unsettling. Brothels used to cherish prostitutes with a missing foot, leg, arm. Some men were sexually attracted to amputees, cripples, and why shouldn't they be? Negative fetishes, fetishes built around the absence of something which should have been present, a phantom fetish, an anatomy of desire based on negative space. So much for the irreducible materiality of the fetish.

The orthopaedic leg was Tristana's orthopaedic leg. Catherine Deneuve came to my mind. Catherine Deneuve playing Tristana, *Tristana*, a horror film where resentment grows into sadism, perhaps into a grotesque loss, the loss of her leg.

You see, Kathy said, for some people absence becomes the only real thing. The negative of something is more real than the positive of something. The absence, the loss, that's what is real.

And the severed head?

There was also a severed head of a bearded man placed on a small shelf.

Tristana's protector, Kathy said. She said that there was a recurrent nightmare of a severed head in that film, the head of Tristana's protector who, abusing his position, had seduced her during her adolescence, hence her poison, her cruelty, the severed head dream was a decapitation wish forecasting her resentment, the fact that she will become bitter, will exact revenge, will allow her sadism full reign. Hatred, a release, a consolation. In some ways, Tristana's protector had mutilated her trust in those around her. Tristana settled the score, she set out to destroy her protector through perpetual humiliation.

There are a couple of severed hands in his films, the Collector said. Even a hand without fingers that is supposed to be the main protagonist's, but in fact is a maimed hand belonging to an extra. Too many severed hands in the surrealist game, too literal, he said, like the mysterious box in *Belle de Jour*. The beheaded head stands there for what it is: a head, maybe also a castration wish. But beheading is the ultimate act, much more threatening than castration. And ultimately, it's the head which is a riddle, not the penis. *Tristana* is like a fantasy of seduction first in its seductive aspect, then in its traumatic form.

The severed head could be read in both ways, I thought. The seventeenth-century painter Artemisia Gentileschi, one of the few female painters to have reached us from that time, came to my head. I thought about her *Judith and Holofernes*, the most powerful painting of beheading I could think of, and about the fact that she had been raped by her mentor. Of course, the beheaded head could be read in both ways, especially if you followed the joke and saw head and penis as interchangeable. Then I remembered a sequence where Tristana showed her breasts to a deaf boy. The deaf boy ran away in horror. Perhaps the deaf boy could hear what others might not want to hear, perhaps he could hear the overwhelming music coming through her breasts.

The last thing which the Collector showed me was a box full of high-heels. He said that all of them had appeared in Buñuel's films, that he was sorry that they were all like that, in a mess, as they were one of the most important parts of his museum of relevant moments. This is all I've got here, he said, but you should visit us in Mexico. There, I've got memorabilia from the films that were shot in Mexico. He then added with a prolonged guffaw that, although not completely apparent, high-heels were a leitmotif in Buñuel's films.

Before we went for dinner, I gave them Nina Chiavelli's shoes, a dull black pair of plain high heels with a double strap. The Collector gave me the cheque, told me to spend it wisely with a smirk which I recognised as his trademark. I couldn't conceal my euphoria, but then felt sadness as well, an absurd feeling that I was selling my mother, stealing from my father. The Collector didn't mention the introduction to Lecour that he had offered me, it was just bait, I thought, and I understood that I was supposed to forget about it. If there was something attractive about the Collector, it was the charlatan in him. We had dinner in a Japanese restaurant, drank warm sake as if it was tea. It was the first time that I ate sushi. I didn't like fish at the time. I wasn't sure about the nori's rubbery texture. I nibbled it while my gaze went into soft-focus mode over Zacharie's seductive features. He was now talking for the first time. He had a perfectly sensual mouth through which he muttered words in English with a husky French accent. He said that high-heels were a symbol of female sexuality and that there was no equivalent symbol for male sexuality, wasn't that interesting? There wasn't any object close to the male body that signalled his sexuality. A gun? He didn't like

the idea of a gun, it signalled male aggression, not virility.
A pipe was the only thing he could think of. But how did
a pipe compare with the sexual impact of a high-heel as a
symbol? Then he said that he was supposed to come to London soon and asked me for my number with an odd gesture
where his tongue hung on his lips while in mid-sentence. It
was an utterly out of place gesture, sort of sexy and disgusting
at once. I had never come across such a gesture before. Nor
afterwards. As I gave him my number, the Collector's coughs
interrupted my erotic reverie. He had a coughing attack. He
pointed to the *wasabi*. Kathy tapped him on the back, said
that he was coughing a lot of late.

Then she talked about Chiapas, the uprisings, the deaths
on both sides, some say a hundred-and-fifty, some five-hun-
dred, she said. She talked with passion. Talked through the
green-tea ice cream about indigenous rights. About the fact
that she didn't like talking about autistic children, I don't like
talking about work, she said. After dinner, we went to the
Red Light District, visited like good tourists the living museum of women displayed in shop windows, yawning, chat-
ting, daydreaming, lost in thought, always somewhere else,
they were there but they were not there. Perhaps for some
people an object became much more real than a person, perhaps in their early days objects were always there, comforting.
But money, money was definitely a fetish. Could a fetishist
love a shoe as much as some people love the smell of money?

The money kindergarten

The orgasmic green, the sheer intensity of the green of the grass, perhaps it was money that made me aware of the orgasmic green, that made me see everything as more luminous on my return. Everything became sharper, more focused. And as I walked along the high streets with my new acquisitive power, I began to see the mesmerising power of fetishism everywhere. Fetishism was a social phenomenon so ubiquitous that it had become invisible. I began to see the energy that emanated from certain objects, from the names of certain labels. It was obvious that labels were fetishised names. But I realised for the first time the euphoria of objects, their glittering celebrity status, some objects, some labels, were known by millions and millions of people, inhabiting the same media as our most cherished or despised stars, appearing gracefully on television in well-lit shots, in magazines, on billboards, photogenically looking at you, seducing through slick sophistication, through humour, even through a no-nonsense strategy that appealed to pragmatic minds. I realised that sometimes I wasn't sure whether I was looking at a thing or at the image of a thing instilled in my head through the endless loop of glossy repetition. I looked at all these people carrying plastic bags full of redemptive objects, a collective ritualised excess that temporarily put them in direct contact with the supreme, dresses for the girls, gadgets for the boys, induced tangible reveries that catered to all sorts of palates. I looked at men with their bags full of prosthetic gadgets, their dull appearance sometimes cancelled out by their glamorous fast cars. I looked at the playful appearance of women with their bags full of libidinal dreams. Inorganic seduction concealed the mechanical beat of the factory, an inaudible song, a song beyond human hearing frequencies. I tried to listen to the fac-

tory beat, see the invisible hands that assembled these objects, the invisible movements and reveries that assembled
everything in the world, it was possible to hear it, to see it,
but it gravitated towards the imperceptible. I realised that
there were no tramps or drunks in the streets anymore, or if
there were, they were not all that eye-catching anymore, all
the attention was absorbed by the sex-appeal of the inorganic,
there were only so many things your brain could focus on at a
time, perhaps whole continents had also been submerged by
the emergence of this new gaze.

Money, such an abstraction. Money could become anything. It could become time, it could become space. My kind
of money could become a present for Mary Jane, a visit to my
father, a red leather jacket, music, books, lipsticks, a sumptuous dinner with a sumptuous tip, a beautiful dress, a cheap
car, a short rest from worrying about money, I had to pulver-
ise this money, materialise it, transform it into visible things.

Toys appealing to all ages were not as ubiquitous as now.
Executives and old ladies playing with electronic pets while
waiting at bus stops hadn't made their appearance yet. But the
trend had already started. And a handful of nostalgia products, products that appealed to our partly regressive nature,
were already making their appearance in the shop windows.
You could see excited middle-aged men kidnapping remote-
control cars from their children's hands, women with rucksacks
in the shape of revoltingly cute bunny rabbits and bankers
wearing Looney-Tunes ties.

As I walked along the high streets, coming in and out of
shops, with more and more bags (I bought a dusty pink dress,
a Walkman, a pair of radiant trainers, a lovely second-hand
pair of platform sandals, a large red hardback linen notebook),
I felt that I had gained the right to enter heaven, to be part of
an enchanting kindergarten. I thought about Mary Jane, the
perpetually uninhabited kindergarten she had created. With
time, I realised that sexual fetishism was just a small bit of the

larger picture of fetishism. Executives didn't lick their electronic pets or their power books, but they did treat them as controlling objects. Novelty was the name of the game. *Goods* were good objects. In horror films they sometimes returned as bad objects, but that was fiction. A secret collective skeleton in the cupboard was highlighted by the sexual fetishist's mystification with the profane world of thought translated into matter. Perhaps the problem of the sexual fetishist was his private fixation on a rigidly specific object, his reluctance to flow with the ever-changing fetishisation of goods.

Multitudes with shopping bags, re-enacting some ancient ritual of excess. I was part of it, I belonged. I bought Mary Jane a soft plastic toy, a pale blue chameleon that faded gradually into pink, then a book, Kafka's collected short stories, maybe she had it already, but this one had an interesting preface. Then I bought her some Yum-Yum dark chocolates, as she called them, some red wine, left the shopping unpacked at home, put on my new radiant trainers and went to visit her.

Mary Jane had moved to the outskirts, to the end of the world, her telephone line had now been disconnected. The journey was tortuous, jumpy, endless. It was impossible to read, so I looked at people, wondering about their hopes, their worries, imagining their all too human lives, imagining their sex lives. Then I indulged in another underground pastime. Sometimes I played this game when I didn't have anything to read, to think about, it was better played with dark sunglasses so the commuters couldn't see your curious gaze, it was a game of detachment, of estrangement. Sometimes I focused on their ears, wondering whether it was true you could guess the size of a penis by looking at men's ears, sometimes I focused on their noses. To isolate a nose and look at it in its noseness was always an inspiring experience, it allowed you to look at the world anew, to perceive a nose as if you had never seen one before. Noses were the strangest of extremities, irregular pyramids with more or less hairy holes at the base, black

pores, little red veins, varying sizes, thin noses, podgy noses, bird noses. On platforms, I would focus on rears, dissim-
ulated rears, some rears were covered up, misguiding, others
stood out with the force of an assertion. Other times I looked
at commuter's watches, deducing from their design the wear-
er's dreams and fears, stealing from them their visible secrets,
then loving the people who just didn't wear a watch. Now my
gaze looked at the world on a level with that point of encounter with the earth, the floor. The world became a continuous
strip of shoes on an uneven and dirty surface made out of ce-
ment and chewing gum.

It was a year or so, since Mary Jane had decided to abandon the world. Sam and she counted the days as a jubilant
sign of achievement, it was possible to abandon the world
with the help of an assistant, it was possible to wave the world
goodbye. The first few months she was visited by quite a few
friends, artists who found her experiment interesting, who
were as fascinated by her experiment as I was. I had been to
Spain a few times visiting my father, then involved in 'Leather-bound Stories,' I had visited Mary Jane a few times, I admired her in her zeal, in her integrity, failed to realise that a
dark force was kidnapping her. Sam had always been encour-
aging. He was determined in helping her abandon the world.
I liked Sam, he was intense, he was mad. It was only later,
much later, that I wondered whether by helping Mary Jane to
cut all links with the world, he had become part of this dark
force kidnapping her, what's worse, kidnapping her with her
full cooperation.

Sam opened the door, fine, fine, they were both fine,
working, working on themselves, so much work. Then Mary
Jane came out of her room, the main protagonist of her own
disappearance, proud of her action. We kissed. We sat in the
kitchen, around the small table with small lit candles, warm
biscuits. We are baking our own bread, our own biscuits, she
said. She opened the bottle of wine, flicked through the Kaf-

ka book, said she loved 'The Great Wall of China,' it must be strange out there in the outside world, when I think about supermarkets, about buildings and signs, when I think about the outside world I see a shattered picture, as if space was sliced up, something about it scares me, something imposing, deadening. I said her area was a bit drab, like mine, but then she said it wasn't just her area, when she remembered the outside world there was something that scared her, she was going to go out for the first time at Christmas, but then she thought about all these paedophiles dressed up as Father Christmas, she just couldn't stand it.

She opened the chocolate box I had brought, savoured one slowly, placed one in Sam's mouth and told him to let it melt slowly into his mouth. Then she smiled. Good boy, you don't believe in unfair trade, but some of the things you like do, she said playing with the soft chameleon. Then putting on an authoritarian, headmistress voice, she said to me: Are you a good girl, Nina? And then to an invisible audience: Are we good children? Do we deserve the toys? Oh, yes we are good children, quiet, obedient, responsive to fear and chocolate bribes.

Then she laughed and took another chocolate. She said she was just being. She said she was learning how to be good, everybody should learn how to be good, how to become a person, she was writing lists about it, it was difficult, you lost sovereignty over yourself. But the only way to repair the world was to start repairing ourselves. Easily said. But if everybody started working on themselves … But was that possible? Didn't violence constitute our world? Was violence an energising force without which we couldn't live? Was she too emotional, too vulnerable for the world? They were working on that, that's why she wasn't ready to come out, not yet, even if everybody had forgotten about her, the more she thought about things, the more she saw coincidences everywhere, it was weeeeeeeird, she said like in the old days, but she knew she was doing the right thing, abandoning the world was the only way of remaining alive, it was kind of written.

Learning how to be good? I believed Mary Jane and I didn't. I realised that nobody cared about her anymore, realised that she didn't care either. If she hadn't lived so far, if more people had known about it, if her telephone hadn't been cut off. But she was so obstinate, Mary Jane. She didn't want anything to do with the world of appearances, or at least, not directly. But how could you live outside this sweet nightmare? I offered to pay the telephone bill, but she said she didn't want a telephone anymore, she didn't need a telephone, nobody ever rang anyway. Electrical appliances were going kaput, she said, but many of them weren't necessary, the kettle wasn't necessary, the toaster wasn't necessary. The television wasn't working any more either. And of course, it had been absurd to abandon the world and carry on watching television. But it was seven months now that they had lived without television, without newspapers, without magazines, completely cut off from the abominable world.

Mary Jane and Sam had written down the precise dates and times on which they had been visited, as if these visits were memorable events. They remembered these dates. I was the first visit they had had in quite a few months. I stayed the night, had breakfast there, they killed me with kindness, perhaps they had decided I would be their last visitor. Mary Jane was keeping a record of her seclusion from the world, a sort of diary, she talked about a damage unforgettably nebulous. When I left it was all lovely words and I had this strange sensation of floating back home, as if I had been outside the earth, on a different planet. Mary Jane's house had become that to me, a place outside the orbit of the earth.

It was within this mindset that I answered the telephone to hear Kathy, the Collector's wife, at the other end. She talked about Amsterdam, about my mutable writing, then she said that she had a little problem, she said that Lecour was too busy to write the piece for The Museum of Relevant Moments, she didn't know how to tell the Collector, how to break it to him, he would be so upset, his health was so fragile already. Then she said that she had this idea, a confidential idea, if she might share it with me. She knew that I was fascinated by Lecour. Lecour was fascinated by The Museum of Relevant Moments. But he already had so many commitments. He was supposed to attend all these conferences, all these interviews and simultaneously be writing away masterpieces at his desk, in his solitary room. The only way to do this was to have multiple bodies, to be able to be in so many places at once. The only way to do it was to have various writing assistants, while he himself attended interviews, supervised the final drafts. Multiple bodies, if only we had multiple bodies to be in so many places of the world at once. But while we had multiple minds, they were all located in a single body. It complicated our lives. It condemned us physically to one point in space, that was one of the limitations of waking reality. Our mind could inhabit a completely different time, even different times, even the time of simultaneity, our body always returned us to a wretched single point in time and space. Tragic. Lecour had eventually suggested that they use an assistant. He already had his own assistant, but his own assistant was already busy writing his latest assignment. I was a good chameleon, she said. Would I like to write under Lecour's name, to do her this secret favour, to absolutely mirror Lecour's style? Had I heard about ghost writers? All these prolific writers and philosophers couldn't live without them, it had always been like that, throughout history, a single name comprehended a whole workshop of artists working quietly away, not to mention servants, mothers, wives, girlfriends, husbands, partners, friends, of course, it would be well remunerated, she said. Just write about things, objects, material things, the secret code of things. You write it in Spanish, and then we'll have it translated into French,

she said. I didn't have to answer straight away, but they wanted around hundred pages, that was what Lecour was going to
write originally.

Ghostwriting. The idea excited me, it was fraudulent, it
was intriguing, a mysterious assignment, a top secret operation. Enveloped by the prospect of paid misdemeanour, the
following days I went out and blew the last money I had on
libidinal dreams, infected by a spending fever that I couldn't
shake off, feeling good, feeling guilty, trying to forget about
the shoes, about Mary Jane, about my father, about myself,
already undergoing my future spectrality.

A headless, small plastic elephant

There were no such things as coincidences. I had bought a fluffy white rug to celebrate ghostwriting. I had caressed it. The image of a white cat copulating with a black fluffy slipper had come to my mind in a flash. As with humans, there were cats and dogs whose brains were wired up to become aroused by the powerful scent of worn shoes. It was probably a well-known fact that slippers fuelled feline passion. I myself had witnessed a few felines passionately mate with slippers, undoubtedly unneutered cats from the time when cats were left to their own devices.

Becoming Lecour meant thinking about my parents secret again. It meant becoming a philosopher. It meant a remunerated alibi to dive head first into the mystery of things. I liked the idea of becoming a female philosopher, there weren't that many of them, I could only think about twentieth-century ones, de Beauvoir, Weil, Luxemburg, Zambrano, Kristeva, Cixous . . . Mae West?

I had to think thing-thoughts, watch my free-falling ideas and make sense of it all. I had to ask questions and questions and questions and questions and questions: philosophy is a geyser that intermittently throws up answers in the air. The questions are mulled over in the question reservoir. Then steam rises from it. Philosophy is both steam and gush. And I hadn't reached the steam phase yet.

This assignment was about ghostwriting, though. Female philosophers? My gaze came across this disturbing dictionary I used to have, a royal blue hardback book compiled by devious creatures from hell. I had acquired it because of its Technicolor pages and its dated feel. It was an Hispano-American Larousse dictionary from the '80s and it had a History, Science and Arts section where with the exception of a few bejewelled queens, barely any women featured. The Technicolor illustrations were mostly of bearded men, no female thinkers thank you. It was a weird object, a reprint from the '70s that hadn't been redesigned during the '80s, so recent and yet there it was: the old tedious misogyny.

The mystery of things?

The secret code of things?

There was no milk in the almost entirely empty fridge. And no coffee in the coffee jar. And no biscuits in the cupboard. And barely any toilet paper in the toilet. As I was hazily getting ready to go to the supermarket, the wail from the phone finally rooted me firmly to this side of the mirror. I salivated and swooned when I recognised Zacharie's voice announcing with his we-can-have-sex-any-time-you-want French accent that he was coming to London in two weeks time to buy some film memorabilia and wouldn't it be great to meet up or would I be too busy ghostwriting Lecour? Kathy has told me all about your new assignment. It'd be *fantastique* to see you, he said. I didn't know what to say. I became the shyest person alive. I actually stuttered: Ka-ka-ka-ka. Then a ventriloquist took over my persona, as my voice speeded up and went up a few decibels and said in an extra-bold move conceived to conceal my sudden bashfulness: You can stay here if you want, I mean, you can sleep on the sofa.

I'm staying in a B&B in Central London, thank you, but I'll bear it in mind, he said laughing. I found myself saying, OK, I have to dash to *le supermarché*, I'll expect your call then, and quickly hanging up. I was amazed at my ridiculous reaction. Was I afraid of my own desire? I had quickly hung up to delimit his exciting presence. I had quickly hung up with a strange inner giggle that was also a wall against the libidinal chaos that already inhabited me.

Zacharie?

Zacharie, the Collector's assistant, an emissary of sensuality whose rubbery mouth was an unaware conduit for unusual unconscious ticks, the very weird-tongue-twister Zacharie.

His voice left me in a state of heightened awareness. I looked in the mirror and caressed my hips. I was dying for some caffeine, though. I thought I'd better go to a café first, have some coffee, ham and eggs, better take a notebook so I can write to my father. I took my new red notebook. Enroute to my destination, I found propped up against a porch a small, headless plastic animal, which on close inspection was a headless elephant. I was fascinated by this find and treated it as a coincidence, another sign in the right direction, whatever that direction was. It was a perfectly mysterious object, almost the size of my hand. It was dark grey and really wrinkled. Had it been designed like that? Without a head? It looked as it had been conceived headless, but this oddity was probably due to some kind of accident or else a sadist child had neatly beheaded it as part of some kind of macabre game. Poor elephant. I looked at it as if it was a mirror, conscious of the fact that seeing is tangled up with our own stories, an encounter, sometimes a collusion, of our own stories with the moods that ricochet off things. The headless elephant seemed to insistently return my gaze. It had been cast in movement, marching in a self-assured way. Its poise was magnificent. It showed determination. This mirroring I felt was strange. It was as if the elephant was speaking to me, but I couldn't hear it because its head had been chopped off. I didn't know whether it was mirroring something I didn't want to know about. I was more than aware of my own limitations. Or so I thought. Was my resolve to take on the ghostwriting assignment foolish, stupid, dim-witted, obtuse? Or was it my own reptile brain whispering into my ear a worrying note to self:

Desire is a headless elephant . . . sometimes . . . sometimes.

I befriended the headless elephant. I liked it. It was cool in its absurd dignity.

The headless elephant became an impromptu muse, my acephale elephant muse as I placed it on the table and im-

mersed myself in its oddity. I had two coffees, devoured some
ham and eggs, tried to mimic Lecour's voice, but soon gave
up in favour of 'whatever comes out, comes out' and scribbled on my red notebook some preliminary notes addressed
to an imaginary reader:

*You know very well that there are things out there looking
sweetly into your ego as they whisper to you: if you buy me,
you'll be both unique and like everyone else.*

You scratch your head, shrug your shoulders and blink.

*You look at a headless small plastic elephant and in-
stantly know that the makers of things can't help but trans-
late the invisible into the tangible. You can't help it if
things trigger off the logic of your unconscious. You know
that some things are tangible simulacra of states of mind
that you seek and other things would like to tell you something that you're on the verge of grasping. Things seduce
you because thought is translated into matter. You spend
a substantial amount of your life dreaming, in outlandish
landscapes where there are no contradictions, where inten-
sities latch on to images in a more or less explicit way. Every night, when you dream, you return to a landscape of
private signs. A subliminal landscape of signs incessantly
worms its way into your unconscious everyday as you watch
TV, browse through magazines and walk past countless
billboards, reminding you of all the things you should own
in order to belong to the tribe you aspire to belong to.*

*Even your dreams feature advertising now. Your dreams
have begun to feature Pot Noodles and vivid literature
from miraculous shampoos. Pot Noodles induce erotic longings. Shampoo ads are so blissfully obscene that they become
comical, shampoos promise unforgettable sex, cars promise
sublime horizons and sophisticated young ladies, a mobile
phone will give you all the energy of the world. Any meaning can be attached to anything, advertising is a Pavlov-
ian system of sorts, it recreates a submerged way of seeing*

where things scintillate with the magic of wishful think-
ing, it mimics the logic of dreams in order to create an al-
gebra of need.

My enquiry into the mystery of things didn't sound anything
like Lecour, but at least it was a start. I ordered another coffee,
thinking about my mother's stilettos, about my father and the
inexplicable allure of shoe fetishism. I wrote him a letter. Just
sweet, soothing words. I had written letters to my father from
this café before. I had started writing letters to him everyday.
I didn't expect an answer. And I didn't get it. Back home, I
phoned him to tell him that I had a job of sorts, a ghostwriting assignment. If your name isn't mentioned, don't do it, but
what is it exactly that you have to do? he said. I have to write
about some memorabilia from Buñuel's films, I said. Memorabilia? he said. High-heels mostly, I said. God forbid us, he
said. What do you mean? I said. Your mother really liked Buñuel. He was so groovy in the '60s, he said. And you? Did
you like his films? I said. Oh yes, everybody liked his films,
when are you coming back? he said. Did you like any film
in particular? I said. I can't remember the titles, he said. I'll
come as soon as I finish this unexpected job. It's well paid, I
said. Work, bloody work, he said, it always gets in the way.

I phoned him a few times afterwards, whispered easeful
words into his ear to make him feel better. I asked him questions and he answered ... yes ... no ... I can't remember.

Did you have a good day?

Yes ... no ... well ... I can't remember.

Have you been with Eva today?

Was I? ... I can't remember

Dad, are you OK?

I'm as fine as health can be.

I'll book a ticket as soon as I can. Are you feeling OK.
Dad?

I'm perennial.

Perennial?

He laughed and said: What does it mean? Perennial?

Anguish and guilt, I tried to shake them off. I could only take the messy reality of life in small doses. I could be there, at El Refugio, I wasn't doing much those days. I was just waiting for Zacharie's visit and the images and video tapes which Kathy said she would send me, while thinking how ill-equipped I was to become Lecour. Lecour smoked a pipe. I couldn't just smoke a pipe to become Lecour. I had to re-read him. I had agreed to the ghostwriting assignment, but in order to write like him I would have had to share the same aspirations and yearnings, dream the same dreams, eat the same food and drink the same drink, have sex or not have sex with the same people, read exactly the same books. I didn't know about the intimate details, but he had grown up with his father's immense library, he wrote his first philosophical treatise when he was three years old, he came from an affluent background, he probably never worried about paying the rent. His life was completely at odds with mine.

Death: a skull asking you to look at its face without blinking.

For the first time ever, I was afraid of death, my father's death. And I knew my father was even more afraid himself. For a long time now, I had been sensing in all my bones his fear of death. I was afraid he would die while I was here doing nothing, nothing relevant or important or essential or unavoidable. Whatever I was doing, this fear was there as a counterpoint punctuating the liquid days. This fear was both inside me and outside of me. Wherever I was, the fear was either there as intimate as an internal shadow or running parallel to my life, ready to flood it with disquiet at any point. A disquiet inflected by unadulterated sadness. Most people my father was surrounded by were probably touched by this fear. Now and again someone would fade away at El Refugio. El Refugio was like the waiting area at an airport, a limbo zone with a confidential priority queue and personalised last calls for the ultimate one-way flight to that legendary destination: Heaven.

Zia Carla's letter

Morbid thoughts, my father, ghostwriting, Lecour. It wasn't the best of combinations, worrying about my father, while trying to become Lecour. And then, a further bubble of tension shot up from my waist upwards and exploded at the top of my head flooding it with migraine molecules, when a Japanese curator assistant phoned to tell me that Nina Chiavelli's shoes, my mother's shoes, had trailed off somewhere along the Toronto-Kyoto route. The Japanese had changed the title of the exhibition from 'Leather-bound Stories' to 'Vintage Fantasies.' My mother's shoes were supposed to fly over the Pacific Ocean and land in Kyoto, but 'Vintage Fantasies' never made it to Kyoto. No amount of phone calls solved the riddle as to their whereabouts. Security was unavailable. Nobody knew anything. Nobody was bothered in the least. The main Japanese curator was on holidays and the assistant curator, whose name I forget except that it had two *k*'s in it, was extremely polite, but I found the coldness that inflected his staccato fast accent quietly exasperating. Sorry, we do not know where the shipping crates are, we are extremely sorry, he said. I'm unsuccessful in tracking. The shipping company says one thing, the airport staff says something completely different, we're extremely sorry, he said. They've been stolen? I said. They can't have been stolen from the storage area. It has 24 hour surveillance. But 3.3% of shipping crates go missing, we're extremely sorry, he said. 3.3%? I said. A few years ago a ship containing our exhibits caught fire and sank, sorry, he said. Great, I said.

There was a long pause, almost infinitely subdivisible.

The man whose name had two *k*'s in it cleared his throat. And then there was a subtle suction sound that made me wonder whether he was smoking a cigarette.

I will ascertain the party responsible. The tour is insured for several thousand pounds, we're extremely sorry, he said. I told him that I didn't care about the fact that the tour was insured for thousands of pounds. They were my mother's shoes. They were sentimental objects but they were also historical objects, they were irreplaceable. Some of them would have been considered subversive forty or fifty years ago, there had been a huge shift in sexual attitudes since then, that was why they were such a chunk of unusual history, fashion designers had found inspiration in fetish shoes like my mother's, the fact that that kind of shoe had now been fully absorbed into mainstream fashion, didn't make them less interesting, I said.

The man whose name had two *k*'s in it agreed with whatever I said with extreme swiftness and kept on saying it will be sorted out, not to worry, sorry. His friendly professional tone unnerved me. I was irritated by the fact that he kept on repeating 'I totally agree with you, sorry, sorry,' when I hadn't even finished what I was saying. Can you give me the name of the shipping company? Who did you hire to do the job? I said. Sorry, he said. I started feeling sorry for him, *arrivederci*, I said and hung up before my pity for him took on full shape.

Fact: 3.3% of shipping crates go missing.

Where did he get that absurd figure from?

Fact: Ships catch fire and sink.

If their ship had sunk, they would know it by now.

Fact: Nothing goes missing in the universe, everything is transformed.

Transformed?

I shuddered at the thought of my mother's shoes transformed into unrecognisable matter.

What to do? There was nothing I could do, except hoping for the best and keep ringing the man whose name had two *k*'s in it. And nothing I could do regarding my father except for visiting him as often as I could. Nothing except for being there as often as I could. In person, or else, on the phone and via sweet letters and postcards. Flights were more expensive back then. You couldn't say, right, I'm off, unless you had deep pockets. A flight was something that had to be planned. If you bought a ticket to fly the following day or two, it was bound to cost a fortune. The shorter the duration of the journey, the more airline companies sucked you dry. A lightning visit was out of the question. Was it? Swallowing saliva, I phoned Dr. Alvarez. Your father is strong, he said, he's well, maybe he's a bit at a low ebb these days, Eva has a new friend, she's always going on walks with him, your father feels abandoned, he's jealous. Jealous?, that's a good sign, I said, life, he's alive, jealousy equals passion equals life. You needn't worry, he said, he's just started organising a mini-jazz festival, he's busy, he's well, he said.

And yet I started looking for a flight. I phoned the man whose name had two *k*'s in it and on hearing he hadn't had any news about my mother's shoes, gave him my contact number in Almería.

It was impossible to get a flight during the Easter holidays, it was almost fully booked and the prices were truly astronomical. The earliest I could go was a few weeks later, so I ended up booking a flight for a month later, then rang my father and told him the date I was coming, stratospheric prices are keeping as away, I said. The gods of greed, the same old fuckers, he said. Yep, I said, same old story.

Pearl, my neighbour, tried to ease my anxiety with a plate of calamari and sweet and sour sauce. That's how she ate calamari, the same way she ate tempura. Now and again she came round with bits of food, her delicious leftovers. She knew I wanted to visit my father as soon as possible. It'll be OK. five big shipping crates full of shoes can't just go poof, she said. Three, it's three crates, I said.

I checked on the man whose name had two *k*'s in it every few hours the following days and then drifted into Lecour's *Selected Works*, ghostwrote as much I could, tidied up my den for Zacharie's visit . . . in other words, I tried to be busy and pack in as much as possible before visiting my father.

When Zacharie rang, I was in such an edgy mood that my receptiveness to his sexy French accent had plummeted to zero. He was listening to French rock. He said he was arriving on Thursday, he was seeing some people that collected film memorabilia and wouldn't it be great to watch the Buñuel tapes together over the weekend. Good films, sofa, wine, good company, that was his idea of a cool evening, he said. Not bad, I said, except for the fact that I haven't received the tapes yet. You should get going with the ghostwriting, write about fetishism, you know about that kind of thing, you're a sexpert, he said. A sexpert? The Collector has told me that his museum of relevant moments isn't related to fetishism, but is he giving me the right directions to get lost? I said. Probably, he said.

The music he was listening to, died off.

The Collector's into things that are worshipped, he's into sacred things, he said, he's interested in the way certain things become sacred, the ritual of giving meaning to things, the way the gift of sense borderlines with magic in so many cases, to what extent some materials and shapes inherently encourage certain associations . . . You know . . . humankind has always bestowed a tremendous power on things. From totems, to magical objects, to crosses, to chalices, to relics, most mythologies and religions have projected an immense spiritual power into the inanimate . . .

Deadly thoughts about death evaporated.

As he was speaking, my dormant desire became bit-by-bit active again. I could almost see his plump lips forming strings of words. Oddly emphasising the word 'given,' he said that sacred things inhabited systems of sense that belonged to *given* cultures, to *given* ideologies, to *given* systems of belief. Outside those systems, the cookie of sense crumbles into dust . . . The voices of time and place decide which things make sense, which don't, he said. Well, I said, every tribe bonds around a knot of likes and prejudices. And it isn't that certain fixations don't make sense, it's that they don't make sense when measured against the fixations adopted by the largest tribe. What now appears as irrational is probably more a measure of our ignorance, dark areas still to be mapped, I said. Did you say *fixations?* he said. A lot of psychobabble about the irrational is undoubtedly a nonsensical testimony to the will to interpret, you should talk to Lecour. Is there anything you'd like from Paris? he said. Oh, a box of *Gauloises blonde légère*, I'll pay for it, I said. You don't have to pay for anything, he said.

Eddies of sensuality lingered around the white plastic telephone and then spun around the whole living room. I gyrated with the eddies, looked in the mirror, bit my ultra thin lips and jumped on my feet. An inner giggle reverberated through every nook and cranny in my body, a caress that went from toes to earlobes as I pulled out one of Lecour's books from the bookcase. The anxious reality I had been inhabiting just before Zacharie's call withdrew to some remote corner of reality atlas. When I opened the book, its pages seemed to come in and out of focus. I had to achieve an extremely porous state, not to desire, but to Lecour, I told myself.

After a light dinner, I finally started cannibalising Lecour's words, trying to make them mine. As a nouveau philosopher, I was excited to realise that in many European languages the same word was used to refer to the sense organs and to refer to sense as meaning. Sense. Senso. Sentido. Sinn. Sense. If something had a shared meaning, it was because it made sense in terms of our senses. There was a template for how the senses should behave. Was it really true that we only had five senses? Hadn't I heard on the radio some scientists claiming that we had somewhere in the region of twenty-one senses? Did the senses of a shoe fetishist behave in a way most people's didn't? Perhaps his olfactory sense, which is the sense most linked to memory retrieval, triggered forbidden associations that had been imprinted on his neural networks from an early age. Or else, a brain chemical messenger confused one part of the body with another one. Or maybe fear was at the centre of the shoe fetishist's libidinal network, the presence of a woman so overpowering that he had to shrink her into a docile object? But what did I know?

If I didn't understand any of these, how was I going to write about The Museum of Relevant Moments, Buñuel's memorabilia? I began talking to female friends about it. It was a shame that I couldn't talk to Mary Jane unless I went to her place, which was on the outskirts of the end of the world. I talked to my neighbour Pearl first, who seemed to solely attract underwear fetishists, you know what I mean, black lace and all that she said. Then she said she'd tell me about a rubber ball that she had been invited to, it was going to be in a club called Fantastique, she wanted to check out that scene, she liked the look, she wanted to have fun, let's be tourists, she said.

Except for Pearl, most of my female friends agreed that most men were fascinated by a part of their bodies rather than a part attached to their body. Thus there were men fascinated by breasts, men fascinated by legs, men fascinated by arses. My female friends also privileged with passion a part of the male body, a bare chest, buttocks, shoulders, veins, especially the penis's main vein. I myself loved Adam's apple. Sheer object fetishism was indeed rare. I found a few stories though. I heard stories about women idealised and dehumanised at once; stories about women who felt humiliated, desecrated, shattered into a garment; stories of seduced cooperation, theatricality, and supreme boredom; stories about people so damaged by other people they could only *literally* fall for objects; I heard a story about a shoe historian so obsessed about footnotes that his lengthy articles consisted of a single paragraph with infinite footnotes; a story about an old woman who ritually wore a fur coat inside out with nothing underneath to check out the black cashier at her local super-market.

There was no such thing as fetishism, there were only fet-ishisms, then degrees, degrees, degrees, it was all a question of degree, that's what I was finding out.

While immersed in all this, I had been waiting for a call from the man whose name had two *k*'s in it. I had also been waiting for Kathy's parcel to arrive. While waiting to be re-leased from waiting, I received a long letter from my mother's sister in Italy, zia Carla. In the letter, she apologised about the delay in writing back, she told me that my mother had always loved nice shoes, that as a child she used to throw herself on the floor in a tantrum if she didn't get the shoes she wanted, that she would rather starve to death than make do without a pair of Ferragamo platforms, that with all the money she spent on shoes, she could have sent me to a public school, but of course, my father didn't believe in public schools, that my father, Jordi Joan, was my mother's butler, that she clicked her fingers once and he brought her a cappuccino, she clicked her fingers twice and immediately, there he was, with a pack-et of cigarettes, a lighter and an ashtray, that my mother had ended up living in a shack, but my father was a good butler, so professional …

It was perfectly ludicrous. I could see in the neatness of her handwriting her spite. I was suffused with an odd mix-ture of anger, incredulity and something akin to laughter. The bitch. Zia Carla. So full of jaundice. She went on to say that my father had always been perfectly useless at providing a proper income, he had always been as if in a dream, maybe a subservient one, that therefore Nina Chiavelli, her sister, my mother, the black sheep of the family, had had to feature in a few films as a foot extra. A foot extra? Didn't I know? I don't know which world I lived in but I didn't know such thing ex-isted. But yes. Some actresses had huge ears, huge feet. And film directors used to prefer actresses with broad facial features but small dainty ears, really tall actresses with small dainty feet. That was the case with Marlene Dietrich. She had huge feet, my aunt informed me, she had always used foot extras. Nina Chiavelli! My mother! My mother's feet must have appeared in a few well-known films, standing in for a few well-known actresses' feet. I wonder now whether I knew all along that my mother had been a foot extra, whether when I received my aunt's letter, it was more a confirmation of something which I somehow already intuited, a piece of evidence that I had chosen to ignore, as one usually ignores so much one knows.

Bodies made out of organs from different owners, different extremities, exquisite Frankensteins, exquisite corpses, dismembered workers. Films were never going to be the same. I started looking at films wondering whether all these bits of body belonged to the same person, whether these bodies were assemblages of so many other bodies, whether some bits could be my mother's. Film is a collection of multiple fragments, twenty truths and lies per second. Photography and film did that, zoomed in on a fragment of reality the way our conscious vision only occasionally zoomed in, our conscious vision often encompassed blurred surroundings, while film, with its close-ups, mirrored the intensity-spot of our gaze, got rid off all those inconsequential blurred bits. My mother inhabited the logic of cinema. Cuts, specific frames, a body made out of multiple bodies, my mother, Nina Chiavelli, a foot extra.

Fast-forward, rewind

Oh well, oh well, my father had never hid from me that my mother had been a strip tease girl, but he had never told me that she had been a shoe model as well. Wasn't that telling? It was, wasn't it? Shoe modelling. What a strange profession. My mother must have got most of her shoes from shoe modelling. All my odd ideas about them, mere reverie. London rainy days were conducive to consolidating fantasies seeded elsewhere. Weeds. Growing up. Becoming aware of fault lines and crevices in the way you interpret the world. Waiting. I was waiting. While waiting, I found myself writing a list about my own relevant moments. I tried to write as many as possible. There were moments from childhood and adulthood all jumbled up and only a couple from my adolescence. Love, death, and the discovery of simple pleasures. And then, also the discovery of cruelty. That's what my relevant moments spoke about. Since then, I have added other relevant moments to my life, but at the time this is what I came up with:

> Making up white lies to a friend about an abandoned
> mansion in the street I lived in as a child.
> A man slightly trembling in my arms
> A young cat dying suddenly in my arms
> An old cat taking to sleeping on my head during the
> months before he died
> Seeing my mother's boots in a film by Buñuel
> Dusting books written in foreign languages when I was
> a child and wondering about their enigmatic content
> Doing the homework from a French school book with
> my mother and going beyond several lessons ahead of
> homework

Discovering a litter of newly born mice in the sand
dunes
Leaving a pair of shoes in a litter bin as a goodbye to a
city and a man
Seeing seagulls dead by the seashore and being suffused
by melancholia for the first time, aged fifteen.
Realising my father could also be a victim when his
wallet was stolen in the market
Returning from school and being greeted by my father
with sheer love
Witnessing as a child sheer cruelty when I saw some
boys spattering some kittens against a wall and asked
them what the hell they are doing and being baffled
by their answer: the kittens won't survive without their
mothers, anyway
Hiding under the blankets and weeping when my father told me that my mother had gone to make films in
heaven
Becoming conscious of the social status of my family
Looking at the stars with my father
Seeing my father crying when he came across a packet
of rizzlas in my bedroom.
Smelling cardamom and smelling cinnamon
Relishing myriad bubbles as a sea wave crushed against
my body
Relishing the undulating effect on my body when div-
ing under a wave.

I was musing on this list, how a moment triggered another moment that contained the same word, when the phone
rang. The call from the man whose name had two *k*'s in it was
manna from heaven. The shipping crates, my mother's shoes
had finally been found. Drug-sniffing specialists at the airport
had indicated to the inspectors that these innocuous crates
full of female shoes needed a closer look. We are extremely sorry. There was this mistake, somebody ticked the wrong

box and officially declared the crates as carriers of 'illegal narcotics.' I had to answer lots of questions as well as writing several statements that declared they were narcotics-free, he said. Carriers of illegal narcotics? I said. The dogs were totally excited, he said. To err is canine too, I said with glee. Airport dogs are odour specialists, they must have found something narcotic in the smell the shoes gave off, he said in a factual manner. I started laughing, but said nothing. My theory is that an officer must have *misread* the alert the dogs gave, these dogs are infallible, he said. The Kyoto show is going to proceed as planned, if that is your wish, we're extremely sorry.

Relieved, I went for a long walk and relished the light drizzle. More often than not drizzle irritated me, but 'the narcotic shoes event' had made me dance on my feet as I walked. Thinking on my feet, my thoughts specialised in how unbelievable reality can be and then I also found myself thinking about Zacharie.

Knowing that he was arriving on Thursday, when Wednesday came, I found myself plucking my eyebrows, shaving my legs, choosing what to wear. The Buñuel tapes arrived in a parcel covered in 'fragile' stickers. When Zacharie rang, I swooned again as he asked me for my address and whispered I'll be at your place three minutes past seven Saturday evening.

Saturday was still two days away but when Saturday came he rang to postpone the meeting to Sunday, same time. I waited for the bell to buzz on Sunday from three minutes past seven onwards, left several messages with the hotel receptionist, but the evening went by in slow motion with no sign of Zacharie. Maybe something's happened to him, maybe he's been abducted by aliens, I thought. Or else, he's *un homme fatal*. I yowled. *Un homme fatal*, I didn't need an homme fatal in my life. And yawning at the thought, I left the phone off the hook.

And yet I felt down.

And down.

And down.

And once in bed, I had the weirdest kitsch sexual fantasies featuring galloping horses emerging from the sea mixed in with Zacharie's face. Was this a prelude to the Buñuel tapes? What kind of man could trigger such lurid fantasies? I started watching the Buñuel tapes *sans* Zacharie, three days after I received them. Became acquainted with most of his work, paying special attention to the sequences where an image would stand out with a trompe-l'oeil effect as an obvious fetish. Buñuel's commercial films were a bit of a rarity. I relished them, realising that even in the commercial films an alibi had been created in order to smuggle in a small disturbing detail, an unsettling image that would afterwards float around in your consciousness like an after-image. Moreover, knowing that my mother, Nina Chiavelli, had been a foot extra, I was looking in particular at women's feet in films, close-ups of feet, but also other close-ups of parts of the body, always wondering whether a beautiful hand belonged to the same body it purported to be part of, whether a neck, a pair of legs belonged to an anonymous extra rather than to the main star. I realised that this kind of intense cutting up of the body was also intrinsic to advertising, a couple of legs advertised tights, a hand, hand cream, a torso, a bustier. But that wasn't all that new. Early advertising already fused consumerism, desire, and female body parts in a bizarre montage. It was me who was new to the world: I was so naïve.

The news about the genocide in Rwanda, which was about a different cutting up of the body, dominated the news at the time. At some point, I decided not to watch the news anymore. It was too gruesome. Human cruelty knew no bounds. I still didn't know that life was an affair interspersed with wars, always wars. I decided not to watch the news until I had gone through all the tapes that I had to watch.

The TV screen became a sheer rectangle of fascination in

the dark. I became a recluse for a while. Didn't understand why they wanted me to ghost-write around a hundred pages when the whole thing could be summarised in a few. I sat on the fluffy white rug, with an improvised ghostwriter's kit: remote control, pen and paper, cigarettes, beer, salted peanuts and cashew nuts which according to the warning on the packet happened to contain traces of nuts. I immersed myself in Buñuel's films, in his world. His neurotically interesting characters kept me good company for quite a few days. That's what I liked about film, the fact that characters didn't look at you. You could see them but they couldn't see you.

I watched the rare films to begin with. I first watched *The Criminal Life of Archibaldo de la Cruz* and was shocked at how abysmal it was. Then I watched it again and thought it was a brilliant macabre comedy, a clever nod to magical thinking. The film was about a traumatised man who surrenders to the police when his powerful psychopathic killing fantasies against women start coinciding with the deaths of those very women. The protagonist reminded me of Zacharie in a vague, ungraspable way. As I was wondering whether they shared anything in common beyond looks and if I would ever see Zacharie again, I wrote about *mental delinquencies* and how they are part of the inner texture of everyone. Would Lecour have thought of that term?

But then pleasure, all that solitary pleasure came to a halt. It came to a sudden halt when I came across this minor film called *El*. It was in this film that I found the image of the shoes that I had sold to the Collector, the innocent high-heels with a double strap. Had my mother been a foot extra in a Buñuel film? Wouldn't my father have told me, wouldn't the Collector have told me? I rewound the tape, looked at the innocent high-heels, those were my mother's shoes, the shoes next to the stilettos the main actress was wearing! There they were. The camera focused first on the innocent high-heels with a double strap, then on a pair of stilettos, then on a pair of male shoes. The main scene was a stiletto and its beautiful shadow. It was a seamless scene travelling upwards to the main actress' face.

My mother was just a pair of anonymous shoes, a pair of innocent shoes without a face. I felt humiliated to see that my mother's shoes were the ones next to the main actress, perhaps the humiliation my mother must have felt at just being a pair of feet. Humiliation? It was a job. A job that must have allowed her to feed me and buy herself more treats, such as more high-heels. She probably learned to enjoy that, the anonymity, the eventual lack of pressure in being an extra, the joyful indifference towards the tyrannical world of achievements. Perhaps not. Nina Chiavelli, an extra like so many other extras in the world. But perhaps there is never such a thing as an extra in the world.

Blood travelled to my head igniting the circuits of anger. I looked carefully at the credits for my mother's name, so many names gathered under one name: Buñuel. My mother's name wasn't there. Had my father fallen in love when he first saw my mother's high-heels, like the guy in the film? I switched off the video, the TV, abandoned myself to my mind's white noise. I rang the Collector straight away. Felt deceived by the whole thing. The Collector had mentioned when I first met him that the black pair of innocent high-heels reminded him of another pair that had appeared in a Buñuel film, but the shoes were identical. He must have known all throughout that Nina Chiavelli had been a foot extra. He should have told me when we first met. A lot of things would have been clearer to me then. But then I thought that it was the shoes which were the same. That didn't imply it was my mother's feet, even if my mother had been a foot extra. Also, why would Kathy have sent me that particular tape?

Kathy answered the telephone. The Collector was indisposed. Said the doctors didn't know what was wrong with him, he was feeling increasingly unwell. I spoke warm words.

Reassured her. I said that I had received Buñuel's tapes but not the images from The Museum of Relevant Moments, she had forgotten to include them in the parcel. I asked about Zacharie and she said she didn't know he was in London, he travelled a lot, she said. Then I made enquiries about my mother's shoes. I didn't know how to put it, but I did. Nina Chiavelli? A foot-extra? Kathy laughed hoots of raucous laughter. And to my surprise, I found myself laughing with her. She then assured me that they had never heard of Nina Chiavelli. There had been a misunderstanding. Yes, the shoes I sold them were almost identical to the ones in the film, but they weren't the original ones, they owned the original ones, they were slightly different, the original ones were completely new, the Collector had been so bemused to encounter an almost identical pair in pristine condition after almost fifty years. Hasn't it occurred to you that at the time they must have manufactured thousands and thousands of shoes identical to your mother's? And what if your mother had a knack of buying shoes inspired by the films she watched? I hesitated. I apologised. Kathy said it was just a misunderstanding, misunderstandings, they were interesting, they created new realities, they happened everyday.

I felt relieved. There was something about Kathy that always calmed me down, something soothing in her intonation. And yet I rewound the tape again. Attentively watched it sequence by sequence. Fast-forward, rewind, fast-forward, rewind. The film started with the protagonist helping in a cleansing ceremony where a priest washed a row of adolescent boys' feet and then kissed them on the instep, a lingering kiss, a rite of passage into something unspoken, a strange ritual. I thought this rite of passage would make more sense if the adolescents had deposited a lingering kiss on the supreme's foot, but then it would have been primarily about power, like kissing a king's ring, a priest's ring. A collective ceremony was followed by a private obsession, foregrounding how collective ritual sanctioned behaviour unacceptable when private: the protagonist's gaze went through the row of adolescent male bare feet, looked quickly at the shoes of the congregation and froze with his gaze a high-heel shoe, its distinct shadow a perfect high-heel silhouette. His passion for the owner of the shoe, crystallised there, with the sight of her high-heel shoe and its beautiful shadow. A passion that crystallises around a foot housed in a beautiful high-heel shoe and its beautiful shadow might not be all that promising. But sometimes things turn out like that, not just the irrational but even the shadow of the irrational.

Ejecting the tape from the video recorder, I reminded myself that thousands and thousands of identical shoes were manufactured at the time.

I continued working, writing, living on coffee, cigarettes, and filmic matter.

As soon as I received the images from The Museum of Relevant Moments, I put them up on the living room walls and immersed myself in each one of them, one at a time. In my endeavours to be a good chameleon, I re-read several times bits of Lecour's oeuvre. I got the mannerisms, the rhythm, the style. Tried to think the way he would think, tried to conjure up the angle he would have taken, utterly freed from any anxiety of influence. I enjoyed that, inhabiting a different way of seeing. It allowed me to be somebody else, it allowed me to consciously incorporate somebody else's vision into my own consciousness, devour it while being devoured by it. I started taking notes about the Collector's museum of relevant moments from Lecour's point of view. Littered my writing with neologisms, mystifying sentences, sentences that went beyond sense, concepts coined with Latin words for the occasion, names of monolithic philosophers, fetish names. I had watched most of the Buñuel tapes. Buñuel's desire was a desire for the knowledge of desire. Middle-class men with established middle-class professions, then, perversely bored wives,

chambermaids, servants, nuns, part-time prostitutes, mannequin models. His eroticised women weren't a mere mirage of
male desire, though. Beyond their appearance, these women
were caught up in their own inner tangles, erotic flights, dis-
cordant liaisons, just as his neurotic men, his often outmod-
ed bearded men.

Beards. I had a phobia about beards, it was like there was
hair where it shouldn't be, but then, it shouldn't be there according to the convention of cleanliness. I found it hard to
sympathise with bearded characters. But was that Lecour's
point of view? Wasn't it more my point of view? Could I escape my own subjectivity? Buñuel's desire was a desire for the
knowledge of desire? In Buñuel, fetishism remained an exclusively male game. Almost all the characters that pointed to it
were men. I realised that in Buñuel's world fetishism was an
exclusively male affair, there weren't any women fetishists in
his films.

A denial? A blind spot?

A memorable long sequence in *L'Âge d'Or* from 1930 came
to my head as a delayed counterpoint to my nagging suspicions. Memorable and hilarious. How I laughed! In this film,
there was this upper-middle-class woman vehemently sucking
a statue's foot for a bewildering long long time. Kathy hadn't
sent me that film. Maybe the Collector didn't own that statue.
That was the first example of Buñuel's foot fetishism, it was a
woman who fetishised, it was related to the absence of her violent lover, her sucking was evocative of another kind of sucking but it only pointed to the absence of her lover, not to any
inherent lack in her. Would Lecour have written about that?

Ghostwriting and film-watching, so perfectly spectral.
I wasn't looking forward to becoming Lecour but I started
scribbling about Buñuel's fascination with unspoken sexual
fantasies, how the Collector's collection of relevant moments
spoke about this fascination, how some of the neurotic characters in his films actually worked like complex case studies,

to what extent other characters were sexual dissidents trapped inside rancid marriages, whether he was stuttering about femininity as mere pretence, a perfect simulacrum, a copy of a copy of a copy going back *ab aeternum* to an original that had never existed. After his first two films, Buñuel had integrated this strange fascination as part of the everyday life of his characters, you could see it in small frozen details that might seem ordinary and yet, at the end of the film, these small frozen details stood out with the over insistent presence of a hallucinated trompe-l'oeil. These were the relevant moments that the Collector had chosen. In many of them, ritual was what invested them with meaning. Yet in others, the way the camera travelled around an object as if caressing it, entailed a compulsive logic. I scribbled about ritual, the ritual of sense, of bestowing sense upon things, about private rituals, about using things as safe conducts to transform the here and now.

Barely registering transitions of daylight, I spent ages and ages scribbling about all this, wondering whether all these films will leave a neural trace of filthy-wanton-lascivious-weird fantasies as side effects. When I finished my scribbling, I realised that I wasn't quite thinking about The Museum of Relevant Moments. The museum dealt mainly with the haunting power of inanimate things, I had been scribbling solely about Buñuel, rather than about the Collector's museum and the voice wasn't quite Lecour's voice, but more like a zealous parody of his style. As a ghostwriting piece it just didn't sound right. It was rubbish. It was crap. It sounded like me trying to sound like somebody else and failing miserably. The contents were more or less OK. but my chameleon abilities were limited. I put half of what I had written through the shredder as a symbolic act of sorts. I felt an immense elation as I saw the paper strips curled up in the bin and could see Buñuel's ghost nodding at me with approval. I saw his face precariously projected on the ceiling. I winked at him with complicity, while warning him mentally that all my scribbling was saved on the laptop and on disquette. I had a cool beer while ignoring my neighbour Pearl knocking on my door: Nina, are you in? I hadn't been out for a million years and maybe Pearl was worrying about me. I rang her and told her that I was alright, just working, fine. It was funny ringing your next door neighbour, hearing the immediate ringing from my own flat.

I was tired-unhappy. I was reluctant to go to the British Library. After the penis nightmare event, I had a developed a phobia towards the building. I improvised an office on the white rug: laptop, hand-written notes, ashtray and a gooseneck desk lamp. I just had to write another sixty-six pages. And yet I spent hours on end looking for split-ended hairs under the crisp clear halogen light. This bout of trichotillomania, the name given to hair-plucking, was interwoven with siestas and power-naps that left me exhausted.

The flat had become so quiet that I learnt to distinguish first each infra-noise made by each electrical appliance: the laptop charger definitely sounded like crickets. Then I tuned into the inner life of the block: the dizzy clanking produced by the lift going up or down, the doors opening with a slash, the hissing rubbish being dragged along the corridor, the arrhythmic breathing of the central heating, the block's regular regurgitation of its inhabitants lives. I was becoming somewhat unhinged. I started thinking about Mary Jane's toys, about the fact that children were convinced that inanimate things were alive. Would Lecour have written about that?

I didn't care about Lecour anymore.

Childhood trance interlude

Surrounded by work and melancholia, no Zacharie, Zach-arie-wherethehellareyou?, I spent ages and ages racking my brain about The Museum of Relevant Moments, thinking that maybe I should be using lateral thinking, whatever that was. Or maybe zigzag thinking. Spiked with vertical, hori-zontal, elliptical and paradoxical thinking, whatever. I had been experiencing linguistic interferences. I was supposed to be writing in Spanish, and English words or turns of phras-es kept cropping up in my head. That was both the curse and blessing of speaking more than one language. At present, it was a curse. I had been locked in for too long. I hadn't had a bath for a zillion years. One of those frustrating mornings, I ran the bath and stayed in the water until it became luke-warm. My hands and feet had shrivelled, the rest of my body dissolved, but I felt like a new born baby. It was sunny out-side and I went out to absorb the luminous particles. There were mini-explosions of vibrant colour bursting from the trees, colourful dots sprouting unsuspected from the ground. I hadn't even realised that it was spring already. I mooched about imbibing the luminosity and befriended a '70s station wagon with wood panelling on the side parked at the end of my street. Then I walked to the charity-shops zone in search of forlorn bargains. You could see last year's fashion hanging on its rails, barely worn. A microcosm of unloved objects and nomadic objects. And also, the objects of the dead. The more you bought, the more you helped Africa, cancer research, the disabled and abandoned animals. The more you bought, the more you saved and helped planet earth. I found a new pair of exquisite shoes for next to nothing, ten times less than their original price. Rescued from oblivion a beaded chok-er that was fifty pence. And a snow-dome with Berlin's bear,

dark and mysterious. Such savings deserved a cappuccino and
a carrot cake in an overpriced sandwich-shop, to compensate.
The willowy waitress understood about such treats.

Lecour? I couldn't become Lecour, but maybe I was becoming a philosopher. Maybe what I enjoyed was the process
of becoming something else, being a dabbler, a perpetual student. It was like living so many lives. Like believing in sus-
pension marks rather than full-stops. I shook the snow-dome
and caught the waitress' blank stare at the snowstorm. There
were poetic objects, rebellious objects, practical objects, and
objects of greed. The snow-dome was a poetic object. The ka-
leidoscope of objects that I had just seen in the charity shops
reconfigured my neural networks creating new unsuspected paths that led me to pen 'Object Hyperballad' there and
then, the first of a series of *Variations* on the subject. I had the
red notebook with me. Stimulated by the aroma of freshly
ground coffee, I opened it and saw the writing slowly emerging from its pages:

'Object Hyperballad'

Some objects are maps of moments and other objects are emotional maps that contain in intricate detail the whole memory of an experience, and then,
there are things that trigger love at first sight, things
that leave you in a lukewarm state of indifference,
things that were desirable a decade ago and have
now become ex-desirable things and things that you
wouldn't mind killing. There are also happy things
full of disturbing potential that can always become
things of horror such as a cheerful clown mask painted in creepy garish colours, and then, there are sickly sweet kitsch figurines that you befriend out of un-
conditional love towards their owner, like the porcelain
little girls and puppies in your aunt's living room.

Then there are all these trashy gifts that you hope to recycle at the earliest opportunity in the near future, objects from hell designed to fill you up with frustration and all the unexpected things that turn up after being in hiding for years in what was an unexplainable emotional exile. And sadly, there are the personal effects of the disappeared. And there are also vicious things of violence that speak about the darkness at the centre of the world such as a machine gun, a beautifully crafted revolver.

There are hilarious things designed by demented people that make you laugh out aloud like for instance a dressed up singing cow that suddenly flashes her udders, lost things that you hope will turn up one day and things that are lost forever: so many gloves, scarves and keys and gloves and umbrellas. There are also things that you just can't throw away in case they are useful in a rather hypothetical future and stolen things that embody a thrilling moment. There are old things that are not old enough and just look old-fashioned, throwaway things that have absolutely nothing redeemable about them and then, there are all these things that will probably outlive you: the bastards.

And there are also dreamlike things, semiotically neutral things whose year of fabrication would be hard to trace and streamlined things of the future encoded in the here and now. Lacklustre things afflicted with a generally depressed aura that ask you for compassion knowing that sometimes they will get it and other times they won't, and then, there are indestructible things that convey unbroken resilience, things of luck that ward off bad mojo and damaged things that remind you of the fragility of life.

And then there are things that can be extremely useful, but can also become things of danger, like a knife or an axe with perfectly sharp blades. And there are promiscuous things such as lighters, pens and paper clips, things that have only been used once and things of nostalgia that your grandmother gave you. There are things that mimic an expensive material in a cheaper material underscoring power and social relations and old damaged things that you can't bring yourself to throw away. Playful things of lust and transformation such as wigs, handcuffs, feathers, and stilettos, and then, there are all these cast-off things on the streets that look back at you longing to be acknowledged.

And then there are things that scream with status.

And things that scream with muteness.

And things that belong to plastic fantastic culture whose fragments end up bursting out of the guts of albatross chicks.

And then, and then, and then.

And then, as I spooned out the last bit of cappuccino froth, I closed the red notebook and saw a little girl take out everything from her mother's handbag. She then touched, licked and rubbed against her body every single item, while her mother smiled approvingly, after checking the suitability of each item to be abused orally: a measuring tape, a set of keys, a mirror, a brush, a book that gave away her mother's interest in things Zen, *The Tao Te Ching*. I wouldn't have found the little girl's actions remarkable if it wasn't for my train of thought. Why had Kathy chosen such an implausible person to ghostwrite Lecour? And why did Buñuel's name keep cropping up in my parents' life?

The little girl came towards me, with amazing resolve, a sturdy mini-presence, tubby, chubby, dumpy, chunky, unflinching hand stretched towards the snow-dome. She had subtle Chinese features and luminous hazelnut brunette hair. She watched it bewitched. Then licked it and yelled in ecstasy: Memema! I considered giving her the magical object. It was smeared with saliva. I cleaned it with a napkin. Felt a bit nasty about not giving it to her, as her apologetic mother took her away. But then her mother said to me with a grin: she loves smashing things, the cathartic power of smash.

Nodding to Memema's mother with an amused smile, I decided that I couldn't let Kathy down, I couldn't afford to anyway. I went back home as if I was returning from a short-holiday. I was determined to finish the ghostwriting. I decided that it would be best to begin with my first encounters with things, to recreate my infancy, putting aside Lecour for the time being.

Memema!

Like a big child trying to solve a five-thousand-year-old puzzle, I sat legs akimbo on the fluffy white rug besieged by pictures from my photo album scattered all over and looked at a picture from when I was a baby, feeling against my skin the sensuality of the things that caressed me from the second I was born. I focused my gaze on the soft blanket, the soft baby suit, the dummy, the nappies, rounded organic surfaces that fitted my body, submissive matter. It must have been amazing to touch these things for the very first time, to smell them, to suck them, to explore the world anew, to come across the first tactile sensations, the first smells, the first flavours, to walk on all fours on the cold fake marble floor. Surgical gloves flashed through my mind. That was probably the first tactile sensation most people born during the last sixty years would have experienced as they came out from the womb. Rubber. Green rubber gloves.

Gently closing my eyelids, I tried to effect a regression

back to my first years: Mary Jane and her baby toys crossed my mind, then my mother's stilettos, Nina Chiavelli's shoes, ninety-five stories which were still in Kyoto. I then sucked my thumb as if that was the fastest route to a nursery rhyme that my mother used to sing. I barely remembered it. I only remembered the refrain. I sang it in a low voice, a whisper:

> Salagadoola mechicka boola bibbidi-bobbidi-boo
> bibbidi-bobbidi-boo
> bibbidi-bobbidi bibbidi-bobbidi bibbidi-bobbidi-boo

I immersed myself in my childhood as if a revelation awaited me there.

I entered it.

Trying to see it as if for the very first time, I looked at a piece of string that was lying on the floor wondering whether when you are a toddler you can fall intensely in love with a mere piece of string. I imagined touching its rough texture in a perpetual trance, sucking it compulsively, then abandoning it for a rubber ball, then abandoning the rubber ball for the logic of endless novelty, the logic of kids.

In childhood, things were undoubtedly connected by secret undercurrents, they could simultaneously be what they were and something else. Anything could become anything. A warm blanket became an absent mother, a broken thermometer invaded the house when my mother told me that the mercury inside reproduced itself, a porcelain figure cannibalised me incorporating me into its tiny body, a slipper whose sole became slightly loose turned into a source of terror: it was going to eat me up, it looked like a devouring mouth, perhaps similar to what my mouth looked like when I devoured my mother's nipple with destructive might. A flat sheet of paper became an aeroplane with the aid of my mother, but a hairbrush could become menacing with no further transformation, there was something lurking in its insistent

presence, something about its erect bristles became suddenly
unsettling, maybe their tense silence. The hairbrush was alive,
it could attack me at any time, but when I crashed it violently against the wall nothing happened, like nothing happened
when I smashed my walking, talking, crying, sleeping, living
doll, dismembered it and searched for its soul. I smashed it
and smashed it and smashed it. Where was its soul? Splattered
against the fake marble tiles? I soon learnt about guilt though.
I learnt that even when there was nobody around, there
was somebody watching me, an internal censor.

Memema!

I smoked another cigarette, while shaking the snow-dome
with Berlin's bear inside, a contained universe that was magical, although after the initial flurry of chaos the snowflakes
seemed to fall in a somewhat pathetic way. My childhood reverie had been punctuated by clusters of random thoughts: I
should call Kathy and tell her to look for somebody else . . . I
really have to get on with it . . . my back is killing me, I should
go swimming . . . there hasn't been anybody in my life for
ages now . . . nobody, you can't count Zacharie as somebody.

Lighting another cigarette with the lit dead-end of the
previous one, I placed on the dining table a string of objects
in a long, minimal line that cut the table into two: the snow-
dome, the beaded choker that I had just bought, the small,
pink helicopter that Mary Jane had given me, a hot-water
bottle, a bottle-opener that didn't open hot-water bottles, the
headless plastic elephant and a golden platform shoe. Each
object branched out into different stories and unsuspected
realms. That was what was at the centre of things: their stories.

Looking at the line of things on the table as a child would,
I thought that at some point in my childhood, I must have
learnt that not everything could become anything. Things
were classified into all sorts of systems, all sorts of hierarchies,
that's what Nina Chiavelli, my mother, a foot extra, must

have taught me. Things had a meaning, a function, a value, things were gendered in my language, some colours had gender too.

To begin with though, there were no categories. Things were simply thrilling matters, you could get lost in them, explore them, abuse them, lick them, suck them, they just lived a different life from us, maybe a thing life, the sub-atomic life of things. The first lesson from things must have taught me to have magical thoughts, the world was an animistic world, if I touched a forbidden key there might be an explosion, if I tread on a doormat the world will disappear, if I was nice to the inanimate world it would soften my fate. Even if a toy didn't break when I crashed it against the fake marble floor, I must have enjoyed that sublime violence, perhaps I even enjoyed the ensuing fear, then feared its revenge. I must have sensed that when something broke, something broke in you, something made you aware that you were also vulnerable, that you were already broken, fractured, that repairing was a solution, but that a repair always carried with it the memory of its fracture, its suture.

The pictures from my childhood spoke about things to sleep with, things not to sleep with, anthropomorphic toys and those with hard edges that belong to the realm of unfriendly things. There was less of a soul in those with no eyes, no mouth, but they also must have had some kind of soul, maybe a more complicated one. A car was on the verge of a table, poor car, it was shaking before the abyss, it had become an anxious car. I couldn't rescue it, couldn't reach the table. And as I leaned on the table leg, the car fell down and I felt the accident, for I already knew what it was to fall down. That was when things were strangely alive. In dreams, in nightmares, the inanimate was also strangely meaningful, everything was strangely possible in dreams.

At some point, my mother, Nina Chiavelli, a secret foot-extra and a drunk, must have told me that things were neither

dead nor alive, they were inert matter, earthlings were higher
entities, if I wanted to become an adult, I had to leave those
fraudulent thoughts behind. Fraudulent thoughts? I encountered again and again the persuasive existence of animated
things, an existence forever growing with multiple meanings
that created tangled associations that entwined with my most
intimate neural paths. I had to abandon my vision of the
world, it was primitive, uncultivated, superstitious, credu-
lous, childish. Then when alone at home I would experience
the uncanny presence of things, things were so quiet, but
sometimes things creaked. I suspended disbelief, I knew they
weren't alive but they were, I knew that the gun a schoolboy
with a cowboy hat carried wasn't real but I covered my face
with my hands. Things were not alive, but they had this endless potential to become vanishing points where secret reveries converged and evaporated in a flash.

The Museum of Relevant Moments? My beloved parents?
Buñuel? Perhaps for some people the intensity of the very
first objects they encountered was the only thing that mattered, maybe each one of us learns a different lesson from the
language of things. I didn't want to be judgemental but then
I thought that the intensity of my first toys was replaced by
other objects, my life was re-written with each new object in
a long game of substitutions, but then I never utterly confused flesh and thing.

Confuse flesh and thing? Don't we confuse flesh with
mere flesh, people with previous souls, the qualities of objects
with their owner's qualities, isn't everything confused to perfection? I looked at another faded colour picture from when I
was a baby wondering about all the pictures that weren't tak-
en, all those possible pictures that could have told a different
story about my childhood and that instead reinstated the circuit of oblivion. Then my mother's black pair of boots with
intricate lacing that looked identical to some boots Jeanne
Moreau wore in *Diary of a Chambermaid* flashed through my

mind.

When I tried to think about my childhood, that was what appeared mainly on the screen of memory, a black pair of high-heel boots. And then questions and questions and questions and questions and questions skidded inside me and some of them were undoubtedly the wrong questions, illicit questions: As a child, did my father play with his mother's shoes? Did a shoe fetishist fixation start when as a toddler he followed on all fours the scent of his mother's shoes? What was the difference between being fixated on a single object and unfocused rampant consumerism? Weren't we accessories to the moods things conjured up? Didn't we chase after them in a vain attempt to recapture the thrill of our first encounters with the inanimate world? Didn't we seek like babies the comfort of things, a new watch, a new car, a new dress, a new whatever, as if they were a warm blanket that sheltered us from the nightmares of the world?

Undoubtedly, the belief in the soul of things was an outlandish belief that was forever kept alive. It was updated with each generation, rekindled in order to be complicit with our own children while disowning it as a silly belief from our own forgotten past, dinosaur beliefs, organic memories made forever present through the double movement of their repetition and subsequent denial. I thought that so many of us were engaged in this double vision, in this oscillation, I know this thing is not what I really want it to be but ... it is. That it was a sleight of hand that belonged to the logic of the unconscious where there were no contradictions, where things existed in a fluid continuum making the persistence of earlier beliefs in the adult mind a fact. Animism was probably the most significant residue of the unconscious that has survived in history, a residue that perpetually returned in fairy tales, cartoons, advertising, films, all sorts of fictions where belief and disbelief in the soul of the inanimate happened in equal measure but were not simultaneous, they occupied different

times, different ways of perceiving the world, with all probability different regions of the brain, older regions.

Dazed, I shook the snow-dome with Berlin's bear inside
and watched the floating snowflakes. The snow-dome was an
object both from the past and the future. It didn't dawn on
me at the time. In my subjective dictionary, Berlin equalled
an unexpected and orgasmic sudden trip, Berlin was Wim
Wenders, Tor Strasse, a couture milliner and mulled wine
served in typically German Christmas stalls. It took a few
years for me to realise that if that snow-dome had captured
my imagination and then my pocket, it was because Berlin
was a keyword that encrypted a story about a woman who
had married the Berlin Wall.

The Berlin Wall, a monument to crushed humanity.

I had forgotten everything about this woman. Maybe it
was just a coincidence, getting this snow-dome, though most
probably a remote neural cluster knew that Berlin was so
many memorable moments, but it was also the Berlin Wall,
and the woman who married it, and thus the snow-dome
symbolised an extreme form of animism.

Memema! I could have met a child sucking objects before
and would have found nothing remarkable about it.

I mentally thank Memema for this long reverie. I felt closer to the secret code of things, even if I knew there wasn't
such thing. I went to bed feeling dizzy that night. I couldn't
sleep for a while. I kept turning and turning, got up and took
a couple of sleeping pills. I heard the phone in the distance
and then the answerphone and then what sounded like Zacharie's voice. Broken toys, dysfunctional bits of colour inhabited my dreams. Then my mother, my father, Mary Jane and
Lecour all merged into an improbable being that woke me up
in the middle of the night.

It was a moonless night, so the living room was completely dark, except for the green glow emanating from the
answerphone. A new message was glowing on the message

counter. I played the PLAY button. You have one new message. Message received today at 2:17 AM: It's me, Zacharie . . . Listen, I could say that I had to urgently return to Tijuana on an undercover operation to prevent narco-traffickers from blowing up a primary school for blind children, but the truth is that my briefcase was nicked by a gang of Southend racketeers and my address book was inside it, so I couldn't contact anybody . . . and then I found *the ultimate movie collectable* . . . My flight back to Paris is the day after tomorrow, in the evening, we could meet up tomorrow, same time at your place . . . I'm staying in a new hotel, the number is . . .

The herbal sleeping tablets I had taken were rubbish.

Half-sleep and half-sleepwalking, I looked at the answerphone and mumbled to it: you must be bleemin crazy, man. I could detect a slight hiccup in his French accent which in the middle of the night sounded as if inflected by Ukrainian intonation. In any case, even if I hadn't detected the hiccup and his patently unbelievable excuses, only a conceited insect like Zacharie could think that it was OK to vanish for aeons and then ring at 2:17 AM. I pressed the DELETE button. I looked at the clock on the wall: 5:11 AM.

Message deleted.

Zacharie deleted.

A wave of well-being flooded my half-sleep consciousness.

The wave of well-being continued the following day.

My flight was that day. Playing the good daughter, the ghost-writing was put on simmering mode. A detour might make something click. I was waiting for that click. I only needed to ghost another thirty pages. And then embrace life again.

Life.

I expected my father to be energised by the mini-jazz festival he was organising, but 'organising' was an exaggeration on Dr. Alvarez's part. The habitual spring heat sapped everybody's energy, including Dr. Alvarez who looked more and more spectral as the months run towards full-blown summer. My father was doing jazz-related activities, repairing an old piano, teaching another old guy how to play the sax, but most of the time he just slept and slept and slept and slept and slept and slept, as if preparing himself for the last sleep, and when he woke up, he would say he had had strange dreams about being suspended in space and seeing the slow movements of the planets.

On a couple of occasions, we went to the beach together, though. We invited Eva but she wouldn't come. My father looked perturbed, but then he said she never wanted to go anywhere, not with him, she's just a spoilt cow, he said. We took a taxi to Cabo de Gata, a natural park of volcanic origin and unspoilt beaches. Walking barefoot by the shore, I challenged him to a swim race, come on, I said, but although he had won a few swimming medals, he wouldn't swim this time. No way, no way, he kept on saying. I could see the fear in his eyes, in his nervous laughter. And for the first time, I saw the child in him, a child frightened by the immensity of the sea. I don't want to get wet, he said, and there is marine life and all those damned jellyfish, he said.

The saltpetre smell.

And the crystal clear water.

We avoided going down The Beach of the Dead. You had to go down a steep hill and then climb up again. My father joked that its name was probably due to that bloody hill. That hill can kill you, he said. Plus it's a nudist beach and the sight of all those naked bodies can probably kill you too, he said. He chuckled at his own joke and I laughed with him. He said he used to dive there looking on the sandy sea floors for flying gurnards. They are like fish-butterflies with wings of incredibly beautiful iridescent colours, they eat crustaceans. they're extraordinary, he said.

We drank iced coffee with brandy, iced carajillo.

Make the most of life on earth, he said. And don't let the bastards get you down.

He sounded so lucid sometimes, but then he slept and slept and slept and slept. When I asked him about my mother, he went silent. And when I asked him whether my mother had been a shoe-extra in films, he just said she did a bit of footwear fashion photography, but on the whole, she only worked occasionally, her ankles were extraordinary, so delicate, he said. El Refugio had become a sleep-inducing building. While he slept and slept and slept and slept, I did bits of ghostwriting sheltered by the shadows on the patio and gazed at a crack inhabited by an intrepid red-tailed lizard.

Pearl, Snow and the insistence of the fetish

I rang Lecour as soon as I got back to London. I couldn't believe I was talking to Lecour! It was the first time I talked to him. I was surprised by his coldness, his robot-like telephone manner at odds with his fragile voice. I said that I loved his work but I couldn't become Lecour, I could only become Lecour my way, a new Lecour. I was surprised to hear a dog barking at the other end. The barking was palpable, sharp-edged, incongruent. I said that I had tried, but I couldn't do it, I couldn't quite become somebody else. Lecour was quiet. It's high time for a new Lecour, he then said. I said that I couldn't write about Sigmund F.'s perverse theory of fetishism, about the penis virus he had inoculated into so much writing through the best-selling marriage of two unhappy words, castration anxiety. That I knew that to touch that name was to leap into the dark, that it hardly clarified the cases of fetishism I had come across. The Collector's museum of relevant moments mainly related to shoe fetishism. I didn't want to use whatshisname's theory. And most of the information I found was somehow infected by the penis virus he had generated. I found myself talking manically because Lecour didn't talk. I heard the dog again, barking in the background, distinct, solitary, filling my ear with something strangely remote, dogged on transmitting a message from outer space, a canine Morse Code that tuned in with my alpha brain waves. Find a new angle, but you'd be better off doing the ghostwriting, than not doing it, noblesse oblige, I was going to plunder Pietz, Lecour finally said. You've left things a bit late, haven't you? he added. Then he said he was busy and hung up. I listened to the dead line for a few minutes, trying to work out the fine line between efficiency and rudeness, thinking that I would have liked to continue listening to the disembodied dog, thinking that Lecour wasn't the most friendly of animals.

Plundering Pietz? Better off? It didn't take long to figure it out. He was right, it was a good deal, it was a privilege, and besides, I had already been squandering, squandering, squandering the little money I had.

That day I read in the paper that a nine-year-old boy had killed an eight-year-old boy to get hold of his Nike trainers. He must have felt the pressure to be like everybody else. To belong. To be part of a clique. To feel excluded no more. He had strangled the younger boy, stoned him, removed the Nike trainers from the dead body and walked off wearing them. It had all been caught on CCTV.

I sat on my armchair with a cup of coffee and quivered internally for a few minutes.

To kill for an object? Well, that happened a lot of the time. Objects bind us and objects separate us. Maybe what surprised me was the age: nine. The news filled me up with a chilled fluid that lingered in my body for a while. In shock, I stuck my nose against the window and looked at the straight lines made out of slow-moving cars. From the seventeenth floor, the traffic looked like a highly organised colony of automaton ants. Sipping lukewarm coffee, I thought about violence and the different types of violence that shatter the world and then about the strange affair we have with objects in general, the dismal fact that sometimes we preferred them to people, that sometimes we brandished them against people, even as a sign of our contempt towards some people, an unsettling sign, an envy-producing sign, that sometimes they occupied a space identical to people, that in any case we objectified each other, sometimes we didn't care about others, we just didn't, we needed a break from others, that lost objects of desire secretly survived in other objects, that sometimes we needed the quietness of objects, we needed objects to daydream, objects fulfilled our lust for unlimited variety, they temporarily enveloped us in a fiction where nothing could go wrong, objects told the stories we couldn't utter to ourselves . . .

. . . But to kill for their sake?

To kill, to abuse, to exploit, to damage, to lie, to accept bribes, all for the sake of the personal prestige encoded in status things.

To maim, to belittle, to bully, to ignore calls for help and all the other petty acts.

I felt a surge of deep disgust towards everything in humanity that makes it inhuman.

I watched the hours go by, my gaze lost in the slow-moving red cranes, then took my red notebook out and began dabbling with the letters of the alphabet.

Maybe it wouldn't sound like Lecour at all, but in the evening I decided that I just had to ramble in my own way for another forty pages or so and then apply the scalpel. I wrote, I wrote, I wrote. I started scribbling about our intricate rapport with things. Sometimes we needed the solace of things, sometimes we needed a break from them. There were austere, thrifty, sober people who abhorred things, as if things were guilty in themselves. Minimalist people in awe of emptiness who refused to use things as tokens of self in a Zen move. And then there were people whose dream was a dream of simplicity, they kept things in check, they gently ignored them. And then, people who could only communicate through gifts, people who enjoyed *l'élan vital* of things and their company, and people who would do anything for their sake.

Things seemed so complex. There was a social life of things. A psychological life of things. A spiritual life of things. A sentimental life of things. A secret life of things. A tyrannical life of things. There were things that were made immortal by being put in museums. Things that became sacred by being used by a priest or by a celebrity. Things that were invested with a power that made me think of the realm of magic.

Things that drew their power from ritual, from context, good luck rituals such as wearing a special tie, a special ring, holding a special pen for special occasions. And then, some people preferred books to people, monuments, ancient buildings to people. Cultural tourism was partly articulated around this fact, as if when visiting a country, the country was ideally un-inhabited, devoid of people, the country being a space only inhabited by monuments, old buildings, classical paintings, sensual sculptures, souvenirs, things.

The string of everyday objects I had placed on the dining table in a long, minimal line was still there: the snow-dome, the beaded choker, the small, pink helicopter that Mary Jane had given me, a hot-water bottle, a bottle-opener, the head-less plastic elephant and a golden platform shoe. There was also a mug stained with coffee tears, no handle and a crack on the rim, a damaged thing that had miraculously survived throughout the years. I found myself re-arranging the things on the table into a semi-circle. I rested my head on the ta-ble and listened to the mystery of everyday things. As soon as the word 'everyday' entered the scene, I started cudding in the present tense, as if the everyday inhabited a perpetual present. My present wasn't my present anymore. In order to ghostwrite, I had to retreat, live life at one remove. I put my life on stand-by.

Find a new angle! Lecour had said.

A new angle, improved with a triple-action effect.

Solitude. But also loneliness. I was failing at love like many philosophers do. I didn't care. I wasn't interested in love. I was now living the life of a philosopher at one re-move, as I was merely a ghost-philosopher. To push Kathy as to the absurdity of my ghostwriting assignment, was to ac-knowledge my insecurities and forego money. I wasn't sure how to connect the genealogy of the word fetish by Wil-liam Pietz with the museum of relevant moments, but then I have always been interested in words, Lecour was interested in words and the word 'fetish' was quite interesting in itself. Yet again, I was led to Mary Jane and her toys. And Mary Jane loved everything to do with witchcraft. As a child, other children would call her 'witch'. It was to do with her beautiful, red, straight, long, hair, with her teeth slightly corroded by endless grinding at night. Mary Jane had appropriated the word 'witch' and made it shine with all the power of subversion. Mary Jane called herself a witch and the word 'fetish' had first emerged in Portugal to hunt the untamed, to delineate the uncivilised ways of that legendary female monster: the witch. The witch, always old and ugly, a prosecuted outsider within Christianity, transferred her demonic power to her amulets, to her fetishes. In witches' hands, charms became fetishes. The fetish stunk of diabolical magic, of heresy, of that most abject of figures, the witch, whose possessed spirit could even infect matter around her. Witchcraft wasn't a burning issue in sixteenth-century Portugal, but the Catholic Church still decreed which cult objects were legitimate, which demonically inspired.

Words travel. Across land, by air, by sea. Portuguese merchants took the word 'fetish' to the West African Coast during the sixteenth century, where for two centuries it was used, drenched with witchcraft notions, to make sense of a religion, a social order based on the worship of religious objects worn on the body, which bore no resemblance to any gods. The word started to appear in travelogues, where Africans were seen as deluded beasts, ignorant of the true faith. Some travelogues were 'sympathetic' accounts where the travellers stated that although misguided, the Africans were harmless. Other travelogues condemned the worship of the fetish as diabolical magic.

I could picture the first encounter. Africans and Portuguese merchants speaking with gestures, with their hands, pointing at things, miming, spontaneously attempting to create a common language beyond speech. I could imagine the nebulous understandings, the humorous misunderstandings, the frustration, the laughter, the mistrust. I could see Africans being suspicious and intrigued at once, seduced by the marvellous novelty of the alien articles white merchants carried, playfully adopting Catholic sacramental objects as fetishes in an inside out game that made the Catholics blush; the Portuguese smug grin when exchanging what they considered trinkets and trifles for real African gold, their fangs growing at the sight of mountains of gold, then the anger at being told they couldn't have everything, some objects were sacred, fetishes. And then the arrival of the Protestants. I could see Africans, Catholics and Protestants repressing their hatred, fear and fascination in the name of trade.

I got immersed in this world of witches, savages, idolaters, Catholics, deluded others lacking in reason that Mary Jane would have loved so much. The West African Coast had become a meeting point for radically different social systems, an encounter of the disparate, the mutually incomprehensible, the irreconcilable: Catholics, Africans and Merchant Capitalists. The Protestants related the African fetish to the Catholic worshipping of sacramental objects, relics, figures, medals of saints, inanimate objects. Both Africans and Catholics were caught up in a primitive and irrational way of thinking that hindered commercial affairs, market activity, the birth of a new god. That was the story the Protestants told.

Fetish, a word that comes about through an intellectual perversion of facts. The job of words. The task of words. How meanings can be created and recreated. Sometimes a word is needed urgently to express a thought begging to be named. At the time, there was a thought begging to be named, the mystery of value. The word 'fetish' came to name that mystery. The fetish was made to embody the riddle of the social and personal value of material objects: the mystery of value.

I got immersed in Willem Bosman's travelogue. At the beginning of the eighteenth century the Dutch trader had published the most influential travelogue of its time, a derisory, scornful account of Guinea presented under the guise of objectivity. Therein the fetish was already posed as a theoretical problem, his ideas on fetishes being the primary source for the Enlightenment intellectuals' development of a general theory of primitive religion: all the alibis to enslave the dark continent were already under elaboration.

Thus, the fetish, from being a word became a sentence. Some words preserve the scandal of history. A fetish, a beneficial or accursed object, depending on who is telling the story. And it was usually the case that the one who told the story spoke from a position of authority, privilege, class, money. For a voice to be heard it has to go through certain networks. For certain networks to open up, the voice must speak in their own language. This was one of the truths of the fetish. A disembodied eye which observed and judged was forever condemning the fetish as a fraudulent object, a false belief, forever endowing it with an abhorrent force that was to last a few centuries.

Then the genealogy inevitably came to the nineteenth century. During the nineteenth century a similar charge was made against commodities. Marx thought of commodities in female terms, he coined the term 'commodity fetishism.' Commodities concealed real social relations among human beings. The ghost of religious fetishism came to inhabit the commodity. Certain beliefs never seem to disappear, they just migrate somewhere else, transmigrate. The symbolic trafficking between thing and spirit had to become sensual. God was dying. A new god had been born: Capital. Metaphysics was diseased. The worship of the spiritual was replaced by the worship of the sensuous as manufactured in the material world. By then capitalism was beginning to learn a precious lesson: an irrational relation to objects didn't hinder it, on the contrary, much was to be gained from the irrational allure of moulded matter. In any case, if there were any survivors throughout these changes, it was objects, the alluring power of objects, objects made or designed by humans onto which we projected our innermost needs. Needs changed. Our capacity to project them onto objects didn't. Needs? Perhaps we should speak of a passion for the object, a soft spot for the human-made.

As I was immersed in this virtual world of printed matter, Pearl popped round and went on about this fetish ball that would take place at the end of the week, Pearl playing at being a bad girl, me playing with her. You're into that kind of thing, you're writing about kinky shoes, she said. We had to buy the appropriate gear, we had to buy it way before, it wasn't the kind of thing you could buy just like that. You have to look the part, there is a strict dress code, she said. I felt lazy. I didn't like to strictly adhere to anything, even if it was just a dress code, I wasn't into dungeons and all that, I was somewhere else, I was busy with The Museum of Relevant Moments, I was a knowledge fetishist, I liked its texture.

I'm really really busy, I said.

Oh shaddap, it'll be fun, we'll be out from dusk till dawn.

Money, time, sex-shops, Pearl and I went shopping. Pearl couldn't get inside the rubber dresses, she was furious she couldn't get a rubber dress size 16, she bought a reduced price inflatable husband hoping it wasn't punctured, she ended up having a tailor-made red rubber dress, expensive but beautiful, perfect for her prodigious hourglass shape. It was fun doing girlish things. I tried on several fetish wear pieces, I didn't want to spend much money, there was this short black shiny pvc dress that had a zip front bustier that looked good, it was cheap. But I was seduced by a red pvc catsuit that left me in the red but hugged you like a dream. My spindly body ceased to feel spindly, my body felt less insubstantial, I felt fictitious in this gear, it felt good, like a second skin, it looked great, a promising encounter, a filmic caress.

Tiger beer, vodka, the noisy vitality of bars, and Pearl's lament about men. When I got back home I couldn't wait to wear the red catsuit. I slipped it on with talcum powder, put lipstick on and played the soundtrack from *The Avengers*. Then laid on my bed like a pvc diva, I was excited about the ball, I wore the catsuit everyday during the following days. The catsuit helped me with The Museum of Relevant Moments, although I realised that I was dying to be seen in it. I had to wait five days, I hadn't been out from dusk till dawn for a long time, I thought that I could go to the supermarket just to be seen in it, but I had to get on with my ghost-writing. Kathy had rung to see how things were going. Was it possible to wear a figure-hugging catsuit and still be Lecour? I was looking forward to the ball, I wasn't sure how to connect the genealogy of the fetish with the Collector's museum of relevant moments, with my mother, with my father, I wasn't sure what the irrational was. Worshipping the sensuous in the material world had its borders. The borders of sense. These borders had changed since my parent's time, which was more or less Buñuel's time. But then at their time the deforming mirror of normality ruled everything. The problem was who defined normality against whom and to what ends. The problem was that certain experiences were defined as deviant instead of being defined as different, even radically different. Black and white, good and bad, even Marx had coined the term 'commodity fetishism' judging Africans unenlightened, savage, low, he had likened it to the feminine, as if femininity was counterfeit, he had judged the sex-appeal of things from a puritanical standpoint, as if sex-appeal equalled depravity. The problem was that the word abnormality was an ugly word, it was tinged with a violently excluding force, whereas other words like 'different' or 'exceptional,' while being more accurate, didn't perform the task of excluding others. If shoe fetishism had been ubiquitous, then my father's behaviour would have been normal.

Excluding, excluding. If grey matter was shaped according to experience, if perception was moulded according to brain matter, if brains could be quite different due to genetics, if there were lesions that affected perception, disinhibition, behaviour, if our vision was distorted and articulated according to our expectations, if the fetish was an embodiment of a forgotten story, a forgotten neural connection or a neural misrecognition still to be mapped, if we all remembered different stories and forgot different stories, intensity and relevance shaping personal memory, then, wasn't there something monumentally perverse about adhering to a norm? My mother, Nina Chiavelli, was different, my father was different, their desire was bound to a different kingdom, the kingdom of things and within it, the footwear species and within it the wildlife of high-heels. I remember them being in love and then the suffering, the hospital visits, the sombre X-rays. I remember my mother's song, her song increased with her illness, she sang the blues to keep death at bay, she sang with a beautiful voice. Then she stopped singing. That pause has always inhabited me.

I played the blues those days.

I knew normality didn't mean anymore what it used to mean a few decades ago. Still some friends told me, it's normal, to reassure me that I wasn't deviant, no matter how bizarre the things that I told them were. And yet most of them went out of their way not to be considered normal. I realised that the meaning of the word 'normal' had expanded and a generalised naughtiness was now the norm. Yet at the end of the day, some people did kill themselves to be normal.

I watched TV those days focusing on the obscenification of everything and the endless parading of deviant behaviour as if they were new steps in our evolution. I noticed that on a new channel the news reader presented the news with a pornographic sparkle in her gaze. The weekend came, the day of the fetish ball came, it will be a night of kinky frenzy, Pearl had said. We went to Fantastique, Pearl, Snow and me. We were late, we just missed the catwalk, we didn't know there was going to be one, there were quite a few women who were wearing the same red catsuit as mine, making us look as mass-produced as the chrome ashtrays on the tables. The red catsuits created intermittent zones of red in the semi-darkness. Instead of witches, African savages and deluded Catholics, there was a pageant of black angels, wasted dogs, post-modern primitives, sharp boys, fetish divas, exotic beasts, corpses in corsets, bored lawyers and suburban blue collar workers totally disguised, people who wanted to inhabit some kind of interstice full-time or part-time, a human gap for urban angst in time and space.

We drank vodka and orange. Then the models from the catwalk made their appearance: rococo white wigs, baroque dresses that revealed unexpected bits of flesh, a nipple, a belly button, a bare chest. It was suddenly like being on a film set, hypnotic music and dangerous liaisons with unexpected bits of pink flesh that introduced a soft suspense into the atmosphere. Perhaps it was the gentle music that initially introduced a soft ecstasy spellbinding the senses, making any hint of aggression impossible, letting people be mesmerised by ocular desire, watch from a cool distance dressed up people who had dressed up to be looked at.

We just watched, and watched, and watched, we probably stared.

There was an old man dressed up as a fairy, virginal dolls, a veteran couple ritually whipping each other, sagging bodies made firm by rubber wear, men with black leather trousers exposing their bare buttocks, some to their benefit, others to their detriment, empty glasses and beer bottles, wasted women and newborn ladies.

Pearl and I shared Snow as a slave. We borrowed from a generous mistress a riding crop. We whipped him softly by turns while he pleaded mercy, mercy, mercy, please. Then Pearl disappeared with a black guy, while Snow and I stayed in a room enraptured by a video projection of anal sex. I told

Snow that anal sex touched within me a point that made blood rush to my head, a point that was a short circuit to my pleasure centre. I don't like it, I find the rectum too narrow, he said. Shame, I said. We then continued watching the video in silence. It was an extreme close up of anal sex. Explicit, mechanical, brutal in its mysterious monotony. It went on and on forever. It was impossible. It was a loop.

As I watched mesmerised, thinking that I hadn't had sex for quite a while, wondering whether I was becoming a bit frigid, whether I was becoming peculiarly unresponsive, I realised that for quite a few months now I had become all eyes. I knew that Snow loved Pearl and that she couldn't care less. I played with Snow's bare buttocks knowing that he wished it was Pearl's hands while he played at being a dog. I played with a guy dressed up as a doctor, played doctors and nurses and patients, had my pulse checked with his stethoscope. I found hoods frightening but talked to a hooded naked guy who said he just wanted to become invisible.

A German blond boy started kissing one of my patent leather boots slowly, conscientiously. Could he detect pheromones emanating from my boots? I wanted to ask him questions. He gave me a gormless smile. Questions? What questions? I didn't want to treat him like an interesting insect. He looked up at me as if I was a monument and saw question marks in my eyes. Then he said that for him high-heel boots became alive, he was trembling when he said that and I wondered whether my father would have trembled as well before my mother's boots. Alive? Yeah, he said, like the dancing teapot in *Alice in Wonderland*. This German boy, he looked so unbelievably schmuck, it actually made me laugh, but then the innocence that lingered on his face confused me.

I went to other fetish clubs with Pearl and Snow, but they weren't like Fantastique, they were harder on the eyes, too much black rubber, perversions were a thing of the past. I got tired of this more or less homogenous world of black-rubber wear and ready-made perversions. It wasn't my thing. It was Pearl's thing, she loved it, she bought different rubber dresses and hair extensions, she bought a riding crop, fur handcuffs and black lace lingerie.

Role-playing, slaves, doctors and nurses, real boot fetishists, everything blended in my head with perfect confusion as I wondered where my blind spot was and unwanted suspicions danced around me creating lateral thoughts: beyond the playful games, the serious reduction of a person to a fragment, was it a question of fear? Of eroticised fear? Of sublimated hatred? What if a woman invested herself in splendour in a leather-bound revenge? What if a woman only allowed her high-heel shoes to be touched as an expression of her contempt towards men as it might indeed happen in the case of a paid dominatrix where a double fantasy is fulfilled? What if certain objects were complex mediators where desire, hostility and fear were inextricably linked?

I knew things were different now, I knew we were now encouraged to attach our desires, anxieties and fears to the kingdom of things, I knew the borders of sense regarding fetishism had blurred. Ideas about plurality exploited by consumerism had changed these borders. Perhaps today, my parents would have gone to a fetish club. They would have been part of a peculiar urban tribe. They would have felt protected by belonging, by sharing their secret. They would have bought other normative accessories, besides shoes. It was a question of borders. At a given time in sexual history, borders were put to the acceptable. So, my parents' dirty secret was a hush-hush subject because of borders. Sense was devised through borders, through limits, more or less strict borders, more or less flexible borders, but like any construction, like anything besieged by borders, it overflowed.

Sense was porous, borders were porous, nothing existed in a pure state of isolation, nothing could be quite contained, the violence of definite sense was counteracted by unexpected flows. I wrote about all of this, mimicking Lecour's voice. I also became interested in neuroscience. Neuroscience was undoubtedly the new science fetish. If individuals with Tourette's Syndrome exhibited high degrees of exhibitionism, it could be that, amongst other things, shoe fetishism was a question of scrambled up chemical messengers, a blip in neurotransmission, a script error created by a fatally deleted gene that shaped up a weird neural convergence whose secret song kept on repeating: *I'll do it myyyyyyyyy way.*

It was an intensely luminous day when I finished scribbling about The Museum of Relevant Moments and queued up at the post office to send it by recorded delivery. And yet, when I came out of the post office, it was all rainy and dark, as if somebody had suddenly stolen the sun.

Anima blandula days

Networks, pathways of objects, flows of objects. Words, sentences I had written glided through my head with the ghostly presence of an afterglow making me smirk, making me anticipate the reactions of their reader, the laughter, the counter-arguments, the bewilderment, the harsh frowns, my words were probably still in the post, but they were already out there, in the world, looking forward to being consumed, waiting for an interpretation, taking up volume in mid-air, exhilarated at the prospect of entering somebody's forehead, at the prospect of creating reverberations in their inner ear.

That is what usually danced around my head for a few days whenever I sent writing through the post. My own words, my song. Except that this time it was somebody else's song, Lecour's song: if writing is a directed daydream, I had been daydreaming somebody else's dream. Even so, mission accomplished. I relaxed. I went through a kind of mild jet-lag phase, a phase where I drifted around the house in a trance, overslept, browsed through books, immersed myself in the TV flow, saw Pearl and Snow, saw friends, did my human things, idled away deliberately, as if I had to squander all the time I had spent purposefully, escape from any useful activity, catch up with all the time I hadn't wasted while I was busy, catch up with all the useless daydreaming I had neglected, as if daydreaming was something I needed in order to survive, my own daydreaming.

Days immersed in reveries, killing time, a necessity.

Days devoted to doing unnecessary things.

During those days, I was surprised to get a box of Gauloises blonde légère through the post with a note from Zacharie: so sorry to have missed you. I also got a small note from Lecour saying that he liked the new Lecour, that I had written an almost veritable forgery, full of talented falsifications, he would have incurred exactly the same misreadings I had incurred, he liked the way I treated rationality as just another tradition, the way I ended the piece talking about cyborgs, maybe I could send him some of my own writing, what I had written was so poetic, exactly the same poetic angle he would have taken. Exactly the same misreadings? And poetic? What did he mean by poetic? Words charged with mysterious power and significance, fetishised words? Was he taking the piss? I also got a cheque from Kathy, a note thanking me so much for the favour, saying the Collector was in good health now, I should go and visit them in Mexico. Well, perhaps I had written a veritable forgery, but after all my searches I felt that I had discovered nothing. There were a few slithers of meaning here and there, but nothing illuminating, I couldn't think beyond the concepts of my own time, I couldn't unthink my thoughts. But that's probably all you could hope for, slithers. I will never fully understand objects, I didn't understand objects at all, perhaps mysteries were better left alone.

The opacity of objects.

The placebo effect of objects: good for the temporary relief of mild pain.

Then the void, then trying to avoid the void.

Blue skies, lost dogs, citrus and petrol fragrance, I went to visit my father for a month. This time he only recognised me now and again, this time the situation exasperated me. His bewildering intermittent memory made me see El Refugio in all its sadness, even if Dr. Alvarez was still his usual enthusiastic self, even if Eva was friends with him again, even if its wild surroundings were an unusual break from a world aggressively branded with advertising. Incontinence, denial of incontinence and its villainous smell, several missing teeth, memory working on and off. I didn't know my father anymore, he didn't know me either. Whenever he recognised me, he wasn't aware that a while ago he had confused me with his sister, a complete stranger, one of the female nurses or a new visiting doctor. When he first saw me he said, so glad to see you, you're everybody's favourite nurse, and touched my long hair, maybe because it was long and there wasn't anybody around with long hair. I just went to the toilet and stood squatted on top of the toilet seat, arms wrapped around my knees, curled up in a ball. The toilet became my retreat. He evaded my questions, he didn't know his name, he didn't speak, he gave me taps on the hand. He read the newspaper with a serious demeanour, don't know how he understood it. There was one day when he walked around the table endlessly, in an automatic ritual whose meaning escaped me. Sometimes he seemed happy, no doubt. When he confused me with somebody else, did he know somewhere in his head that it was me, his dear daughter? That's the question that hovered over my head to begin with. Then after a few days, I started hiding my grief, it affected him, I just went to the toilet and stood squatted on top of the toilet seat. I started smiling at his confusions, they were often funny, what could I do but smile?

Grief, fear, acceptance and non-acceptance, in the evenings we sat together on the terrace and looked at the stars in silence.

The stars.

He gazed at the immensity of the starry night with reverential wonder.

He already felt part of the stellar dust.

During those days, I stayed with my cousin Antonio, his flat full of glittering fabrics now, latex, wires, hat moulds, solid wooden blocks. He didn't have time for cartoon animation anymore, he had a job making theatre props for a small company in Madrid, he designed hats, made them out of papier-mâché, he designed accessories for the costumes, for the sets, he loved working with his hands, being an artisan, the patience, the love. He had inherited this from his mother, the ingenuity of knowing how to make things. Many things he didn't buy, he usually made them, it saved him money, but above all, making things by hand equalled pleasure. All the hats, all the accessories were tailor made for a few performances, he had to meet the actors, the actresses, but some of them were so fussy, he detested them, found them unbearable, could only bear them on stage, when they were playing a different role, when they weren't playing the stars. He had a motorbike now, we went out everywhere with it, bars, the beach, flea-markets with their chaotic promise of reveries conjured up by a provisional map of sacrificed objects. One evening I rode his bike, feeling the physical exhilaration of speed against my face, the fusion of my lower torso with the seat, the fusion of my hands with the handlebars, my temporary status as a hybrid, part human, part machine. Cyborgs? I was sleeping on it, I had started to think about it when I was ghostwriting for Lecour.

During those days, I told Antonio endless tales about my mother's shoes, their comings and goings, their weird disappearance, about the Collector. Antonio, dirty suede shoes. I did desire Antonio, it was a mild desire, it found no echo, it disappeared the day that he decided to get rid off his long black hair and have his head shaved, thus going from gypsy king to Buddhist monk.

He was going out a lot, coming back at dawn, and when I wasn't with my father, I wrote aphorisms about chaos and about forgetfulness and death. This time I hadn't taken my laptop. I wanted to explore life without it. I took a liking to writing by hand, watching the ink slowly dry out, holding the pen between my thumb and my index, writing with just one hand rather than six fingers, writing in silence rather than listening to the mechanical sound of the keyboard, savouring my variable handwriting, the rustling of paper. I also savoured the language. Listening to my native language, listening to certain expressions, stimulated me, it energised me, like foreign languages do, but it had to do with remembering forgotten expressions, forgotten words that activated my intimate neural paths, not with the jouissance of the unknown, of learning.

Foreign words, forgotten words, the pleasure of sounds reconfigured in a previously unknown way, the sudden pleasure of a cluster of sounds unearthed from the remote land of oblivion resonated within me on a physical level. Shopkeepers, people in the street, bus conductors brought me by chance this complex pleasure. I also relished that, the spontaneity, the kindness of strangers. The fact that they talked to you, made friendly, conflicting, wearied, flattering remarks, told you personal stories, shared with you part of their consciousness. I missed that feeling of spontaneity. But I realised at the same time that after a while I would want privacy, as if I could only endure the spontaneity in small doses, as if I felt that small chat in public spaces wasn't conducive to introspection, to living in your own head, to hiding inside your own train of thought. I had become used to living at the centre of my consciousness while in London, even in public spaces, perhaps that's why I always ended up in the land of non-eye contact, I had become accustomed to that, to invisibility, to a different notion of personal space, where personal space wasn't pushed to the edge of mind when in public.

Perhaps that was why during those days I relished talking to strangers so much: I had been starved. It also distracted me from El Refugio, from my father, from myself. I discovered new ways of communicating with my father. Whenever he strode around the table compulsively, I waited at one of the corners and tapped his hand. He liked that. He also liked it when I manically pulled my tongue out. He just laughed. I said quack, quack, moo, moo. I didn't know whether he remembered that he had initiated that joke himself, but he laughed. Dr. Alvarez said that my father seemed happier when I treated him as an infant, that he had lost his mental abilities in exactly the opposite order that children gain them.

Nobody wanted to treat old patients as children, but that was when they were the happiest. He plays hide and seek with Eva, I just let them enjoy themselves, he said.

Antonio came with me to visit him sometimes. On one visit, he wore my father's navy blue stripy suit. The one I had stripped from his body with my own hands. I didn't say anything, behaved as if that suit didn't mean anything, perhaps I blushed. Definitely blushed the day he told me an unpalatable story about my mother, my mother the hysteric. I couldn't believe him. He was probably tired of my stories about my mother's shoes, perhaps it was an unconscious revenge, maybe working with actors and actresses created a negative neural circuit that connected to similar memories from an earlier time. My mother sang the blues so well, he said. She was such a star my mother, he said. My father was completely dominated by her, she needed a lackey, his mother used to say, my father was her lackey, she always had to be the centre of attention, she would sing, she would tell endless stories, but then they had a gagging effect on you these stories, she talked too much. Then now and again she would spark off a scandal, she had to get all the attention, even if it was negative attention, whatever the means. One day she shook the whole street out of its torpor. That was one of his strangest childhood memories. A memory about my mother. Seeing my mother in the middle of the street, with no clothes on, hysterical naked, with a folded gown hanging on her arm, wearing just a pair of yellow stilettos, definitely drunk, she used to say wine was good for the blood, she was so pale. That was one of the things he remembered about my mother, my mother asking passers-by to look at her yellow stilettos, shouting that her husband didn't like yellow stilettos, that's what she was shouting. Until my father came out, put the gown on her, and took her back inside the house. The whole street knew about it. Didn't you know? Your mother slapped your father on the face, like in the films. Your father had been asking for a long time for an amicable separation, but your mother wouldn't have it and then really he really didn't want it, at least that's what my mother told me. That's what my cousin Antonio said. He told me all this in the mist of sincere exchanges on family burdens. Yellow stilettos, my forgotten childhood, I knew the yellow stilettos he was talking about.

My father slapped, insulted, as my mother had probably felt insulted. From love to insult. And perhaps back to love again? And now all that existed were words, the words my cousin Antonio had uttered.

My father now existed as he had existed way before I was born, slapped, insulted, my mother, hysterical, naked. I changed my flight, felt useless being there. I realised I would not be part of my father's landscape anymore, he inhabited a landscape from a different era, the present had become a discontinuous landscape, the past a map full of gaps. On my last visit to El Refugio, he was wearing two shirts, one on top of the other, he was absent. I waved goodbye to my father, to my cousin Antonio, to Dr. Alvarez, waved goodbye to blue skies, went back to unpredictable skies, white, grey, black, rain, white, knowing that on my return I would have to find a storage place for Nina Chiavelli's shoes.

This time I couldn't keep all these shoes, Nina Chiavelli's shoes, they took up too much space, I couldn't live with them forever, I wanted to live my own life. Their touring was about to end, they had been little stars, these shoes. They were also still useful these shoes, women could wear them, but I couldn't exactly give them away. I could hide them in a loft, like my father had done, forget about them. I could then occasionally show them to friends, they would become my ambivalent treasure, these shoes, but I didn't have a loft. Maybe I could even lose them. But where could I lose ninety-five pairs of shoes, when they were so conspicuous, so obviously from a different time, maybe in a second-hand market amongst forlorn and radiant trash? I wasn't interested in

a private collector, I called the Collector for advice, talked to
Kathy, they weren't interested in buying them either, perhaps
I should push the gallery that first showed them, make them
work harder, suggest a sale for the permanent collection of
a museum. I myself could write letters to fashion museums,
back them up with reviews from their touring, go solo if the
gallery proved useless. It was a good idea, then they would be
outside of my life, but I could still visit them. I plunged into
letter writing, burned my ears on the phone, almost persuaded the unpersuadable.

'Leather-bound Stories' came back from their tour before
I had found a place to store them. I looked for the yellow stilettos my cousin Antonio had mentioned. They were completely worn out, both of them had substantial holes on the
soles. My mother had worn to death my father's least favourite shoes. I could feel my mother's scorn on the cracked soles.
Her anger.

I welcomed the ninety-five pairs of shoes, they had
brought me luck, but I knew their time had come, they had
become my impossible friends. Mary Jane had a huge loft,
perhaps she could keep them there while I sorted out their
fate. I had completely lost touch with her, with Sam. Their
telephone line had never been reconnected, the only way to
see them was to visit them, travel all those miles, knock on
their door.

One drizzling afternoon I ended up there, knocked on the
door, but there was no answer. The lights were on. I knew
that Mary Jane was in, Mary Jane and Sam were in. I saw
through the blinds a silhouette moving fast. I knocked and
knocked, waited in vain, there was only silence. In the silence
I whispered:

Mary Jane? Mary Jane?

Sam?

Mary Jane?

During those elongated anima blandula days, I wrote a

letter to Mary Jane asking her how she was, how everything was, whether she was fine, apologizing I had not been in touch, then I wrote aphorisms about loss and impossible friends. Then wrote about cyborgs, got immersed in a piece about cyborgs I had envisaged when I was ghostwriting for Lecour. I tried to shed Lecour, wrote about all the things that had been trapped on my mind, sealed in my tongue. I wrote what Lecour would have written if he could have gone beyond his world. I became aware of my own hubris, tried to go beyond it and tried my best to bypass my pathetic self. Then as I was immersed in this strange world of cyborgs, I was contacted by the Victoria and Albert Museum with an enquiry to hire Nina Chiavelli's shoes as part of the extension to the loan collection.

It was there, that I met Chris, Chris Hamlyn, their occasional archive photographer, an olive-skinned male with dishevelled hair and small holes in his shrunken jumpers. I went to the Victoria and Albert Museum everyday. It wasn't necessary, but I wanted to make sure they put a face to my mother's shoes. I met Chris at one of the back EXITS, while having a cigarette. He was having a rummage through some old objects in a skip, he was looking at a large tin box. He had a tiny freckle on his right ear, wore interesting trousers such as jodhpurs, and V-neck jumpers that emphasised the line of his neck. He touched my thoughts, something to do with the small holes in his jumpers, something in his voice, in the depth of his gaze. I developed an instantaneous addiction to Chris's smell. We started following each other's scent. Was your mother a model? Well, yes, no, I mean. I told him snatches of what I knew. Intriguing mother, he said. Excuses, excuses, and excuses to bump into Chris and share nicotine time.

What are the most relevant moments you've ever lived, like seeing a ball of dust and fluff and having an epiphany? I said. Some of the pictures I take ... I take them to grasp the inner beauty of a moment, climbing, reaching the sum-

mit of Mont Blanc, I bought a Leika recently, that was quite
a special moment, he said. I'm writing about cyborgs, how
some gadgets become extensions of people's bodies, it's weird,
we're becoming a new species, part human, part technology,
I said. Do you know Maplins? he said. Maplins? The world
of electronics and beyond, he said, they sell all these interesting gadgets, I had this strange experience the other day, I was
looking at Maplins's shop-window, and then I experienced
a slight erection, he said. You did? You didn't, I said. It just
happened, honestly, he said. I told him about my father being so old, I said I was ringing him everyday, it was difficult,
sometimes I just said to him moo moo, it was the only way to
get a response out of him. Chris put his hand on my shoulder, left it there for a long time, the first time he touched
me. But then he said after a while: did you know that cows
in Bengali don't go moo? Honestly, in Bengali cows don't say
moo, they go: *hamba*!

I didn't believe anything he said. He surprised me in his
passion for gadgets, he was forever buying them, claimed his
interest was purely historical. I thought that my new interest
in cyborgs was partly what drew me to him at first, when really the meeting point was at the level of everything.

Oh, the holes in his jumpers, his dazzling tattered shoes,
the recurrent halo around his head and then he was such a
cunnilingus virtuoso.

Chris was also a great skipologist. His flat was a skip-mu-
seum extravaganza where the most amazing archaeological
remains from the 1940s to the mid 1990s could be found.
Aviation goggles from the Second World War, an inflatable
hair-dryer, a transparent Perspex chair, a collectible foldable
bicycle, a round trampoline. Whenever we went for a walk,
we would come back with something or other: a ridiculous
Ascot hat, an L.C. Smith & Corona typewriter.

Time changed. It became feverish. It became Chris. A free-
floating desire originally activated by the clubs I went to, still

enveloped me. It attached itself to Chris. He picked it up. Pondered it. Teased me. Surrendered. Chris and I. My life became Chris. Nothing existed but Chris. I became we. Time became idyllic time. Chris took pictures of everything. He clicked away all the time. He took a series of pictures of odd warning signs, deserted motorways, apocalyptic industrial horizons. He called them *pictures from the future.* Blew them up to gigantic sizes, life size. They were splendid, majestic in their own unpredictable way, like him. He took astounding portraits of me. He somehow managed to capture my inner beauty through my unappealing face, as if the blindness of love could be captured in film. 'Leather-bound Stories,' my mother's shoes, were documented by him, I shared them with him, with him I narrated my own story as if for the first time, although somehow I didn't tell him about my father being a shoe-fetishist of sorts, about my strange findings.

Sex

Sex

Sex

Sex

Sex

Sex

Sex

Sex

Sex

Relentlessly

All over the universe, excluding black holes

We danced to its music, we had vanilla sex, mint sex, chocolate orange sex, smoothie sex, vindaloo sex, Thai curry sex, sushi sex, mango ice-cream sex. We danced to exhaustion until we abolished time. Then we danced around my mother's shoes. The Victoria and Albert loaned Nina Chiavelli's shoes. Their offer wasn't brilliant. But Chris and I celebrated. Had dinner out a lot, bought rare second-hand trash and gadgets, new technologies. Visited a few times the new extension of the loan collection at the Victoria and Albert Museum. The shoes were arranged chronologically through the help of a Canadian footwear historian who analysed their shape, colour, and material according to the socio-economics of the day. The analysis was interesting. It had been placed underneath each pair. Chris and I found something sad about these labels and the chronological arrangement, though. Would shoe lovers still look at them in awe, would they still blush like they might do in front of some shoe-shop windows? Would anybody ever suspect their stories?

I had written my mother's story as a shoe extra for the big explanatory placard placed to the right of her shoes. I had written about the lack of records, was proud to see her name printed in big letters:

> ## NINA CHIAVELLI, A SHOE EXTRA

I couldn't vindicate my father's story, the story of a shoe fetishist. Not for the Victoria and Albert Museum. But my mother's story had been vindicated. And with her story, the story of so many extras in the world. Or so I wanted to believe.

A double full stop

I had wanted to go to Mexico for a long time. But then, things happened, got in the way, I ended up in other places, places I had never thought of visiting and then I was visiting my father all the time. Whenever I thought of Mexico I could never afford it and now that I could, Mexico had become remote in my mind. In any case, where were Jeanne Moreau's ankle boots? I could picture the Collector yet again set against a new background, this time a protecting blue sky with a fierce white sun, the Collector introducing me to a burnt mannequin, showing me a shiny black high-heel shoe, saying this is a classical example from Buñuel's famous shoe fetishism, it comes from a minor commercial film, *El*, Buñuel told me that of all his films, this is the one he felt closer to.

I had just met Chris, Chris was to become my other half, don't know how long the spell will last for, but this is another story, a story I am still finding out about, a story about finding bliss in domestic happiness. I was with Chris the day the Collector died. Still remember the ominous sounding words: cardio-respiratory failure due to probable pulmonary embolism. That day, I had had an idyllic time on the heath with Chris, we had open-air sex hidden by the long grass. When we got home, there was this phone call. It was Zacharie, telling me the news with his lovely French accent perfectly at odds with what he was saying, saying that the Collector would have liked me to be at his funeral, Kathy and him had become so fond of me, if I could take the first flight to Mexico, he would book and organise everything for me.

The flight was eternally uneventful, except I could hear bits of Spanglish around me. I love Spanglish, its humour, its subversiveness. And in a way, it distracted me from mournful thoughts. Mournful thoughts are difficult to utter. When

Kathy opened the house's gate dressed in navy blue, I didn't know what to say. I hugged her. Said my father was ill. Then kept silent. The house was smaller than I thought it would be, as if in their last years they had decided to build a simplified, intimate world. There were lots of cats running around in the courtyard. I counted twelve. Some of them, the young ones, must have been from the same litter, the others were all different ages, there were two angoras sitting on top of a small shelf of books on the Tibetans, Ainu, the Maori, the Cree, the Yup'ik. She offered me toasted grasshoppers, they're like chips, she said. They were crunchy and I smiled at her and spat them on a serviette with an I'm-sorry-this-is-truly-disgusting-gesture.

Kathy, her long silver fringe. Her long silver fringe concealed her red eyes this time. To begin with, she didn't talk about the Collector's death. She talked about the cats, beautiful creatures, about their elegance, about their fur, their different personalities, their perfection over non-feline friends, the fact that a relationship was established purely through touch. Then she remained in silence for a long time. Then said her husband saw himself as the saviour of objects that might otherwise be lost, she talked about The Museum of Relevant Moments, the convent the Collector had bought to reunite his Buñuel memorabilia, his endless search for Jeanne Moreau's little boots, the last item that would have completed the collection. During the last months of his life, he was changing his mind all the time. Kathy thought that he would end up destroying the collection, like many collectors do. Burn it in a ritualised fire. But he didn't do that. At first, he had gone off the idea of gathering The Museum of Relevant Moments under the convent walls. Had said it didn't make any sense. A convent didn't make any sense. And gathering everything in one place didn't make any sense either. It was more interesting like that, dispersed throughout the world, preserved moments scattered through space. It was lighter like that. These things derived their power from being part of a secret every-day life, rather than being subjected to the rigid taxonomy of a single point in space. Besides, one of the interesting things about Buñuel was that his life was nomadic, there were trac-es of that in his work, of not quite belonging to a single place. Then the Collector had the idea about the auction she said, he wanted to auction everything, to donate the proceeds to different social causes. But he didn't want the collection to be acquired by a single collector, he had put down the condition that only one piece could be acquired and kept by a single in-dividual. In the end, he had gone back to the idea of the con-vent, the museum. He couldn't help gathering everything in one point in space. The building was already there. He had already created a fund for it. He died before he changed his mind again. So that had been his last wish, the original one.

There were quite a few people at the funeral. Kathy was dressed in radiant white. Except for her, I didn't know any of the mourners. They all looked elegant, a distinguished breed dressed in dark tones that complicated the vibrant life of the flowers. Then I saw a man wearing dark glasses that looked like Lecour. It was Lecour. He had grown a beard. I glanced at him awkwardly, wondering whether I had been thinking the thoughts of a bearded man. He hadn't seen me before, he nodded, acknowledging me as his ghostwriter not knowing that for me he had become a skin that I had shed. Then I saw Zacharie. We looked at each other for a long time, kissed hel-lo, touched hands, then looked at each other for a long time again.

As the coffin went down, I sensed that the world the Col-lector represented was coming to an end. I looked at Zacha-rie's Doc Martens. I looked at Kathy wondering whether she would project the loss onto an object, perhaps the museum will become that object, perhaps one day she would bump into a person, that person would suddenly become a mag-netic field for loss and she will start a new life. I thought about my mother, my father, about some of the characters in Buñuel's films. I thought that for some people absence did make the heart, absence and disavowal, but disavowal of the supreme loss: death. Separation and the unspeakable loss were sometimes projected into an object, a blurring of the person in favour of the object. I thought that objects don't usually go away, you can quietly carry them with you, that if you lose them, you're the only one to blame. I thought about the Collector's film fetishes, about the fetish. The fetish was in many cases a reassuring survival tool, an unstable object open to vertiginous interpretation as well as to the possibility of a meaning so hidden in the personal circuits of a brain as to be the most incommunicable cipher. Loss was at the centre of the fetish. How could one deal with death? Perhaps the fetish was an interim object that in some cases remained transitional forever, perhaps it was a different way of mourning. As the coffin went down, I started crying, feeling a fundamental disconnection with the world. Slow tears, tears of loss, then a deluge. I wept incessantly, I took over the funeral, I was perplexed, I didn't know what to do with my sudden discharge. My tears were tears for our finitude, they were abstract tears, but in essence they were mainly early tears for my father.

After the funeral, we went back to the house to have lunch. The seats around the table were toilet seats, replicating a scene from another of Buñuel's films where a group of people go to restaurants and dinner parties but the food forever fails to materialise. I thought that Kathy wasn't going to offer the elegant breed of mourners any food. But she did. Food, drink, and the scent of death in the air. I ate and drunk as if death didn't change the taste of things, but it did to begin with. To begin with, something happened to time too, time passed in a strangely still way. But it did to begin with, after a few morsels and drinks, death retired to the background. It was there, but waiting for the wake to end. Lecour tried to bring it back to the centre. I was sitting opposite him.

I talked to him. Or rather he talked at me. Or rather he talked at the whole table of mourners pretending he was talking to me, slowly raising his delicate voice above the rest, slowly sinking other voices into murmur, looking at me while looking at everybody else. He philosophised at length about death. He was the type of person who always needed an audience. He said that death was but a moment. Like when a pebble falls into a bottomless lake. The moment we were living was death's ripple effect. It was a moment that would expand indefinitely, transforming life continuously, death was a limit that rearranged boundaries.

He was gradually silenced by a guitar. A man from Tijuana started to sing old songs, a mix of American and Mexican songs I didn't know. Then Zacharie started singing as well, his husky French accent making the songs imperfect, perfectly human. A chorus was formed. Life had to be reaffirmed. As it was reaffirmed that night with Zacharie.

Zacharie's blue eyes became black that night. There was this erotic encounter in the dark. Something to do with desire, life and death. Something to do with the purity of desire. I could barely see him. It's the lateral night, when you have to strain your eyes to see what is happening, he said. I'm flying back first thing in the morning. My briefcase was *really* stolen that weekend we were supposed to meet up, I couldn't contact you. Admittedly, I was a bit pissed when I rang you, but what I told you was roughly what happened, he said.

I turned away from him. I felt no desire towards him. My chemistry was only receptive to Chris's. Or so I thought . . . When I woke up Zacharie was gone. And the encounter took on the blurred consistency of a wet dream where we had suddenly become carnal creatures. Something to do with desire, life and death. I didn't feel any guilt. It was something that was supposed to have happened before I met Chris. And it just happened to happen afterwards. It was a knee-jerk reaction to death, a blip in my consciousness.

During the day of the funeral we inhabited the time warp
of death, pierced by alcohol, laughter and song. Kathy must
have inhabited it quite a few days longer, probably countless
days. A couple of days after the funeral, she showed me the
Collector's last acquisition. He had been restoring it during
the last weeks before his death, he was going to get in touch
with Lecour so that he would include it in the written piece
for the museum. It had been her idea to get the scarecrow
that appeared in the film *Robinson Crusoe,* but the Collector
was also really into it. Buñuel had told them at a dinner party that he himself was like Robinson Crusoe when he saw the
scarecrow dressed with female clothes, if for him desire took
the shape of a woman, female clothes were a woman. Buñuel,
she said, had made all these films about desire, but kept his
wife locked in a cage! He kept her apart from all his friends,
completely irrational, he was a jealous man. He gave her beloved piano away just for a bet!

Kathy had placed the scarecrow in the garden. I walked
around the dressed up scarecrow, overwhelmed by its presence
against the violently pink strands in the sky. I haven't seen that
film, I said. She told me about it. She said that in the loneliness of his island, old Robinson Crusoe, with youthful Friday
as his only companion, had made a scarecrow with female
clothes he had found in a trunk. The wind blew the female
clothes suggesting the presence of a woman. Robinson Crusoe looked at the scarecrow and then looked away. Friday, a
savage man, had never seen western female clothes before and
fascinated by them playfully tried them on. Robinson Crusoe blushed. Furiously asked Friday to take these clothes off,
never to wear them again. Friday's playful innocence revealed
that he couldn't read certain cultural signs. Diabolical sexual
attraction for dressed-up Friday, that's what Robinson Crusoe experienced. Sexual attraction not as a welcome release
but mixed with unspeakable shame, shame mixed in turn
with the awareness that that was what he desired, coloured

bits of fabric, colour, life.

That was the Collector's last sigh, a dressed-up scarecrow, dressed up in colourful female clothes, a preserved moment about the outlandish importance of female masquerade, Kathy said. I walked around the dressed-up scarecrow again, thinking about the impossibility of returning to a pure natural state, a pure natural body, about cultural signs having taken complete precedence over nature, about the exacerbated confusion of flesh and thing. Was it a scandal, this confusion? We were all complicit with it, then there were degrees, degrees, degrees.

We drove to the museum the following day, Kathy, Lecour and I. I knew all the contents inside out. I knew them as images, not as tangible objects. I had written about them. But then I had written about them as Lecour. I caught a glimpse of his nose evenly patterned with blackheads on the rear-view mirror. There was something shifty about him, he had been asking me in the car about my writing on cyborgs, gave me a micro-lecture on the reshaping of the human body by modern technology, talked about military cyborgs and invisible blood while I looked from the car window at the discontinuous strip of resplendent buildings. Then he went silent, barely talked again. I realised that he was either silent or talked in lengthy monologues limiting himself to a reassuring professional script, keeping chitchat at bay, talking mainly about intellectual work. Work. I kept quiet, so quiet, but Kathy never commissioned any further ghostwriting again. I took some snapshots of the museum, I hadn't taken snapshots of Mexico City, felt the circumstances weren't appropriate, must say I was amazed by some mountains made out of fridges on the way from the airport and the sheer carnival of colour on entering Mexico City itself.

The Museum of Relevant Moments spoke about the Collector's lifelong obsession with Buñuel. I recognised the music box with the ballerina, the wedding dress, the orthopaedic leg, the numerous high-heels. High-heels, with their emphasis on gravity and minimal contact with the earth, were multiply charged objects that in Buñuel's world were fused to beautiful legs to refer to a sexuality that transcended nature through culture. But in the museum these high-heels were fused to nothing.

It was strange seeing these things in their three-dimensionality for the first time, isolated from their context. Strange to see the black pair of innocent high-heels that looked like the ones that I had sold them. I gazed at them for a long time, couldn't tell any difference at all, they were identical to my mother's. I took a picture. I thought of stealing them, so easy to just slip them into my handbag. Then Kathy came. We walked together towards the ballerina music box. She wound it up. The ballerina spun monotonously around to the haunting melody. I gyrated around the space, listening to the melody, listening to the Collector's museum of relevant moments. I listened to the cross with female heads of hair, the wedding dress, the orthopaedic leg.

Kathy was immersed in silence, she was smiling, as if with her smile she could dispel the smell of death. The sheer silence became audible. We listened to the silence. Only banality could break that pure substance. Lecour spoke. Black holes, that's what you ghostwrote about, he said looking into my eyes. You ghostwrote that the Collector's relevant moments were fugues of meaning, black holes that devoured all meaning, opening into vertiginous interpretation, into the possibility of things meaning nothing, into the sheer materiality of things. But as Kathy says these objects are entities dancing on the edge of the abyss. The Collector's stolen relevant moments are borderline objects that speak of more or less about untameable objects, a resistance on the part of certain objects, certain fragments, the history of a permanent insurrection led by dissident objects.

Dissident objects? Perhaps they are dissident objects, I replied, but then they also have a signature: Buñuel's. In the

Collector's world these objects were exiled from their film-ic habitat, isolated as Buñuel-embodiments, sheer moulded matter imbued with the fascination for a name. The Collec-tor's obsession was with the acquisition of the Buñuel object, as if with this acquisition he acquired the mystery of a name. A mystery often intensified by the allure of a film-still where sex-ual fetishism was highly codified, deeply urban, inextricably linked to culture, to consumerism as an image of refinement, of sophistication, historically different from contemporary rubber as a collective sign of dissent or an ironic comment re-ducing fetishism to one of the many lifestyles you can buy. The Collector's relevant moments weren't his moments. They were mediated. They were fictional moments that he had made his. The Museum of Relevant Moments is a nice con-cept, but this, this is just Buñuel.

As I was saying all this, Kathy rested her head on Lecour's shoulder, then kissed him on the neck, an act that radical-ly altered the moment, an intimate light kiss that presup-posed years of intimacy. I blushed. The ballerina stopped spinning. The melody stopped abruptly. When the melody stopped Kathy sighed. At last he's at rest, she said, thousands of light years away, he always was anyway. Then she held Le-cour's hand, leaving a long silence before she confessed that she didn't want to become a slave to her husband's collection, she didn't want anything to do with it anymore, she didn't want to be a saviour of objects, she was going to sell it, she was going to give the proceeds to the forgotten little ones, the prosecuted, autistic children, los Zapatistas, her husband would have liked that, she had been persuading him for years, he would have liked her to get her own way in the end, she always did. She looked at Lecour. Lecour assented. She then wound up the ballerina music box again, left me wondering, her display of intimacy with Lecour had brought me close to her, but her voice had sounded remote, as if she was talking to me from the other side of things.

Mexico City, a splendid and chaotic epic scripted by twenty million people against a multi-colour backdrop of palaces, slums and sky-scrapers swathed by smoky haze.

I developed an exotic cough after three days. I walked away from the museum, Mexico City, the Collector's world, as if closing a chapter, unaware that the story hadn't quite finished. Perhaps stories never quite finish, they are always there waiting for the right moment, to be taken up again, to be re-interpreted on details, to be rewritten, to show you their demonic laughter.

It was my mother's shoes, Nina Chiavelli's shoes, a foot extra, that had brought me to the steps of this Mexican convent. The convent had become a museum, a shrine to some of Buñuel's relics, doubly consecrated by the shelter of its holy walls. The hope was that it would become a point of pilgrimage for cinephiles from all over the world, for stiletto lovers, definitely a place to visit for unsuspecting tourists. A pilgrimage is always plagued by unexplainable visions, small miracles of perception. A pilgrimage always enhances the senses as travelling does, making visible the previously invisible. I had done my job. I had put in context through somebody else's voice all these fascinating objects that shone forth with the power of dreamt images. It's always difficult to close a chapter, to start a new one. But in a way, the Collector's death had done that. It had created a definite discontinuity, released me from the mesmerising power of a world, written a full stop from which to say before and after.

I thought that it was all over, and in a sense, it was. Mary Jane had disappeared. Buñuel's museum was finished. The Collector had died. And I knew that it was my father's turn.

I called Chris, said I would be going straight to Almería, once back at Heathrow.

I panicked, I changed my flight in order to be there ten days earlier, a farewell visit that allowed me to be with my father during his last weeks, to give him the last kiss. I knew that he had become a ghost of himself. He needed intensive, around-the-clock help, he was chair-bound and then by the time I arrived, bedridden. He just slept and slept and slept and slept for longer periods than ever, enveloped in a tired sour smell. A male nurse changed his position every two hours to relieve the pressure of his body and dealt with the bed pads that he had to wear at night. Mealtimes lasted an eternity, as if by treating each morsel as an everlasting onus, his departure to everlasting peace was justifiably delayed. A couple of times I saw a toothless childlike smile that spoke about cheating death. I sat there for hours on end through his diet of cheese, chicken nuggets and mashes. He would just have a bite and slowly chew it forever. The room was kept in semi-darkness, except for meal times, when the sun particles invaded the room in a sudden apotheosis of light. It was painful to see him wincing, his insomnia, his wan thinness, his vacant presence in front of the small TV that the nurses had put in his room. He told me with his eyes that he was tired, that he wanted to die, but I saw something in him that didn't want to die, something that struggled. He thought I was one of the nurses. And he confused Dr. Alvarez with his brother. He went on life-sustaining treatment while I was there, mainly artificial nutrition and hydration which mainly sustained the transition between life and death. Eva brought in a chair and sat next to him everyday. She kept repeating that the tangle of transparent tubes were a torture for him, that he was ready to enter the tunnel of light. And there was a time I thought of disconnecting the drips. I couldn't disconnect my father's life. It was his life. The only thing I could do was hold his hand, tell him about Eva, about how lucky he was to have met her, about Mexico, about Chris.

He was slowly forgetting to exist.

And then he forgot to exist.

He forgot to pump his heart.

He embraced the general collapse.

His head was turned towards the bedside table, his vacant eyes gazing blankly at an empty glass of water, his set of false teeth resting next to a pinewood knot. That was the last thing he saw: false teeth resting on a pinewood knot, a transparent glass.

Eva had heard that people sick with forgetfulness eventually forget to breathe and that's what she kept muttering. He bloody forgot to breathe, she kept repeating. But he didn't forget to breathe. It's impossible to forget to breathe. It's a legend about the destructive power of oblivion.

My dad forgot to exist.

His fragile heart forgot to beat.

His blood drained out making his skin pale. His flesh succumbed to gravity. His body cooled. His muscles relaxed and then stiffened. Then putrefaction began, endowing his skin with a greenish colour. That is what death is: the foul-smelling gas of active microbes, the devouring bacteria at their noisy feast, the breaking down of the cells, more foul-smelling gases which turn the body purple, then black. Then the body bloats. Then more advanced decay, putrid blisters, the swelling of selected body-parts, the bulging out of the eyes. Then the body liquefies until decomposition leaves only skeletal remains which eventually turn into dust.

Mortality sucks

In a way, my father's longevity had already been dissolved by the Collector's death. I had buried him at the Collector's funeral. The inner pause, the endless sorrow I had experienced during the following weeks, was an anticipation of the sorrow I should have felt at my father's death. And when my father died two months afterwards, I knew I had already mourned him, had already gone through all the inner motions, the implosion and liberation that comes with a parent's death. And so I didn't shed a tear at my father's funeral. A pathetic melodrama could make me cry. My father's funeral, didn't. Dead? He wasn't dead. He was walking with me. All the rest was charade. Death says: And now what? And that was a question whose answer had to be delayed. Infinitely.

Chris came to Spain, that was the first time he met my father, a corpse. He could only stay one week, but he helped me to focus on practical details, to choose my father's best suit, his best shoes for that most special of occasions. Sometimes tears are not shed at the right time. They are shed just before, often way afterwards. Mourning is often out of joint. It was severely so with me. My grief happened ahead of its time, to then resurface with a series of dreams which prefigured my collapse, perhaps my mourning was condensed in a single word: *papá*.

I muttered the word *papá* with a hapless voice, as if a voice was speaking through me. It was the voice I had as a kid. That voice re-emerged intact from the depths of time, that discarded voice re-emerged from the oldest memory path to conjure up a repeated syllable that condensed my helplessness.

But then I had done what I had promised myself to do. I had found his story, my mother's story, a dignifying place, the Victoria and Albert Museum. These shoes had been at the centre of their passion. These shoes contained endless stories. They had survived my mother. They would be in the world well after my father's body had disintegrated, ninety-five pairs of shoes, ninety-five stories.

A dignifying place? Still have doubts about it. In any case, the loan is temporary. In any case, I also did something that I thought my father would have liked: I wore a splendid pair of red shoes for his funeral.

I didn't cry at my father's funeral, but then something strange happened to my gaze: it went into filmic state. I saw the whole funeral as if I was making a film, I saw everything frame by frame, all with natural lighting, starting with a close-up of the visual attack from the vibrant flowers sold by gypsies, then a general shot of a gypsy flower stall, then a long shot of the long wall that separated the dead from the alive, then a cut, the camera was inside the hearse looking at a woman almost identical to me, a sort of double accompanied by a double of Chris, then another cut, an abstract shot at the strangely uniform architecture of the cemetery, at the people around me looking at my splendid red shoes, at Eva nodding at the coffin, at Dr. Alvarez who had put weight on, at Antonio who was holding my hand, at neighbours saying your father was a saint, then back to the houses of the dead, all this in slow motion, as if to strange the gaze from consciousness. Then a series of soft focus flashbacks into my childhood gently fading into each other, my parents smiling at me, talking to me, me hiding underneath my parents' bed, knocking on their bedroom door at weekends, my mother holding a book, her odd beauty, my mother teaching me to read and write, teaching me sweet words in Italian, *ciccia, bambina*, a minute girl raising her head in admiration, with huge wide eyes opened, clear olive skin, intensely red lips, the camera slowly following my eyes, travelling up to their monumental bodies as if they were awesome monuments, thinking my parents were the most extraordinary human beings in the world.

Then, as their faces faded, I saw myself dropping a black pair of stilettos softly on their coffins, heard myself outside my body muttering to people, saying it was some of their belongings, they would protect them on the other side. Then a dramatically lit close-up of my dead mother with Jeanne Moreau's boots on, that was the footwear she had borne for her own funeral, that's why I had never found them, she had died in January, my mother, my memory of my father hugging these boots in his sleep after she had died had probably been an inaccurate memory, an error had entered my memory, it must have done, it must have done.

An error.

I paused the black boots' image, dazzled by their shine. But didn't my father just hug one boot? Could it be that she was buried with just one boot? It could very well be. I'll never know. It had never occurred to me that the boots would be in her coffin, it had never occurred to me that she was one with them. The black ankle boots dissolved into a close up of my shaky hand with a handful of soil throwing it on their coffins, the soil in mid-air, the soil landing softly on the wood. Then a shot of their joint grave. Then another flash back to my filmic childhood reverie: running, running, running.

Then the end. But is there ever a clear-cut end? The promising pleasure of a new beginning, a clean slate? Isn't the possibility of a clean slate forever foreclosed? I was ringing Chris everyday, he was my lifeline. My cousin Antonio was a lifeline as well, but he was now living in Madrid, he was going to open up a high-class hat shop, he definitely surprised me when he told me that he had moved in with a man.

It was good that Chris had come to my father's funeral. He was amazed at verifying with his own eyes that the landscape of Almería indeed doubled for the American West. It was like Arizona, he said. You just expected a blue-eyed cowboy to turn up any minute, strike a match on his bearded cheek and light a cigarette. I had never seen Almería sole-

ly in terms of westerns and that's how tourists saw it. Chris
took pictures of the arid hinterland, the hazy mountains, lad-
der-snakes. We drove around the Tabernas desert, a cross between Arizona and a lunar landscape that spoke of barren
beauty. We stopped at the immense solar-energy plant, a subservient assembly of hundreds of shimmering mirrors looking up to the central tower, reflecting the sun's rays into it,
working relentlessly to supply sustainable, clean, world energy. The solar plant was like a shorthand for the future, Chris
said. He was awestruck. He took pictures of the heliostats,
the parabolic dishes and troughs, undoubtedly pictures from
the future. I insisted that we visited the remnants of studio
sets at Mini-Hollywood and Texas-Hollywood near the town
of Tabernas, but the mood dictated otherwise and we had left
it too late. We also walked around the old parts of Almería.
And Chris went inside a religious shop that I had seen many
times but never gone into. It was a religious shop that had diversified into a joke shop. So, there were statues of virgins,
saints, liturgical candles and bibles on one side of the premis-
es, and on the other side plaster turds, huge curvaceous plastic cocks, aprons with sculpted pink tits and fake ice-cubes
with flies inside. The shop-keeper, a balding middle-aged
woman, was imperviously reading one of the Pope's biogra-
phies for sale. It was the first time that I laughed out aloud
since my father's passing away. And I was shocked to discover
that you could laugh so truly while being under death's sway.

I got a meagre amount for my father's house. It was in
a complete state of disrepair. And after dealing with the car
fines, the bailiffs' fees, the inland revenue, and the water
charges he had forgotten about for the last ten years, there was
just enough to pay for the funeral, buy a secondhand car for
Chris and to keep me going a few months while I half-heart-
edly looked for work. I discovered that the main provision
my father made was to hide from me that he was ill while he
was still alive. When I went to El Refugio to collect my fa-

ther's things and visited Dr. Alvarez in his office for the last time, he told me in the softest of voices, that my father had made him promise not to say anything about his condition. He had been diagnosed with Alzheimer's when he agreed to go to El Refugio. He didn't want me to know anything. Immersed in the mist of disbelief, I looked at a filing cabinet for a long time and said nothing. So all the time you reassured me he was fine, you were lying? I said at last. Just white lies, he said. It was a grand gesture on your father's part. He wanted his illness to be invisible to you, and also, to himself, when he heard of his diagnosis, he actually asked me to remind him as well every so often that he wasn't ill, he just didn't want you to worry, he said with a balsamic smile.

White lies. I felt I had been protected from the truth, it made a difference, even if my father's death was a fact foretold by his age. I whispered: *thank you, dad.* The pain was still there, though. Then the insistence of things came back to muffle the pain, to silence the possible crisis. It came back as I was collecting the things my father had left and found inside the breast-pocket of his jacket a pocket-size photo album stuffed with snap shots of my mother's shoes. I felt tired, resigned, touched. I had never seen it before. I browsed through the plastic sleeves going from black and white to Technicolor to the orangey ageing chemicals from the seventies. My mother's shoes hadn't been forgotten after all. Maybe he had put them in the loft and buried their memory with her, but couldn't help but keep the snapshots as souvenirs of his foible? Was that the only memory Alzheimer's had not disintegrated? Did that survive further than the memories from the war and Durruti's memorable words? I didn't dare ask Dr. Alvarez, although it would have been an interesting point to raise. I had no way of knowing. Perhaps he had kept the photo album out of habit, maybe the last thing that Alzheimer's deleted was a privileged part of the unconscious.

I recognised many of the shoes, I saw again the black pair

of boots that looked like Jeanne Moreau's, the ones that I saw
my mother wearing at her own funeral during my reverie, the
ones that with time made me realise that I wasn't the protagonist in my childhood, my parents were, I was their audience. I
watched *Diary of a Chambermaid* again, compared the album's
photograph with a paused still, then with a close-up sequence
where those boots walked up and down. In this close-up
sequence you could only see the boots and a bit of leg. There
was no reason to think Jeanne Moreau would need a foot extra, an extra that would pace up and down on her behalf.
There was no reason to think those were Jeanne Moreau's
feet. There was no reason to think they were not my mother's. During the following days I looked at the photograph
and that bit of film countless times. I oscillated. That bit of
film, those legs and feet housed in a black pair of boots could
be anybody's. To me, the way of walking pointed towards my
mother, Nina Chiavelli, oscillating between my mother and
the unknown.

The small photo album, old pyjamas and old-fashioned
clothes, an old shoe box, the insistence of things also came
back under the guise of an old postcard. This old postcard
became a proof. I relished the find with infinite pleasure. It
was a trace from the real, a piece of evidence that confirmed
my buried suspicions. The postcard was in an old shoe box
with old family pictures. It was there that I found this postcard that my mother had sent to my father. It was there that
I found a proof. It had a colourful sugar skull printed on it.
The postmark was from Mexico City, you could just about
make it out, the year 1952, exactly the same year as the film
El was made, one year before my parents married. My mother had written: *My beloved Jordi, love from the Aztec gods, travelling to Chihuahua next week.* And she had drawn a small
slanted heart ♥. My mother, Nina Chiavelli, must have appeared in that film, a film by Buñuel. The innocent high-
heels that I had sold to the Collector must have been the ones

that had appeared in that film. That was what that postcard meant. That was what it pointed to. No doubt about it now.

But why hide it? Why hide from everybody the fact that my mother had been a foot extra, that she had appeared in that film by Buñuel, possibly also in *Diary of a Chambermaid*? The only reason I could think of was fear, my parents living in fear of being discovered. Undoubtedly, Franco's Spain was a country suffused by fear. Anybody who had links with the wrong side could suffer an incident. And Buñuel was an unorthodox film-maker, he had been a communist sympathiser for a while. Maybe at the time she appeared in the film, it was necessary to hide that link. But my parents had been clandestine anarchists themselves and by the late '60s made no effort to hide it. My mother's occasional job as a foot extra was the secret of secrets, a secret now partly dissolved by the traces from the real, a secret that must have been known by the Collector. For a while, I tried to unravel it further, the secret, but found a resistance made out of solid silence, a dead letter, there were no records of my mother having been a foot extra, the actors on the Buñuel's film credits that I contacted didn't remember any of the extras, I found nothing but a perfect circle of irresolvable suspense.

Nothing.

I heard this nothing coming from my mother's grave, from my father's grave.

I wrote a letter to my aunt in Italy, zia Carla, saying my father had died and did she know whether my mother had ever appeared in a film by Buñuel?

I was alone in the world.

I wasn't alone.

I was with Chris.

After so many incomplete revelations, so many losses, my life continued in an essentially meaningless sequence of random occurrences. Chris, the seasons, appearing and disappearing friends, disappointments, failures, contradictions, waiting endlessly for things to happen, trying to learn not to wait, not to expect, trying to dissolve the intoxicating power of expectations, learning the purpose of these expectations was to dissolve the present. In short: living.

Of course, I never wanted to acknowledge that, the randomness, the meaninglessness, couldn't look at it for long time in the face, told myself that randomness is only a form of temporary ignorance, while meaning is something that emerges with time. Meaningful things did happen, stories that proliferated in other directions, stories that have not come visible yet, but they are stories unrelated to this story, mainly stories about finding meaning in small pleasures, stories about the small publication of my book on cyborgs which was ignored by the entire planet, stories about Chris and I having a small tiger tattooed on our buttocks, about struggling with daily life, always struggling, about Chris becoming a centre of meaning for me.

I probably also found meaning in Mary Jane's radical disappearance. An oscillating meaning where sometimes an abominable world didn't deserve but to be abandoned and other times, the futility of such a radical act could only lead to a majestic private gesture of self-destruction. The increasing presence of toys everywhere I went made me think about her. I saw toy-like things leisurely sneaking in everywhere, like a sweet lullaby slowly taking over the world. I kept telling Chris about Mary Jane, about what she had done, about her wilful disappearance, he was as mystified as I was, although he came up with this fable of Aesop about a Miss True which ran more or less like this:

> A wayfaring man travelling in the desert met a woman standing alone and terribly dejected. He inquired of her, 'Who art thou?'
> 'My name is Truth,' she replied.
> 'And for what cause,' he asked, 'have you left the

city, to dwell alone here in the wilderness?'

She answered, 'Because in former times, falsehood was with the few, but is now with all men, whether you would hear or speak.'

There are lies and lies, Chris said. Not everybody lies. Some people lie to survive, but for some people lying becomes a habit, he said. It's vital to have integrity, but you also have to survive, survival makes people lie, self-interest that doesn't give a fuck about anybody, that's the problem, why don't you visit her? he said. That fable is right, Mary Jane is indeed Miss True, though her disappearance doesn't solve anything, except for signalling the strongest of dissent, I said. A world cut up by wars, by manifold violence and greed, and daily petty deeds carried out by innocent people who practised innocent violence, was indeed a hard pill to swallow. I knew that I could always visit Mary Jane, but her place had become a no-go area. I just hoped that at some point there would be a sign telling me that she was well. I am still waiting for that sign, I know she is working away in the dark, she never replied to my letter. I've learnt that things develop over years and years. Films, fictions, technology, concentrate time distorting it. An interminable war, the events of a century, become a thirty minute documentary. A long book, a quotation. A life's time, an epitaph. We are surrounded by things that happen instantaneously. More and more, we expect things to happen that way. But life is made out of time, understanding takes time, absorbing understanding takes time too, our mental beat is still too slow for the world.

Or at least mine is. I was slow to weep the way I felt I should have wept. I could only cry in my dreams. In waking life, it was a gradual thing. It took a few months for me to weep the way I felt I should have wept. One day I wept a clumsy tear, the next week a few more, the next month, a flood. I thought that I had slowly assimilated that my father was going to die, but with death there is no such thing, it leaves a dent that keeps changing shape. I had been dreaming about him, day in and day out, about my mother's shoes. I thought about him everyday. I started weeping everyday. Sadness becomes you, Chris said on a few occasions to make me feel at ease with myself. I started staying at his flat more and more. I lost touch with Pearl who really got into S&M clubs and told me dark things that made me squeamish and made her laugh at me. Chris wanted me to move in with him, but I wasn't ready to leave my little den. Are you afraid we won't get on? he would say. No, it's not that, I would say. I'll wait 1001 nights, but not a single one more, he would say. My relationships don't last, I would say. You're hard work, he would say. But you enjoy it, don't you, I would say.

Chris became my sentinel between job assignment and job assignment. He was a freelance. Maybe freelance was another name for precariousness. London is like that, fifty thousand people for one lousy job. All the people we knew were doing juggling acts. Chris was by my side. He would say he was going to collect my tears in small bottles, he found sexy the wet zigzags on my eyelashes. He would come round with small toys, a tiny PC guardian angel, a small red hot water bottle with a white heart on it. It was funny seeing such a tall man offering such small things. He cooked me heavenly meals that I barely touched, with the exception of what he called *skrumptious carrot cake* and *gorgasmic cheese cake*. With these irresistible cakes, I couldn't help having a break from my loss of appetite and lick clean the plate, the spoon, the cake-tin, my fingers, my nails, and even the cake crumbs on the table. The halo around Chris's head became a permanent feature. He was like a mountain. Solid. Huge. He was there, he was always there. He was the man who had turned me into a sexual animal, who called me nonsensical, silly names and treated me as if he was reading my mind. My father was gone.

Gone.

A swirl of white dust.

A persistent memory and a handful of photographs.

The death of others creates a hole in time, a no-place. In this no-place, I received a condolence card from my aunt zia Carla. It had a large daisy printed on it and didn't say anything about my mother.

I tore up the card and wept.

I was happy with Chris and yet I couldn't quite shake out of mourning and melancholia. He kept asking me to move in with him and I kept saying that I wasn't ready to move from the no-place that I found myself in.

The cloning passion, a sort of footnote

In this no-place where there were no certain answers, where possible realities hovered suspended in opposition to brutal certainties, life continued. Chris got less and less work as time went by contradicting the idea of the future as progress, while I wrote less and less as crippling forces gulped my energy. Time is a bastard, we have to face up to it, we have to annihilate it, he said. We looked at time intensely in the face until it withdrew into the background. It was the only thing we could do. Time made impossible contortions in self-defence. We blanked it. We turned our backs to it until it vanished. We put our feet on its gnarly torso claiming an illusory victory designed to keep our minds at rest. We obliterated time until we became time. We built a cocoon against time. We had sex day and night, we worked day and night, Chris took dazzling pictures of shadows and related phenomena and I wound up rescuing the red notebook and started scribbling some of these pages. Time whizzed by in a flash. We just killed time before it killed us. Then time came back as it does to add a footnote to a scrap from my past. It happened as Chris and I were planning to move in together. And it happened by chance, as it does. I had been a dupe in a convoluted game, an involuntary accomplice in an ingenious swindle that now shook me out from the sweet cocoon we had built back into the real world.

Time delivers footnotes to stories, amendments that jolt foundations unearthing dirt and wonder. Something happened recently that altered the Collector's story, a sort of footnote, a postscript, an unbelievable twist if you want. This footnote appeared in a newspaper, in *El Mundo*. I was browsing through it, suffering the traces from the real, accidents, natural catastrophes, but mostly man-made barbarities attesting to the will to destroy which hadn't changed in the least with the new millennium. I always shivered when I read the newspapers. I was browsing through the culture section when I recognised a small picture of The Museum of Relevant Moments, with an intriguing headline: F FOR FRAUDULENT? There was a small article about it. The article said that this new Mecca for cinephiles was under investigation for claims of forgery. It wasn't exactly forgery that was at stake though, it was more a case of 'inauthenticity'. A prop manager who had worked in a couple of Buñuel's films claimed to own the original orthopaedic leg that had appeared in the film *Tristana*, the orthopaedic leg that Catherine Deneuve was supposed to have worn, he claimed that a replica of the orthopaedic leg was shown at the Buñuel museum, not the original one.

I raised my eyebrows and scratched my head.

I frowned.

I read the article again.

I raised my eyebrows again and carefully folded the newspaper.

Eventually, I rang Kathy not knowing whether it would be the same number. Left a message on an answering machine that had an anonymous message on it. And when she didn't return my messages, I sent her an email mentioning the orthopaedic leg story, asking her whether it was true. I also rang Zacharie a few times. But he wasn't in either. Zacharie! Felt a tingly high while listening to his French accent on the answer-phone, a chemical turbulence, an urgent desire to have sex with him again. This sudden heat wave transformed my day, filling it with erotic reveries, erotic encounters outside time and space that fuelled my passion with Chris that night. The message that I left didn't mention anything about the orthopaedic leg story. Did it matter if one of the exhibits was a copy? Didn't copies usually glow with the power of the original? Was there a difference? I recalled the discussions with Mary Jane about the Mona Lisa that we used to have lunch in front of. It was the place where it was, a cheap café, that precluded it from being an original. The Louvre could house a copy of the Mona Lisa. But it could never be perceived as a copy. The Louvre was supposed to be a site of authenticity. Nobody wanted to believe otherwise.

Kathy eventually returned my call. Rumours, somebody had been spreading rumours. And rumours sometimes found their way into newspapers, into the perpetual disinformation machine that the media is. It was now solved. But she had to talk to solicitors. Pay through the nose. Avoid the poison. The Buñuel family had issued a statement disengaging themselves from the whole issue, saying that film props were always re-turned, they knew nothing about what happened to them af-terwards. But the rumour had generated a lot of free publici-ty for the museum. Notoriousness is always good. There were then local rumours that the museum itself had been responsi-ble for the first rumour in an attempt to generate free public-ity. In short, visitors had increased tenfold. The museum had found new audiences. Audiences seduced by the appeal of the counterfeit, accomplices. The rumour had created an air of ambiguity that appealed to these new audiences. It seemed nobody wanted to resolve this ambiguity. It was preferred. And that's how the Collector would have wanted it. Dissimu-lation. Complicity. From others. But then the ambiguity dis-solved. Everything went back to normal. Kathy sighed, then coughed.

Zacharie returned my call two weeks afterwards, that's to say, about a month ago. He had been away in Vietnam, talked about the incredible people there, the incredible food, the political changes. Then he went silly. He flirted, laughed, explored my limits. He reminded me that the Collector's fu-neral had ended up as a reaffirmation of life. But wasn't that what you did when somebody died? He suggested that there was no reason not to duplicate the experience. To *duplicate*? I brought up the orthopaedic leg story, the fake prop I had read about. We talked for a long time. I thought that he was joking at first. Still think sometimes he made it all up. Zacharie's sense of humour, we haven't talked since. The Museum of Relevant Moments was the Collector's labour of love, his wayward baby, he said. The Collector devoted all his time to it, he had all the time in the world, nothing else mattered. He loved Buñuel's films. He was sure that Buñuel would have loved The Museum of Relevant Moments. Didn't Dalí just sign empty pieces of paper, of canvas, to be filled in at leisure by anybody with the guarantee they were signed by the master? You see, he said, the Collector felt there was something false in authentic objects. He liked that and he didn't, he was intrigued by it. By the fact that throughout history we had immortalised objects by giving them ludicrous properties, through the magical aura of their illustrious owners, fabricating impossible stories about them, stories that miraculously defied all evidence. He thought that something perverse lurked there. Became obsessed with confusing the signs. He was interested in the Turin shroud, the crop circles, that kind of thing. When he discovered that in most films they have to have replicas of the main props and costumes, in case they get damaged or they need the same item but worn out, he became excited. He knew his collection of fake memorabilia would survive him. He wanted it to survive him, thus the convent, the museum. Do we need authentic things to assure us that all this is not a fiction? That the past did actually exist? Doesn't the physical presence of things add a realistic touch to the blurred nature of our lives? As if things were more real? Sometimes more definite than us? Real? Didn't the world consist of a cacophony of multiple realities?

Initially, the Collector had wanted the Buñuel museum to be in Amsterdam, Zacharie said. But Amsterdam had so many other museums full of fakes already. Then the Collector decided on Mexico City. He had spent the last twenty years of his life looking for exact copies of what he considered to be the most revealing moments in Buñuel's films, forging them when necessary as with the case of the cross of female heads of hair that had appeared in *L'Âge d'Or*, the wedding dress in *Viridiana*, looking for the exact cloth from the exact time, coming across the exact paper and typewriter used at the time, preparing a catalogue with pertinent explanations, certificates of authenticity, documenting everything elegantly, rummaging endlessly through secondhand markets, old factories, finding the most perfect of replicas, creating the perfect *crime passionnel*. The museum was the Collector's oeuvre. A meticulous forgery to which he had devoted endless days, year after year. Was it a revenge against the tyranny of the real? The real? Did it exist in an unadulterated state? Wasn't the real a confused space made out of all these unspeakable dimensions? Was the Collector seeking justice? Building a desperate affirmation which emphasised that ultimately all these fragments of reality upon which we build our precarious certainties might be secondhand, fraudulent, seductive shams? Aren't museums brimming with quiet forgeries, quietly complicit with that most ancient of urges, the urge to forge, to copy, to pass as truthful that which only came afterwards, haunted by a morphic resonance, where a successful entity screams persuasively for reproduction? Wasn't there a cloning passion at the heart of our endeavours? An obsession with origins or rather with faking origins if necessary? All these Rembrandts, Picassos, all these Van Goghs and Modiglianis, did anybody believe they were *all* authentic? And wasn't authenticity a snobbish concept that art collectors had created to distinguish themselves?

The Collector had aspired to create genuine fakes. He knew that these replicas would soon be taken as the real thing. Our strange thirst for the real knew no boundaries. He knew that all throughout. Yes, Nina Chiavelli's shoes were the ones exhibited at the Buñuel museum. Nobody knew what had happened to the original ones. And if anybody did, they had kept quiet. Nobody had shared their secrets with anyone, the whole contents of the museum were copies. Nobody had uttered a word. Only that prop manager had come up with the orthopaedic leg story. But money alters people's stories, people's perception of events. The guy had retracted his story, the collection's value had gone up. Kathy already had a couple of commercial propositions, she wanted to give the proceeds to children's charities, she had always wanted to do that, that would also keep everybody quiet.

Zacharie sounded as if he wanted to convince me of something, when I didn't need to be convinced. My mother's shoes were real. All the other objects were real. It was only the circumstances around them that were different. I saw the convent in my head. In my memory, it was a tenuous image. An image that could have come from a dream. An image, not a tangible, three dimensional thing. And yet the museum was there, a figment of place on the edge of Mexico City, under Mexican clouds, surrounded by chaotic buildings, traffic, noise, pollution and occasional trees, visited by hundreds of people, like so many other museums full of fakes in so many other cities, treated with the reverence that only authentic things received, but also ignored by monumental crowds indifferent to what others called culture.

I felt conned, deceived.

I didn't say anything.

I needed time to absorb everything.

I said: shit.

I said: I don't believe you.

Nonsense, utter nonsense, I said.

And yet I understood the whole logic and was awestruck by the monumentality and absurdity of the Collector's project. He wanted to be remembered, not for replicas, but for meticulous forgeries, which was where most art theories foundered. But why call it The Museum of Relevant Moments?

I asked Zacharie. That's a good question, he said, I don't know, you'll have to get a ouija board and ask him. He was probably fixated on a few moments in Buñuel's films and just expanded on that. He saw himself as a magician, a magus, he just wanted to posit the world as a question mark.

He then said that in any case I had been paid a lot of money out of the blue, that the Collector and Kathy liked the idea of giving money to a bum like me, a talented bum, they thought that it was money well-spent, that they wanted me to know, but they wanted me to know in my own time. In my own time? I couldn't help feeling the naïve victim of a kind of candid-camera trick. But it wasn't cruel or hilarious. It was a metaphysical trick that released a warmth through my head that exploded slowly, then imploded into a kind of inexplicable chaos.

I felt conned.

The image of the shoes I had sold them flashed through my mind.

Then I laughed. It was a sublime laughter. And with my laughter I heard Nina Chiavelli's demonic laughter emerging from her coffin, then my father's joining in. They were convulsing, they were moving up and down splitting their sides, rolling on the soil of the neglected cemetery with an unlimited *ha ha ha ha* that reverberated across the universe. Could it be that the Collector really didn't know who Nina Chiavelli had been, that he had bought these shoes unaware that they were the real ones, unaware that my mother had appeared as a foot extra in the film that Buñuel identified with the most and that something authentic had slipped into his secret museum of replicas, that the fake museum contained an original, my mother's innocent high-heels?

Zacharie had always been an emissary of unreality.

He loved it, it was his game. I didn't fantasise about him at all this time, as if my fantasy switchboard was already clogged up with what he had told me. To return to reality, I rang

Chris. We were planning to move in together, to his place, and I had already packed most of my things. I was laughing when I told him about the whole thing, although it was a laughter I hadn't experienced before, an awkward laughter. The whole museum was a fake. Everything was bogus except for my mother's shoes, but they didn't know that, they thought they were bogus too! I didn't say anything to Zacharie. In any case, maybe there was a time when copies were seen as monstrous, but that time had been left behind long ago.

Chance had the last word.

And if in a genuine collection fakes could sneak in, there was always the chance that in a collection of fakes, something genuine could slip in.

That's crazy, write about it, Chris said, it'll make a good story and it's based on reality, he said. I feel a strange loyalty to Kathy and the Collector and the whole idea, I don't want to stir things up, it's perfect like that, I said. Like a perfect cake with a tiny fly on it, he said. I said the whole thing left me feeling as if I was in a no-place. Talking about the museum Zacharie had said, of course it's real. And then, of course it isn't. Whether it was or not, the possible fiasco had installed in my head an oscillation between different types of reality. Going through one to the other, there was this gap, this no-place, this no-place that had unwittingly been trespassed by the real, everything criss-crossed, everything intermingled, the Collector should have known.

Another no-place? Chris said. Well, it's a different type of no-place, it's a metaphysical no-place, I said. A metaphysical no-place? he said. He was going to kidnap me when I least expected it and hide me in his no-flat, tied up to a no-bed post, he said. I liked the idea, except that his bed didn't have a no-bed post. You'll have to buy a new no-bed, and a lot of no-rope, I said. I've just found a new four-poster bed outside a house, just the frame, I'm going to disinfect it with Dettol Multi Action Trigger . . . but I was thinking about painful handcuffs and ankle-cuffs rather than rope, he said. Would you rather have rope? he asked. It's up to you, whatever you want, you're the master with the masterful hands, I said. We'll go for a special dinner before the abduction, he said. Don't forget the blindfold! And the gag! I said. Did Lecour know that it was all a sophisticated forgery? he said. I hadn't thought about Lecour. He must have done, he's Kathy's lover, I said. Who's Zacharie? he said. A guy who's into playing games, I had a crush on him, I had a one-night stand with him, I said. Do you still fancy him? he said. Why? Are you jealous? I said. Of course, he said. I can't believe it, I said. That I'm jealous? he said. No, the museum thing, have you ever heard anything like it? I said. You can be a bit of a fantasist sometimes. Are you really sure that your mother's shoes really appeared in that film by Buñuel? he said. Pretty certain, I suppose I'd rather my mother was connected to Buñuel's films, I said. And as I said that, I wasn't sure about anything anymore. It all had the disconcerting logic of a long and convoluted dream.

After Chris hung up, I was in this no-place for a while, then I went for a walk. In general, the weather seemed to be getting warmer. The streets, always so real to me, took a while to acquire reality. Things became focused gradually. Toys proliferating everywhere, multiplying, like a varied vegetation gone out of control, things shouting: buy me, buy me, buy me, take me with you, rescue me, I will fulfil your deepest psychological needs, with me you will be more. I was enveloped by the euphoria of things. Apparently submissive things. I walked along ignoring them while my brain released a sensation of infinite gratitude. I was grateful to chance for slipping this footnote into my life. It was good that Kathy was going to sell the museum and give the proceeds to charities, but this footnote also gave me access to this no-place, an oscillating angle from which to look at life. Life, I suppose that's the word, an increasing minefield for fictions of all kinds, we need these fictions, we cannot bear facts for long, but then who and what decides on fictions, on which fictions are allowed, which not, which realities, which not?

Questions and questions and questions and questions and questions.

I walked back home thinking that I should ring Kathy for a reality-check.

But I didn't do it.

The ubiquitous lullaby

To posit the world as a question mark implies the adventure of answers. I didn't seem to find plausible answers to things, I only seemed to find questions, I wasn't sure they were the right questions or interesting ones. All I knew was how important it was to keep asking questions, to sharpen them, to breathe life into the world, to X-ray it, scan it, inhale it, taste it, gobble it up, digest it. As I was walking back home, I looked at the world around me, then thought about the small world that Chris and I had managed to build, when suddenly Mary Jane's whispering voice appeared melodiously in my head like an intrusive jingle:

> Are we good children?
> Do we deserve the toys?
> Oh yes, we are good children.
> Quiet.
> Obedient.
> Responsive to fear and chocolate bribes.

Mary Jane's words had been popping in my head for quite a while now. Toys were the trigger. Toys everywhere. That's why I called the cluster of words here *Philosophical Toys*, because of Mary Jane, because of the neural web she had drawn in my head, a neural tangle of connections that was now constantly being triggered.

Initially, I had seen this new trend in art, artists using toys in their work, exhibiting beautifully manufactured plastic playhouses where you wished you could get in, where suddenly you were too big and cumbersome, realistic playhouses with roomy interiors including homely furniture and pretend phones, the toy industry was reproducing the whole of empirical reality in vibrant plastic, initially for children, but more and more for adults: extraordinary toy-like Hoovers, computers and robots, the whole western world was becoming a play world, a playful cartography. Advertising used friendlier and friendlier cartoons to represent the world, cutesy graphic design to animate it. Packaging used the same euphoric rhetoric the toy industry used. Car design was becoming more toy-like, promising a stylish ride back to our early days. Everyday objects were made more and more from the same substance as toys, the same playful plastic, the same translucent materials, the same rounded appearance. That's what made me see a toy-like aesthetic at play, the materials, the smooth and curvy lines. Perhaps artists were creating metaphors about a world still in its infancy, they were pointing to an unprecedented regression comparable to the dark ages, but this time a happy one, a regression muffled by a cotton-wool world of comfort and safety, where the ride will be smooth, the landing soft.

It was strange seeing so many artists producing work so similar to Mary Jane's, so many years later. It struck me that maybe she was working under a pseudonym, camouflaged by this new trend. So many artists tuning into the same reality, and then there was one and only one artist elevated as the brainchild who had the brilliant idea of using toys in her work, this artist being given everything she hadn't been given, even if the work was an unresolved echo of Mary Jane's.

Mary Jane hadn't been given a chance, she had got lost, she had lost her sanity, she had decided to defect from the planet knowing that other forces were working on it, she had decided to eclipse herself before she was thrown into the pit with all the others. Perhaps the pain she felt, was close to the pain my mother must have felt at not being given a chance, at becoming a foot extra. Mary Jane. With time, I realised the repercussion of her actions over me, a repercussion that had come in slow motion, slowly insinuating itself in my neural circuits, dancing around them, seducing them, leaving a bittersweet trace. For a long time, every time I saw pale pink, every time I saw pale blue, I saw her face, her large velvety mole, her red hair. And then I saw her in her mad decision. I had been a voyeur to her collapse. I had done nothing but watch. Hypnotised by her presence. By her obsessions. By her idea of abandoning the world. It seemed such a great idea. And then the horror. The horror and the fascination of seeing her doing it. And then the distance. And then the silence. Her collapse? Sometimes I wondered what the difference was between abandoning the world and burying your head in the sand, hiding from everything, becoming an ostrich, other times I thought she had done the right thing, her fragile survival depended on inhabiting her own will, her own fiction.

Bit by bit, her absence thickened as new seductive toys crept all around us. Like so many people my age, Chris and I lived with plastic trinkets, the trinkets from kinder eggs, from film merchandise, miniature toys from cereal packets, red hippopotami and purple ghosts. We certainly couldn't afford mortgages, so we had turned trinkets into big things. A three-eyed monster talking lamp sat in my bedroom, trashy toys lightened up our houses, sweet babies, we loved these small things, they made us smile, they kept us warm, they approved our vulnerabilities giving us eternal youth.

But was it just my reality, were there really toy-like objects everywhere or were my eyes more attuned to them, to the point I had made a social phenomenon out of it? Had my perception gone literal? Too literal? It was a fact that the toy industry had diversified its market with a whole range of toys for all ages, that the amount of objects absorbing the qualities of toys was multiplying. There was no doubt these would be the objects that would sit in future museums, in rooms adjacent to archaeological remains, these toys attested to our needs and disavowals, to our new status as vertiginously lost subjects. On the whole, those fixated on austerity hated the logic of this new landscape. Perhaps, we would end up hat-ing it too. But at the time, we celebrated it with a simulacrum of laughter. There was something about this toy world that we liked, it was playful, it was about cynically accepting where we were, we probably suspected a mischievous unconscious voraciously in need of protection, maybe something had come to the surface under the guise of irony, an irony containing a kernel of despair, somewhere we didn't know anymore who we were, we had to keep on marching, like an army of docile children asking for nurture, for reassurance, perpetually mesmerised by a sense of powerlessness disguised as play.

Benevolent objects.

Consumerist missiles.

Chris kept giving me these toy-like curios, absurd offerings, tokens of love, something genuine was inscribed on their surface, something that made us kind-hearted, that put us in touch with something inextricably human, nostalgia for idiotic times, for the supreme nonsensical, there was empathy in these objects, something ticklish was inscribed in them, there was humour. We started buying whatever brand of cereals gave away free toys, knowing that these trinkets that appeared in your cereal packet, to be consumed in that blurred time, breakfast time, were a kind of cosmic joke that fused juvenile happiness, consumerism and fairy-tale dissolution of contradictions in a single stroke.

Babies? My generation didn't have babies. We had substituted the experience for the company of friendly bibelots, organic design, thinking toys, plastic trinkets. And yet we knew that the myth of the happy world they embodied, where happiness could be bought even at a modicum price, was precisely that, a myth, and that there came a time when the pretence of innocence was no longer possible.

No longer.

And yet these trinkets were good for the temporary relief of mild pain.

I wrote everything in my red notebook.

I realised that I wouldn't have met Chris if it wasn't for my mother's stilettos. My mother, a failed actress who became a striptease girl, a babbling head who drank and sang the blues, a woman who towards the end of her life wore yellow high-heel shoes defiantly against my father without whom she couldn't live, a woman who loved me and ignored me, Nina Chiavelli, a stranger who had become ninety-five pairs of shoes, ninety-five stories. Her shoes had taken me round the world, to Amsterdam, to Toronto, to Mexico City, to a convent where an eccentric collector had decided to gather a series of forged mementoes from Buñuel's films, some strange objects, mostly shoes, but also anthropological objects, objects I had ended up writing about as a ghostwriter, like my mother had been a foot extra, although I had done it my way. The objects in The Museum of Relevant Moments were so serious, so sober, so ritualistic. They were historical objects. They had gravitas. Even if they were of doubtful origin. The toy-like objects now proliferating everywhere belonged to the realm of the light-hearted, the disposable joke, tacky optimism. Perhaps we needed this sparkling philosophy, maybe it made things more bearable, since darkness was always there, lurking behind the shadows of toys, unpredictable, real, smothering.

Chris and I worked hard. We worked and worked for peanuts and we struggled and then played and collapsed exhausted. We walked on a precarious rope created by forces we couldn't control. On weekends, we occasionally got caught up in the traffic jams that proliferated everywhere maliciously blocking the main streets and motorways, everybody was doing it, driving towards supermarkets, DIY centres, furniture stores, driving towards pleasurable encounters with objects, buying things for the house, a space that could be renovated forever, traffic jams that lulled us into dullness, a dullness that might have something to do with us, a bovine will, a collective ritual dullness, as if waiting, queuing, waiting, was always worth the sacrifice, as if by putting ourselves through waiting a trauma was re-enacted where obstacles had to be surmounted before the final reunion with the object of our affection.

Have you realised how more and more people are walking around with lollipops in their mouths? Chris said recently. Look, he said. And looking out of the car window, stuck in the endless wait, I saw a man in his forties sucking a lollipop. Then I saw an old woman sucking a lollipop, then a happy family, then a dustman collecting the endless trail of waste. It's true, it must be a new fashion, I said while I took out a couple of chocolate kinder eggs from my handbag and peeled the aluminium foil. Then we started building the free toy inside the yellow capsules. I got a tiny green dwarf wearing a long, conical hat and Chris got a spaceship. These small polymer things, these trashy trinkets, there is a kind of spell in them, I said. My father used to call them Hong Kong rubbish, Chris said. Then a fragile adolescent running on stilettos crossed the street majestically.

Stilettos were about to become as ubiquitous as plastic toys. Like everything in this endless recycling of the past where time is choreographed through appearance and contagious tunes, stilettos were back in fashion. You could see teenagers suspended from needles walking awkwardly down the streets, dancing in the dark, they must have rehearsed at home, practiced walking on stilts, following an imaginary line, one step after the other, slowly, gradually building up to a steady pace, turning walking into a performance, learning to be señoritas, like my mother must have done.

I didn't think about my mother's stilettos anymore, Nina Chiavelli's high-heel shoes. Sometimes I thought that their comings and goings were a distraction from my father's slow and irreversible illness, a way of warding off the inevitable, sometimes I saw a fleeting image of my father's ghost using a stiletto as a telephone, sometimes I dreamt about them,

strange dreams. I knew that all these shoes told as many stories as they concealed, I knew that the more I explored the
kingdom of things, the larger the parable of the unknown became. What did I really see? Was I a little girl who liked spying
on her mum and dad? It was none of my business. I became
a philosopher, a minor one. Everyday things were the trigger.
There were things proliferating everywhere, multiplying, like
a varied vegetation gone out of control.

I continued writing in the red notebook. I wrote about the
sex-appeal of the inorganic, the infantilisation of the times we
live in, and the dark side of plastic fantastic culture. I also
wrote a tragicomic story, 'Dyson DC 04, Mon Amour' about
falling in love with an aloof Hoover, but was shattered when
writing about 'objectum sexuality,' a term coined by Eija-Riitta Berliner-Mauer, the woman who married the Berlin Wall.
Eija-Riitta had coined the term to define people who fall in
love with objects and are convinced that their love is reciprocated, a conviction that was often a drastic survival strategy set off by abuse, rape, severe cruelty, unimaginable sorrow.
Objectum sexuality was another name for *damage*, a survival
ploy adopted by Asperger sufferers and by people so fucked
up by other people that they could only engage in passionate
sexual romance with objects unrelated to the human body: a
woman who secretly copulates with the Eiffel Tower, a woman who has a cosy romantic liaison with a banister, a man
who is married to a picture frame.

Some say that the task of the philosopher is to speak about
death. But I found that I had nothing to say about death. Except that it should be abolished. So instead of death, I focused on objects. Objects are suffused with life. The life of
those who designed them, made them and consumed them.
And they are also suffused with the many small deaths that
people go through life.

I now write in English, making occasional mistakes with
the prepositions, unexpected stupid mistakes. Sometimes I

am unsure about the nuance of the new words I use, whether a word really means the thing I am using it for or whether it's wildly out of tune with all the other words around it. There are so many shades to words, so many undercurrents and layers. I am now aware of the little lies bilingual dictionaries tell. Nuance. Atmosphere. Every word is wrapped up in its own atmosphere. Bilingual dictionaries don't give you the nuance of words, their atmosphere. They are the first traitors in the *traduttore-traditore* equation. They are guilty of giving you the illusion of equivalence, of telling you that a word has an equivalent word in other languages, when it just doesn't. And I now dream of grasping the atmosphere of words. And I know that in most languages words can be angelic but they can also be real rogues.

I also started decorating our nest with stuff from skips, cereal packets, charity shops and car-boot sales. I tried to tell Chris the full story about my mother's shoes the night he kidnapped me, but felt that it wasn't the right time. The kidnap was fully successful, although it was a slightly messy venture. The night he kidnapped me, we went to a Thai restaurant and indulged in swordsmanship with the chopsticks while waiting for the lemon grass rice, the king tiger prawns, and the hot hand towels called *oshibori*. Then we went back to my place and he put all my belongings on his car's roof rack. I said bye to Pearl, who gave me a smoking piglet as a forget-me-not and then, a key ring with an oblong, bald-headed silver alien which lies forgotten in a drawer. Then I stayed very still while Chris gagged and blindfolded me with black silk scarves, tied me up with a piece of rough rope and absconded me to his place. But then, he didn't tie up the knots hard enough, and they became undone while I was on the back seat of the car. He also kept asking me whether I was OK, so in the end I had to remove the gag in order to say: yeah, I'm OK, how can you be *so* useless as an abductor? He did tie me up to his four-poster bed, but not permanently. I also tied him up now and again, blindfolded him with my bra and tortured him a bit, it's the kind of game the bed suggests, it just hurt a bit on the wrists. Living with him is bliss, it's smooth, no tension, no crap, no cracks, the only recurrent problem is money, but what is money?

Yesterday, when we went to bed, I finally told him that it was none of my business but that my father was in love with my mother's stilettos. Undoubtedly, my mother's shoes were magical objects, enchanted shoes, I said. They had taken over my parents' lives and even my own life. Her shoes, my father's sentimental museum, Mary Jane's toys, they had all merged in my head leading me to muse on the material world. I have been writing about all these things, they all kind of add up to a story, I said. I propped the pillow up against the wall and said that yep, my family was perfectly dysfunctional, perfectly normal, that it wasn't a big deal but that my mother was a dominatrix married to a submissive shoe-fetishist. That she dominated him through her stilettos and he was a hopeless case.

A shoe fetishist, your father, no he wasn't, he said, was he? His eyes beamed back a surprised sparkle. How do you know? he said. I know, I said. But how do you *really* know? he said. There were so many hints, I said. Did you ask him? he said. How can you ask that? I said. It didn't surprise him, nothing surprised him these days. There are shoe-fetishists out there, it's not harmful, just really depraved, he said. It reminded him of the story of Emperor Charlemagne, he said. Fetishism, necrophilia, homosexuality and contemplation, condensed into a few lines. Do you know that story? It's about a magical ring, an object that took over Charlemagne's life, he said. It rings a bell, but I can't quite remember it, it's hazy in my mind, I said. Well, at least your parents were interesting, my parents were so ordinary, he said. You know, sometimes I think my father knew I'd find my mother's shoes in the loft and become busy with them, he pretended he'd forgotten about them, so I'll be

busy with them, he knew all these shoes would intrigue and
challenge me, I said. From what you've told me, your father
was always really considerate, telling his doctors to keep quiet
about his illness, I'd love to have met him, he said. That's the
way he was. Would you tell me Charlemagne's story as a bed-
time story? I said placing my head on his shoulder.

It's 3:18 AM, he said pointing at the red-light-emitting di-
ode alarm clock. But then he put on a storytelling voice and
told me the medieval story in a whisper while yawning now
and again: At the end of his life, he said, Charlemagne fell for
a young lady so much so that his fervour made him neglect
the affairs of state. His courtiers became extremely worried.
And when the girl died suddenly, they were greatly relieved.
But not for long. Charlemagne's love didn't die with her.
He had the body embalmed and carried to his bedchamber,
where he refused to be parted from it. Disturbed by this macabre turn of events, the Archbishop decided to examine the
corpse. Hidden under the girl's tongue, a ring was found. An
enchanted ring! But as soon as the ring was in the Archbishop's hands, Charlemagne fell passionately in love with him.
It was embarrassing. And the Archbishop flung the ring into
Lake Constance. But then Charlemagne fell in love with the
lake and remained there in contemplation until the day of his
death.

It comes to show that the pull of things goes back a long
time, it's probably innate to the human species, maybe it's
as ancient as the first Neanderthal that shaped a bone into a
bead and became hypnotised by its beauty, maybe we carry
thing-codes in our genes, I said. Chris nodded and yawned
a long, satisfied yawn. He kissed me on the shoulder, pulled
down the pillow from behind us and we slid inside the duvet.
There was a prolonged silence. Things, and then, there are so
many other things besides things, he said with a voice from
the land of Zzzzz. True, there is everything else, I sighed, the
whole world. Obvious, he said. I'd love to go to the desert, I

said, I miss the silence, the horizon line. We'll go this spring, at Easter, he whispered. He curled up his body and I moulded mine around his. It's the best time, I whispered. There was a prolonged silence. Can you switch off the lamp, please? . . . I'm falling into deep time, he whispered. Me too, I sighed.

Sweet Dreams

Sweet REM

SUSANA MEDINA writes both in Spanish, her native language, and in English. She has been awarded several literary prizes. She is the author of *Red Tales Cuentos Rojos*, *Souvenirs del Accidente* and two short films: *Buñuel's Philosophical Toys* and *Leather-bound Stories* (co-directed with Derek Ogbourne). Her writing has been featured in *Best European Fiction*. She also has curated international art shows, written art catalogues, exhibited at Tate Modern and collaborated with artists.